Witch Is Where Cats Always Win

Published by Implode Publishing Ltd

Chapter 1

"I am not wearing one of those things," I said.

"Come on, Jill, they look great." Jack grinned.

"You have to wear it, Mummy. They won't let you in if you don't."

My husband and daughter were both sporting purple wigs that Jack had bought from Grandma's wig shop, WiFY. He had purchased three of them and they were trying to persuade me to join their insanity.

"I can't believe you put good money into my grandmother's pocket to buy those ugly things."

"We won't get into the Purple Festival without them."

"And that's a bad thing, why?"

"Come on, Jill, it looks like it's going to be great fun. There are local bands, a funfair, and loads of food stalls."

"What kind of food?"

"Everything you could imagine."

"Can't you get a refund on the wig if I don't go?"

"No, your grandmother was quite clear on that point."

"In that case, I suppose I might as well give it a look, at least."

"Great. Try it on, then." He held out the third purple wig.

"No."

"Try it on! Try it on!" Florence began to chant.

"Okay, okay."

I put the wig on, and before I could object, Jack had taken a selfie of the three of us.

"Don't you dare put that photo online."

"Why not?"

"Because I don't want anyone seeing me with this

stupid thing on my head." I pulled off the wig and threw it on the kitchen table.

"I'm going to play at Bluebottle Girl," Florence said.

"Okay. Try not to get too dirty."

She went buzzing out into the garden.

"I'll be glad when this Bluebottle Girl phase passes," I said to Jack.

"Have you heard any more from Martin?"

"Not yet. He's still trying to track down Braxmore."

"Do you think he knows?"

"Do I think *who* knows *what*?"

"Could Braxmore know that you have all four compass stones? That would explain why he's suddenly disappeared."

"It's possible, I suppose. The timing is a bit of a coincidence otherwise. Either way, it won't do him any good because I'm going to catch up with him sooner or later. I meant to ask yesterday, have you had any second thoughts about working with me?"

"No. I thought it was a good idea at the time, but I now realise it was a mistake."

"I did warn you that we could never work together."

"Honestly, it's not that. It's just too much like my old job."

"Duh, isn't that the point? You have the right experience."

"I know, but when I was sitting in that car, watching the travel agent for hours on end, I realised that I want to do something completely different."

"Such as?"

"I don't know, but working as a PI seems like taking a step backwards."

"Gee, thanks."

"I didn't mean it like that. There's nothing wrong with being a PI. It's just not for me."

"So, it's back to the job search?"

"Looks like it."

***

Thankfully, they had finished work on my regular car park, so I didn't have to park at the other side of town. Walking back and forth from there several times a day had been exhausting.

I'd just stepped out of the car when a little voice called my name.

"Jill!"

I glanced all around, but I couldn't see anyone. Maybe I'd imagined it.

"Under here."

Mine was the only car in the car park, so I crouched down and peered underneath. Holding onto the subframe was a small red creature. When he saw me, he released his grip and tumbled onto the ground.

"Are you okay?" I said.

"My hands are numb from the cold, but that's all. I thought I was going to fall off a couple of times."

"Were you under there all the way on my drive in?"

"Yes, I had intended talking to you when you came out of the house, but I must have fallen asleep under your car. When you set off, all I could think to do was to grab onto the underside. I must admit I didn't expect the journey to be quite so long."

When he stepped out from under the car, I got a much

better look at him, but I was still no wiser as to what he was.

"Who are you?"

"My name is Ralph." He winked at me. "I'm very pleased to make your acquaintance."

"Likewise, I'm sure. I don't mean to sound rude, but what—err—?"

"What am I?"

"Yeah."

"I'm a Yella."

"But you're red?"

"Not *yellow*, the colour. Yella. Y-E-L-L-A."

"Oh, right. Sorry. Where did you come from?"

"Yellaville." He winked again. "It's a suburb of Candlefield."

"I had no idea. Why did you want to talk to me?"

"I was sent to see you by Princess Stella. She's heir to the Yella throne."

"Stella the Yella?"

"That's right. Her mother, Queen Bella, is critically ill."

"I'm very sorry to hear that, but I'm not really sure how I can help."

"The queen appears to be in perfect health, but she's been asleep for several weeks."

"Do you mean she's in a coma?"

"Our doctors say not." Yet another wink. "According to them, she's simply asleep."

"For weeks?"

"Yes, that's why the princess asked me to come and see you."

"But I'm not a doctor. I have no medical training."

"The princess is convinced that if we could find out

what caused the queen to fall into this deep sleep, then we'd be able to awaken her. Princess Stella asked the wisest minds in Candlefield who they thought would be able to help her solve the mystery, and your name came up time after time."

"I'm flattered of course and if I can help, I'll be only too glad to."

"Excellent, that's what I was hoping you would say. With your permission, I'll return to Yellaville and set up a time for your audience with the princess. When would be good for you?"

"I'm not super busy at the moment, so any day this week would work."

"Great." He winked. "I'll get back to you as soon as possible."

By now, I was beginning to think that he wasn't actually winking at me but that he had some kind of nervous twitch which just made it look like he was.

"Okay. It was nice to meet—" Before I could finish the sentence, the little red guy had disappeared in a puff of smoke.

"Who are you talking to?" A passing policeman shot me a puzzled look.

"I—err—no one. Just talking to myself."

"Have you been drinking this morning, madam?"

"Certainly not." I went over to him, so he could see I was able to walk in a straight line. "Don't you ever talk to yourself, officer?"

"Of course, but I don't usually hold such a long conversation."

"You should try it sometime. I find it helps reduce my stress levels."

"Okay, well have a nice day, madam."

"You too."

I really should be more careful when talking to creatures that only I could see. In better news, though, my fame was obviously spreading. Why else would so many people have put my name forward to the princess of the Yellas?

Mrs V didn't look happy.

"Good morning, Mrs V."

"It was until that husband of mine spoiled it."

"Oh dear. What did Armi do? Isn't today his birthday?"

"It is. You remember how much thought I put into his present, don't you, Jill?"

"Yes, you decided on socks, didn't you?"

"That was my initial idea, but then I settled on nose-hair clippers."

"Oh, yeah. I remember now."

"You'd have thought he'd be delighted, given the amount of hair accumulating in his nostrils."

"I take it he wasn't."

"He hated them. He actually had the nerve to tell me that he didn't have any need of them. I was literally staring at his nose hair while he was telling me he didn't have any."

"Oh dear."

"We aren't speaking."

"It is his birthday, though. Maybe you should give him a call and—"

"I'm not apologising."

"I was going to say you could suggest you both go out for a nice meal tonight."

"I'll have to think about it."

"Have there been any calls?"

"A Mr Bones called and asked if we sold skeletons. I think it was a wrong number."

"Right. Anything else?"

"Oh yes, a Mr Brown called and asked if he could come and talk to you about his son."

"What about his son?"

"He wouldn't go into detail over the phone, but I got the impression that his son is in some kind of trouble."

"Did he make an appointment?"

"No, but he said he could do any day this week except today."

"Okay, call him back and see if you can set up a meeting for tomorrow, would you?"

"Will do. Cup of tea?"

"Yes, please."

"Socks arrives today," Winky said. He looked more excited than I'd seen him in a long time.

"Whoop-de-doo! Who cares?"

"Nothing you can say is going to dampen my mood."

"Look, I'm really pleased for you, but just remember what I said: This office is a Socks-free zone."

"What about when you're not here? Can he come over then?"

"I suppose so. Hold on, though, does he still pilot that microlite of his?"

"No, he traded it in for an e-scooter."

"Those things are dangerous too."

"So, can he come over when you're not here?"

"Yes, but if he makes any trouble, he'll be banned

completely."

"You're the best. I've always said so."

"Hmm."

"Have you seen what's going on across the road?"

"Where?"

"On top of that office block."

"What's that they're constructing on the roof?"

"If I'm not mistaken, it's going to be a heliport."

"I think you're right. That entire office block has been empty for almost three years. Someone must have bought it."

"Someone with some serious money, by the looks of it."

Halfway through the morning, Mrs V popped her head around the door.

"Mr Brown is coming in tomorrow morning at ten o'clock."

"Excellent."

"And your sister is here to see you."

"Kathy? Is she okay?"

"She does seem a little flustered."

"Send her through, would you?"

Mrs V was right, Kathy did look out of sorts.

"What's up? Are you alright?"

"Not really." She took a seat next to my desk.

"What's wrong?"

"You'll think I'm crazy."

"I already think that. What is it?"

"You know how Lizzie used to bang on about ghosts?"

"Err—yeah. Is she still—"

"No, she hasn't mentioned them for ages. I think she must have grown out of it."

I knew for a fact that Lizzie did still see ghosts, and that she was actually studying with Mad.

"So, what is it?"

"Promise not to laugh?"

"I promise."

"I think I've got a ghost in my shop."

I definitely hadn't seen that coming.

"You don't even believe in ghosts."

"Of course I don't. They're not real."

"But you just said you've got one."

"I know. I don't know. I mean, I—"

"I think I should get Mrs V to make us both a cup of tea, then you can tell me all about it."

"Okay. I don't suppose you have any biscuits, do you?"

"Only *my* custard creams."

"They'll do. Just a couple, though."

Chapter 2

Once we had our drinks, Kathy started to tell me about her ghost, but I was a little distracted because she had just taken her fourth biscuit from the packet.

"It was last Wednesday, when—"

"I thought you just wanted a couple of biscuits?"

"That's all I've had."

"A couple means two. That's your fourth."

"What are you, the custard cream police? Do you want to hear about this ghost or not?"

"Of course I do. I took a biscuit from the packet and then moved it out of her reach. All subtle like.

"Like I was saying, it started last Wednesday."

"Which one of your shops are we talking about? You have so many."

"The original one, just off the high street."

"You've been in that shop for ages."

"I know. That's what makes it even weirder. Do you think it's been there all the time?"

"Hang on. First, can we at least establish if you do or don't believe in ghosts?"

"I don't. Except for maybe this one."

"Okay, I'm glad we've got that sorted out. What exactly do you want me to do?"

"Get rid of it of course."

"In case you hadn't noticed, I'm a private investigator, not a ghostbuster."

"I realise that, but you've taken on all kinds of weird cases over the years, so I thought you might be able to do something."

If she'd known the full extent of weird cases that I'd

been involved with, it would have blown her mind.

"Were you planning on paying me for my services?"

"What? No, of course not. You wouldn't charge family, would you?"

"So, by that same token, if I wanted a wedding dress, would you let me have it for free?"

"You're already married."

"Don't be obtuse. You know what I mean."

"Of course I wouldn't. Those dresses cost a small fortune."

"Whereas my services are as cheap as chips, I suppose?"

"I didn't say that. It's different, that's all. By the way, what was the story behind that free dress you got from Harmony Fashion?"

"There is no story."

"It said you were getting a medal from the king."

"It was just an advert. It wasn't supposed to be taken seriously."

"It read as though it was actually happening."

"You were telling me about your ghost."

"Right. The manager of that store was on holiday for a couple of days, so I had to stand in for her."

"Poor you. Did you actually have to do some real work?"

"Jill!"

"Sorry, carry on."

"It was a quiet day, so I decided to sort out the stockroom. I'd been at it for about half an hour when I saw a woman standing at the very back of the room, behind some boxes."

"What was she doing?"

"Nothing. She was just standing there, looking at me."

"What did you do?"

"I asked who she was and what she was doing."

"What did she say?"

"Nothing, she just seemed to disappear."

"Isn't it possible that a customer found the shop empty and just wandered into the stockroom?"

"I don't see how. To get to the back of the stockroom, they would have had to walk right by me, and I didn't see anyone do that."

"I assume you went out and checked the shop?"

"Yeah, but there was no one there. If it had only been the one time, I might not have thought anymore about it, but it happened again about an hour later."

"Same thing?"

"Exactly the same. One minute, she was there. The next, she'd gone."

"If it happened last Wednesday, how come you're only telling me now?"

"I told Pete about it that night, and he said I should talk to you, but I just wanted to forget about it. When nothing else happened over the next few days, I thought that was it."

"But—?"

"But then, yesterday, I got a call from Marilyn. She's the manager of the shop. I'd told her that I'd reorganised the stockroom, so she went in there to check it out. She saw it too and rang me in tears. She was scared silly, so I had to go over there to calm her down."

"Did you see it again when you got there?"

"No, I hung around for a couple of hours, in case it came back, but there was no sign of it. Marilyn is threatening to hand in her notice if it happens again. She's one of my best managers and I can't afford to lose her. That's why I'm here. Will you help?"

"I'm not really sure what you expect me to do. Like I said before, I don't know any more about ghosts than you do."

"That's just it. It might not be a ghost. What if it's a competitor, trying to scare me?"

"Why would they do that?"

"The bridal industry is absolutely cutthroat. You have no idea."

"Clearly not."

"Will you help? It's not like I ask you for many favours."

"Okay, I'll see what I can do, but don't go getting your hopes up."

"Thanks, Jill. You're the best sister in the world."

"I still can't believe your own sister hasn't worked out you're a witch," Winky said.

"That's because I'm very discreet."

"Yeah, that can't possibly be the reason. She's probably too self-absorbed."

"You might be right."

"Just like you."

"I am not self-absorbed."

"Keep telling yourself that. Anyway, I'd love to stick around and chat, but I've just had a text from Socks. He's arrived in Washbridge, so I'm going to help him to settle in."

Winky was right about Kathy. She had always been self-absorbed. But to suggest the same was true about me was one of the most ridiculous things I'd ever heard. I am without doubt one of the most selfless, altruistic individuals you're ever likely to meet.

As I'm sure you'll all agree.

What was I to make of Kathy's claim to have a ghost in her shop? If it hadn't been for the fact that her manager also claimed to have seen it, I would have put it down to my sister's overactive imagination. When we were kids, she was convinced there were aliens living in our garden shed. The aliens were actually garden gnomes.

Although I could see ghosts and regularly conversed with them, I wasn't able to sense their presence as well as an experienced ghost hunter like Mad, so I gave her a call.

"Hey, Jill, I believe congrats are in order."

"For what?"

"I heard on the grapevine that you were going to be presented with a medal by the king of the gnomes."

"Right, yeah, I got it last week."

"How come I didn't see anything in the Candlefield press?"

"It was a pretty low-key event. To be completely honest, I think the king had forgotten all about it until I arrived there."

"Typical gnome. Anyway, you called me. What can I do for you?"

I told her what Kathy had said about seeing a ghost, and I asked if she would have time to check it out.

"I'm really sorry, Jill. Any other week, and I'd have been happy to do it, but I'm on an outward bound course in GT, and we're not allowed to leave the grounds until it's over."

"Not to worry. I'll nip around there myself."

"Why don't you ask Lizzie to have a nosey around? If a

ghost has been there, she'll be able to sense it."

"I would, but I'm not sure how I'd explain it to Kathy."

"Does she need to know?"

"Maybe not. I'll give it some thought. Good luck with your course."

"Thanks. I've got a feeling I'm going to need it."

"I've taken your advice, Jill," Mrs V said, as I was on my way out of the office.

"About what?"

"I've booked a table for two this evening at The Cuckoo's Nest, Armi's favourite restaurant."

"That's great. Have you told him?"

"No, I thought it would be a nice surprise for him."

"It's a strange name, isn't it? Cuckoo's Nest?"

"Why do you say that?"

"Isn't the whole thing about cuckoos that they lay their eggs in other birds' nests?"

"That is a bit weird, but the food is good, so that's all that matters."

"I hope you both have a great evening."

***

Jack was standing in the front garden, looking at a large pile of boxes that had been stacked on the front path. Had he ordered something without telling me? It was probably those stupid display cabinets he'd been threatening to buy for ages.

"What have you bought now?" I said.

"I haven't bought anything." He rolled his eyes. "These are for you."

"Me? They can't be. I haven't ordered anything recently."

"UCU? Ring any bells?"

"*UCU*? Isn't that a wrestling thing?"

"Here. Look." He handed me a sheet of paper.

Only then did the penny drop. UCU stood for Unhealthy Cereals Unlimited. The Stock sisters had taken the decision to stop selling my favourite cereals without consulting me, so I'd been forced to source them elsewhere.

"Ringing any bells yet?" Jack said.

"Yeah, but why have they sent so many?"

"Because that's what you ordered, apparently."

"I didn't order that many."

"That's what I tried to tell the delivery driver, but he had a copy of your order to prove it."

"That's nonsense. I distinctly remember ordering three boxes of Strawberrycandy Pops, three boxes of Chococandy Pops, and three boxes of ChocONut Pops."

"What did you understand a box to mean?"

"What do you mean? You've seen the boxes they come in."

"Yes, I have, but that's not what you ordered. It's true you ordered nine boxes in total, but each one contains forty-eight boxes of cereal."

"Nine boxes of forty-eight? That's—"

"A lot of cereal."

Oh bum!

"It was clearly a mistake. They must have realised that when they received the order."

"Why would they? They're a wholesaler. How much did this lot cost?"

"I didn't notice. I was just so pleased to find a stockist. Not many people carry this cereal now."

"I wonder why."

"Look on the bright side. I won't have to buy any more cereal for ages."

"Decades probably. Where on earth are we going to put them all?"

"How about the spare bedroom?" I suggested.

"Are you joking? It's full to bursting already."

"I'll think of something. Anyway, where's Florence?"

"She went straight up to her bedroom after she came back from CASS."

"What did they do there today?"

"She didn't say."

"Didn't you ask her?"

"I—err—"

"She could be up to anything up there. Stay here and watch these boxes while I go and check on her." I hurried into the house and up to Florence's bedroom. Nervous of what I might discover, I opened the door, only to find her standing there, all innocent-like.

All ten of her!

"Hello, Mummy!" all ten Florences said in perfect unison.

"What's going on, Florence?"

"We learned the doopcake spell," they chorused.

"Okay, I need you to reverse the spell right now."

"Aww!" they all groaned.

"I mean it."

Nine of the ten Florences evaporated, leaving just one standing there. "I like the doopcake spell. It's fun."

"It's called duplicate, not doopcake."

It was a spell I'd seen in the spell book, but never actually used.

"Mr Tomdrum said he'd never seen anyone make as many doopcakes as I made."

It seemed like Florence had a new teacher every time she visited CASS, and they all had the most ridiculous names.

"What else did you do at CASS today?"

"Just boring stuff. Genevieve has got a dragon egg."

"They're dangerous. Do the teachers know she has it?"

"It isn't a real one, silly. She bought it at the CASS shop."

Since when did the school have a shop? I'd never seen it, but then I hadn't been aware of the broomstick riding simulator either.

"Can I have a toy dragon's egg, Mummy?"

"You'll have to use your pocket money."

"But I'm going to buy a Bluebottle Girl book with that."

"Then you'll just have to wait for the egg."

"Can I doopcake again?"

"I suppose so, but when it's dinnertime, I only want to see one of you at the table."

"Yay!" said all ten Florences.

When I went back downstairs, Jack was in the kitchen.

"I thought you said you were going to keep an eye on the cereal?"

"No, you said that. I needed to start dinner."

"But what if someone steals them?"

"Who's going to steal four-hundred and thirty-two packets of teeth-rotting cereal? What was Florence up to? Nothing crazy, I hope?"

"She's fine. All ten of her."

"Huh?"

"I'll explain later. I'd better go and sort the cereal out."

"Good luck with that."

Little did Jack know that while I'd been upstairs, I'd come up with a cunning solution to the cereal problem. And, just in case you were wondering, a cunning solution is a close relative to a cunning plan. Sort of a cunning plan-lite.

Chapter 3

"I'm going to get a dragon egg," said both Florences.

Earlier, there had been a slight altercation when ten Florences had turned up for breakfast. I'd insisted she reverse the spell completely, but she'd argued that Mr Tomdrum (possible made-up name) had said they had to practise every morning. As a compromise, I'd agreed that she could recast the spell so that there was only one doopcake (as she still insisted on calling it).

"You're going to buy a dragon's egg instead of the Bluebottle Girl book?"

"Yes. I'll get the book next week."

"Okay."

Jack hadn't said more than a couple of words over breakfast, so I asked him if he was alright.

"Yeah, it's just—" He nodded towards the two Florences. "I don't know which one of them I should be speaking to."

"You should speak to me, Daddy," said both of them.

When the two girls had finished their cereal, one bowl between them—I drew the line at feeding a doopcake—they went back upstairs.

"That really freaked you out, didn't it?" I said to Jack.

"Yeah. That's my least favourite spell. I liked it better when she turned herself into a mouse."

"Interesting."

"So, are you going to tell me?"

"Tell you what?" I shrugged.

"You know what. Where did you put all those boxes?"

"You weren't interested in helping me last night, so why do you care where they are now?"

"I'm just curious to know what you did with nine humongous boxes of cereal packets, that's all."

"It's on a cereal to know basis, and you don't cereal to know."

"Very funny. I thought I might have a drive into Washbridge today while Florence is at school."

"For anything in particular?"

"Not really. I don't often get the chance to look around by myself."

"Go for it. Just don't go spending all of our money."

"I can't. You've already spent it on cereal."

"You're hilarious."

I was just about to get into the car when a removal van drove past me. Donna and family were moving out today, but I still had no idea who would be moving into their house. Florence didn't seem unduly upset at losing her bestest friend, but then she had so many of them.

"Jill!" The little voice came from under the car.

I stooped down, looked underneath, and found Ralph, the red Yella, standing there.

"Hello again." He winked. "I managed to stay awake this time, thank goodness. I wouldn't have wanted another trip like last time. I managed to speak to Princess Stella, and she wondered if you'd be able to pop over Thursday morning?"

"Sure, that works for me."

"Great. Is nine-thirty okay?"

"Yeah, but I'll need directions to Yellaville."

"I have them here." He took out a sheet of paper and handed it to me. "I'll be waiting at the doors to the palace for you."

"Okay, I'll see you on Thursday."

"Are you okay, Jill?"

I spun around to see the vicar standing there.

"Good morning, Vicar. Yeah, I'm fine, thanks."

"You seemed to be talking to someone."

"The cat. Didn't you see it?"

"Cat?" He stooped down and peered under the car. "It's not there now."

"It must have shot off. Typical. I'd been trying to coax it out for ages."

"Right." He looked unconvinced, but he obviously had other things on his mind. "I was hoping you might have time to show me your Roomba."

"Sorry, but I can't dance, Vicar. Jack's the dancer in our family."

"No, not rumba. I meant your vacuum cleaner. The robot one you told me about."

Oh bum! I'd lied about the vacuum cleaner when I'd been trying to distract the vicar from an approaching zombie.

"It's broken."

"Oh dear. I'd heard they were very reliable."

"They are, but not if you drop a sack of potatoes on them."

"Sorry?"

"Jack has always been a little clumsy. He carried in a sack of potatoes from the car and dropped it in the hallway. He didn't see the little guy until it was too late."

"Can't you get it repaired?"

"Unfortunately not. It was a really heavy sack of potatoes. Sorry."

"Never mind. I'd better not keep you."

"Bye, Vicar."

As I was approaching my office building, something caught my eye. Sitting on the window ledge of my office was a cat—and it wasn't Winky. I would recognise that particular feline anywhere. Socks! After all the warnings I'd given to Winky too.

I hurried into the building and up the stairs, but when I walked into the outer office, I stopped dead in my tracks.

"Armi?"

"Good morning, Jill."

"Where's Mrs V? Is she okay?"

"She's a little under the weather, I'm afraid. Food poisoning, I think."

"Oh no."

"She booked us a table at my favourite restaurant last night."

"Yeah, she said. Belated happy birthday, by the way."

"Thanks. I had the lamb—I usually do. Annabel went for the trout. She was feeling queasy on the drive home, and she spent most of the night in the loo."

"How is she now?"

"Much better, but quite exhausted. I told her to stay in bed."

"You did right, but why—err—why are you here?"

"She insisted I stand in for her. She said you wouldn't have time to get a temp."

"You should be at home with her."

"That's what I tried to tell her, but—well, you know how she can be."

"I certainly do, but I insist you get back to her. I'll be fine here for a day or two."

"Are you sure?"

"Positive, and don't let her come back until she's completely better."

"Okay, thanks, Jill."

"What about you, Armi?" I pointed to the plaster on his nose. "Are you okay?"

"This? Yeah, it's—err—nothing."

"You have to let me do it now," Winky said.

I had no idea what he was talking about, so I ignored him while I searched the office for Socks.

"What are you looking for?" He jumped on the desk.

"That brother of yours. I saw him on the window ledge."

"He's gone."

"Hmm." I continued my search until I was happy the office was Socks-free.

"You said it was okay for him to visit when you weren't here. He just left."

"You were cutting it fine."

"So, will you let me do it?"

"Let you do what?"

"Work on reception of course. I doubt the old bag lady will recover from this one."

"Don't be ridiculous. It's just food poisoning."

"Yes, but at her age, anything can tip her over the edge."

"She'll be fine. I've no doubt she'll be back in a few days' time."

"Let me do it until then, at least."

"Are you completely out of your mind? How is a cat going to work reception? You can't communicate with my clients."

"I can use text to speech on the computer."

"Stop! Enough! I can't believe I'm even having this conversation with you."

"How about you turn me into a two-legged? That would work."

"I—err—"

"Come on. You know that would work. I know as much about your business as anyone. And, if I'm a two-legged, no one will give me a second glance."

"I suppose that could work."

"Yes!" He gave a paw pump. "Let's do it."

"Okay, but only until Mrs V returns. Agreed?"

"Sure. Come on, I can't wait."

I cast the spell.

"This feels kind of weird," he said. "How do you guys stand on two legs like this all day?"

"You wanted the job, so get out there and do it."

Once he had left my office, I began to count. I'd only got to twenty when I heard the scream. Moments later, the door flew open.

"How could you do it?"

"You said you wanted to be a two-legged."

"Yes, but why did you have to turn me into the old bag lady?"

"This way makes most sense. People are expecting to see Mrs V sitting there, so they won't stop to wonder if you're really a cat."

"Why can't you make me look like Jules? At least she's pleasing to the eye."

"It's Mrs V or no one."

"Okay, but I won't forget this."

"Neither will I." I laughed.

At a few minutes before ten o'clock, Mrs V (AKA Winky) popped her/his head around the door.

"Mr Brown is here."

He even had the voice off to a tee.

"Send him through, please."

Mr Brown had a lived-in face, which is a polite way of saying he was looking rough.

"Thank you for seeing me, Mrs Maxwell."

"It's Jill. Would you like a drink?"

"What do you have?"

"Tea, coffee, hot chocolate."

"A tea would be great."

"Two teas, please, Mrs V."

"Coming right up." Winky scowled.

"So, Mr Brown, what brings you here today?"

"Please call me Charles. I'm here about my son, Max."

"Okay?"

"I don't really know where to begin. You're probably going to think I'm wasting your time."

"That's very unlikely. I get all kinds of cases."

"My wife, Max's mother, died when he was only a toddler."

"I'm sorry."

"Thank you. It was very hard, as you might imagine, but it formed a very strong bond between the two of us. That bond continued even through what were supposed to be the difficult teen years. Don't get me wrong, we had our moments, but we always remained close. That all changed about a month ago."

We were interrupted by the door flying open. Although

Winky looked like Mrs V, he clearly didn't feel comfortable walking on two legs, so I watched with some trepidation as he carried the tray of drinks across the room. To give him his due, he'd had the foresight to bring in a bowl of sugar and a small jug of milk.

"Thank you, Mrs V."

"My pleasure, *dear*."

Never had the word 'dear' carried such venom.

I waited until Charles had poured a splash of milk into his tea, and then encouraged him to continue.

"You were saying that things changed about a month ago?"

"That's right. It was so sudden and so dramatic. Even now, I find it hard to believe that it's happened."

"You said *everything* changed, but can you be more specific?"

"The first thing will sound ridiculously trivial."

"That doesn't matter. If I'm going to help you, I'll need to know everything."

"It was Sunday morning and Max didn't come down for breakfast at the usual time."

"Just back up a second. Is Max still living at home with you?"

"Yes."

"How old is he now?"

"He was twenty last month."

"Right. You said he didn't come down for breakfast at the usual time."

"I told you it would sound trivial, but Sunday breakfasts were like a thing for us. In the week, we both work, or at least we did—Max lost his job a couple of weeks ago."

"Let's stick with that Sunday morning for now."

"We always have a fry-up for Sunday breakfast. We've done the same thing ever since Max was a kid. He loves them, or at least, he used to."

"So, it was unusual for him not to get up for breakfast on a Sunday?"

"Not unusual. Unheard of. I assumed he must be ill, so I went to check on him, but he wasn't in his bedroom."

"Did he often stay out overnight?"

"Hardly ever, but whenever he did, he always called or texted me."

"Right."

"He came home late at night, looking like death. When I asked him where he'd been, he practically bit my head off, and went straight to bed."

"Isn't it possible that he went out on that Saturday night and got completely wasted?"

"Max doesn't drink. He never has. He is—err—was into sports in a big way."

"He isn't now?"

"He lost all interest in it on that day. He hasn't played since then."

"What else has changed?"

"Everything. He rarely speaks to me, or anyone else for that matter. He comes and goes at all hours of the night, but never comes out of his bedroom during the daytime. I only discovered he'd lost his job because I bumped into one of the people he used to work with. I'm really worried about him, Jill, but I don't know how to help him."

"I can't help but think that some kind of medical intervention might be needed."

"You're probably right, but I can't persuade him to do

anything these days. I certainly wouldn't be able to get him to see a doctor. That's why I'm here today. I just need to know what's going on. Maybe if I did, I'd be able to help. Will you take the case?"

It was more a plea than a question, and I was keen to help, but not before we had discussed the elephant in the room.

"Before I commit myself to anything I have to ask if you've considered the possibility that Max has started taking drugs?"

"Of course, but I don't believe he would ever do that. He has always been so anti-drugs."

"You didn't believe he'd do some of the other things he's been doing recently either."

"That's true, and despite what you might think, I'm not naïve. I've searched the house high and low for any evidence that he might be using, but I've found nothing."

"But if I were to find evidence that he is?"

"Then at least I'll know, and I can try to help him get off them. I just need to know."

"Okay." I took out the usual paperwork from my desk. "If you're okay with this, please sign on the last page."

He barely skimmed the paperwork before signing and passing it back to me.

"Okay, Charles, here's how this is going to work. You've told me a few things about Max today, but I need to know much more. I'd like you to go home and prepare me a file on your son. I want you to put as much information in there about him as possible. I'll need photographs too. A recent one is essential. Can you do that?"

"Of course. I'll make a start as soon as I get home. And

thank you."

"When the file is ready, drop it in to my receptionist and I'll get straight onto it."

Chapter 4

Not long after Mr Brown had left, Mrs V/Winky came through to collect the tray and cups.

"Why are you walking around barefooted?" I said.

"Those shoes were crippling me. I don't know how you lot put up with them."

"If you're going to be my receptionist, you have to wear the appropriate footwear."

"You're enjoying this, aren't you?"

"You were the one who asked to do it, remember?"

"I didn't ask to be the old bag lady."

"Think yourself lucky. If I'd turned you into Jules, you'd have had to wear high heels. Were there any calls while I was with Mr Brown?"

"A woman called Gemma Four called to ask if we sold flags. Why do you get all these weird calls?"

"I've always thought you were behind them."

"I have much better things to do with my time."

My phone rang with an unknown number.

"Auntie Jill?"

"Lizzie? Are you okay?"

"Yeah, I wondered if I could see you for a few minutes? I'd normally call Mad but she's away on a course."

"Sure, where are you?"

"In Washbridge."

"Okay, do you know Coffee Animal on the high street?"

"Yeah."

"Great. I'll see you outside there in a few minutes."

"I take it you're going out?" Mrs V/Winky said.

"Yeah. I'll be back after lunch."

"I'll ask Socks to pop over while you're gone."

"Okay, but make sure he's not here when I get back." I started for the door.

"Hold on, before you go, you have to change me back into myself."

"Sorry, no time. Got to rush."

I was sniggering all the way down the stairs, as I imagined Socks' reaction to seeing his brother in Mrs V's body. I was almost tempted to stay back to witness it, but I needed to find out what Lizzie wanted.

She was waiting for me outside Coffee Animal.

"Are you sure you're okay, Lizzie?"

"Yes, I promise."

"Okay, let's get a drink and then we can talk."

I was a little surprised when Lizzie asked for a latte, but I guess that was a sign she was growing up. She had a strawberry cupcake, and she looked quite appalled at my Eccles cake.

"Mum calls those dead-fly cakes."

"Have you ever tried one?"

"No." She pulled a face. "They look horrible."

"They're delicious. The funny thing is I didn't used to like them, but now I adore them."

"What are we supposed to do with these hamsters?" Lizzie asked.

We had both been handed a cage with a hamster in it. Lizzie's was a pleasing shade of brown, and mine was beige (my favourite colour).

Before I could answer, my hamster chipped in, "How about feeding us?"

"You look like you should lay off the cakes," I said.

"Pot. Kettle."

"Cheek."

"Are you talking to the hamster, Auntie Jill?"

Oh bum! I'd totally forgotten that although Lizzie knew Mad was a ghost hunter, she had no idea I was a witch, and that I could talk to animals.

"Err, yeah. I've always talked to my pets."

"Right? Do you think they'd like some cake?"

"I'm sure they would."

She broke off a small piece of her cupcake and dropped it in her cage. The hamster scooped it up and made short work of it. I was about to give my hamster some of my Eccles cake when he said, "I don't want dead-fly cake. I want some of what she's got."

"Lizzie, would you mind giving my hamster some of your cupcake? I don't think they're supposed to eat currants."

"Okay, sure."

"So, what was it you wanted to talk to me about?"

"Did my mum come and see you about her ghost?"

"Yeah, she did, actually. She thinks it might be someone messing around, and she asked me to investigate."

"It isn't. Someone messing around, I mean."

"How do you know?"

"I was in the garden, and I overheard Mum telling Dad about it. I was curious, so I made an excuse to drop by the shop, and while she was serving a customer, I went into the stockroom."

"And you saw it?"

"No, but I got a really strong feeling that the room was haunted."

"What I don't understand is why it has suddenly appeared. Your mother has had that shop for ages with no problems."

"I don't know, but the ghost is very sad."

"I thought you said you hadn't seen it?"

"I haven't, but the presence is so strong I can tell."

"I'm not sure what I'm going to tell your mother. If I tell her that the shop is haunted, she'll freak out."

"I know. That's why I wanted to talk to Mad, to see what she thought I should do."

"It's a pity she's not around this week."

"I do have one idea, Auntie Jill."

"What's that?"

"I could try talking to the ghost, to see if I can find out why she has suddenly appeared. Maybe I'll even be able to persuade her to leave."

"I'm not sure about that. It could be dangerous."

"She isn't dangerous."

"You can sense that too?"

"Yeah, if anything, I'd say she seems afraid."

"How are you going to speak to the ghost when your mum is always in the shop, and you don't even know when it will appear."

"I don't know. I was hoping you might be able to help me do it."

"I was afraid you were going to say that. I tell you what, why don't you leave it with me for a day or two, and I'll see if I can come up with any bright ideas."

"Okay." She glanced down at the cages. "The hamsters still look hungry. Shall I give them the rest of this cake?"

"Nah, those two have had enough cake for one day."

Ignoring the hamsters' protests, I returned them to the counter on our way out.

"By the way, shouldn't you be at school today?"

"No, it's an inset day. I'm meeting some friends later."

"Okay, have a good day, and I'll be in touch."

Mrs V/Winky was pacing around the outer office.

"Has Socks gone?" I said.

"Yes, and thanks to you, I'm now the laughingstock of the whole feline community."

"Why?"

"Why do you think? Just look at me."

"You were the one who wanted to be my receptionist."

"You could at least have reversed the spell while Socks was here."

"Sorry about that." Not. "How did it go?"

"How do you think? It took me five minutes just to convince him it was me. Then, he spent the rest of the time mocking me."

"I thought you had a thick skin."

"I can take anything Socks has to throw at me, but he posted a photo on Feline Social. Now everyone is going to see it."

"I told you that brother of yours was bad news."

"I quit as your receptionist. Change me back."

"Already? But you were so keen."

"Do it now. I have some serious damage limitation to do."

"As you wish." I reversed the spell, and Winky went running through to my office. I followed.

"What are you going to do?"

"Post on Feline Social."

"And say what?"

"That it was all a set-up, and that Socks fell for it, hook, line and sinker."

"Do you think that will work?"

"It better had, or I'll never be able to show my face again."

***

When I arrived home, Florence was in the lounge playing snakes and ladders with Jay. I popped my head around the door, hoping for a kiss or a hug, but all she could manage was a 'hi'.

"How come they're playing in the lounge?" I asked Jack.

"Apparently, the new wall colour in Florence's bedroom is still making him queasy."

"We're not changing it."

"I know. I've told him we'll get him some sunglasses."

"Did you have a drive into Washbridge?"

"I did."

"Did you buy anything?"

"No, but I did see a job that I might go for."

"Oh?"

"They're advertising for parking wardens."

"You've got to be kidding."

"I quite like the idea. Plenty of fresh air and exercise."

"And abuse. You do realise that everyone hates parking wardens, don't you?"

"That's not true. It's only the people who get a ticket for parking on double yellow lines who hate them." He shot me an accusing look.

"I told you, that wasn't my fault. They'd been tarmacked over. You haven't actually applied for a job, have you?"

"No, but I'm giving it serious consideration. Anyway,

how was your day?"

I told him about Mrs V's food poisoning and how Winky had stood in for her.

"Let me get this right. You turned your cat into Mrs V, so he could work on reception?"

"Yeah, but he didn't last long in the job. He made me turn him back halfway through the afternoon. Apparently, he was worried about his street cred."

"Just when I think nothing else you could do would surprise me, you come up with this."

"I've got a new case. A man wants me to find out why his adult son has changed."

"Changed how?"

"Completely, apparently. I'm worried I might discover that he's started taking drugs, but we'll see. I've also got a meeting with Princess Stella."

"More gnome royalty?"

"No, she's a Yella. Spelt Y-E-L-L-A. I'd never heard of them until Ralph contacted me."

"Ralph's another Yella, I'm guessing?"

"Correct. Apparently, the princess's mother, Queen Bella, has been asleep for several weeks and no one knows why. They want me to investigate."

"There's never a dull moment with you, is there?"

"Not lately. Oh, and Kathy has a ghost."

"I didn't know she believed in them."

She doesn't. At least, she didn't until one showed up in the stockroom of her shop. She asked me to find out what's going on."

"It sounds like you've got a lot on your plate again. Do you need me to help with anything?"

"No, I'm okay. Lizzie is going to help with Kathy's

ghost."

"I'm surprised you've got her involved."

"*She* was the one who contacted *me*. She'd heard Kathy talking to Peter about the ghost and decided to check it out for herself. She hasn't actually seen the ghost, but she can sense its presence."

"I assume you won't be telling Kathy that Lizzie is involved."

"No way. She'd string me up. I suppose I ought to get changed."

"Before you do, we need to talk about your lying."

"What do you mean?"

"You're going to start providing me with a list of all the whoppers you tell people, so that I'm not caught off-guard like I was today when I bumped into the vicar."

"Why, what happened?"

"He said he was sorry to hear about the Roomba. Needless to say, I didn't have the first clue what he was talking about."

"What did you say?"

"Luckily, I was able to get the gist of what he was talking about. What I don't understand is why you told him we had a Roomba in the first place."

"It was all the zombie's fault."

"Obviously, I should have realised."

"It's true. I was trying to deal with a zombie when the vicar came to the house. I managed to cut him off at the gate before he saw anything, but then the Z began to head our way. I had to tell the vicar something so that I could get away."

"So, you told him we had a Roomba?"

"Not in so many words, but that's the conclusion he

came to. Next thing I knew, he was asking to see it."

"So, you told him that I'd dropped a sack of potatoes on it?"

"Yeah."

Jack put his head in his hands and made a strange groaning noise.

"What?"

Chapter 5

"I'm getting a dragon egg, I'm getting a dragon egg," Florence was chanting, in between spoonsful of muesli.

It was almost as bad as the long-lamented hot tub song.

"Don't forget to take your pocket money with you," I said. "Did you miss Wendy at school yesterday?"

She shrugged. "I'm going to get a red dragon's egg. They're the best."

"Wasn't it yesterday that Donna was moving out?" Jack said.

"Yeah, I saw their removal van arrive in the morning."

"It's a shame they had to leave. Any word on who has bought their place?"

"None. I just hope it doesn't turn out to be Grandma."

"Judging by how popular the Purple Festival seems to be, she'll be able to afford it."

I'd finished my cereal, but I was still peckish, so I went to the cupboard to get the custard creams.

"Where are my biscuits?"

"Why are you asking me?"

"We don't have any in here."

"Then you must have eaten them. Florence and I prefer Garibaldi. We've got plenty of those in the cupboard."

"*Garibaldi*? Are you serious?"

"Why not?"

"Because they aren't custard creams. I can't believe there aren't any left."

"You had some with your cup of tea last night. Didn't you notice then?"

"I finished a packet, but I just assumed there were more in the cupboard."

"I'll be going to the store later. I can get you some then."

"That's no good. I've psyched myself up for some right now. Will the store be open yet?"

"Yeah, since they started selling magazines, they open at six o'clock."

"Great. I won't be long."

"Ever the optimist."

I was halfway to the village store when someone called out to me.

"You're an early bird, Jill."

"Good morning, Mr Ivers."

He was wearing a long overcoat, and if I wasn't mistaken, he had his pyjamas on underneath. His arm was still in a sling.

"Are you taking your early morning constitutional too?" he asked.

"No, I'm just off to the store for some essentials."

"I'm headed back there, so I'll walk with you if that's okay?"

"Sure. How are you finding living above the store?"

"It's okay. A little on the small side, as you saw, but enough for my needs. And I don't have far to go when I run out of supplies."

"How's your shoulder?"

"Much better. I can't wait to get back to work."

"Don't rush it. You need to make sure it's fully healed."

"Of course, but you know what it's like when you're self-employed. If you don't work, you don't get paid."

"I really am sorry about what happened."

"Don't be. It was just an unfortunate accident."

For such a weird little man, he could be remarkably

understanding. He could easily have blamed me for what happened to him, but he didn't.

So why do you lot?

When we reached the store, Mr Ivers went around the side of the building, to a separate door to his flat. Both sisters were on duty, but neither of them looked fully awake.

"Good morning, ladies."

Judging by the way they both jumped, they may actually have been dozing.

"Good morning, Jill." Cynthia yawned.

"What time is it?" Marjorie checked her watch.

"Are you two okay?"

"Just a little tired. These early mornings are starting to take their toll," Cynthia said.

"I told you the magazines were a bad idea," Marjorie sniped at her sister.

"No, you didn't. We both agreed it was a good idea."

"That's not how I remember it."

Just when I thought they'd buried the hatchet over the love triangle, it seemed they had found something else to squabble about.

"I'm just here for some—"

"If it's your cereal you're after, we have some good news for you," Marjorie said.

"Oh?"

"We had a bit of a rethink and came to the conclusion that not everyone wants to eat healthily, so we relented and have restocked on Strawberrycandy Pops. Not the other two flavours, though."

"Actually, I managed to get some from somewhere else."

"Not to worry. At least you know we have them the next time you run out."

"Where are the custard creams this week?"

"Custard creams?" They exchanged a look, and then Cynthia said, "I'm sorry to tell you this but—"

No! This could not be happening.

"Just kidding." She laughed. "They're at the far end of aisle five. In fact, we've increased our monthly order of them, just for you."

Phew!

"Did you get some?" Jack said and then glanced up. "Oh yeah, I see you've already eaten half a packet of them."

"Don't exaggerate. I've had three."

"So far."

"I saw Mr Ivers. He was taking an early morning walk. In his pyjamas."

"*Pyjamas*? In the street?"

"He had an overcoat over them."

"How is he?"

"Okay. He's keen to get back to work."

"It'll probably be a while yet."

"That's what I said. Guess what? The Stock sisters have decided to stock Strawberrycandy Pops again."

"It's a pity they didn't do that before you bought ten years' supply. Are you ever going to tell me where you've put them?"

"No."

***

The real Mrs V was back behind her desk.

"I wasn't expecting to see you for a few days. Are you sure you're okay?"

"Fit as a fiddle, dear. Once I'd purged that awful fish, I was okay."

"Even so, you should take it easy for the next few days."

"I will."

"A cup of tea would be nice."

What? She wouldn't have come into work if she couldn't make a brew, would she?

"I had such great hopes too." Winky sighed.

"About what?"

"I really thought the old bag lady had cast off her last stitch this time."

"That's an awful thing to say. You should be ashamed of yourself."

"I'm only saying out loud what you were thinking. I've seen the draft obituary, you wrote for her, in your drawer."

"That's a blatant lie. I did no such thing."

"Perhaps it's time to think about writing one."

"Be quiet. Don't you have damage limitation to do on Feline Social?"

"Nah, I got ahead of the game there. Everyone thinks Socks fell for one of my practical jokes."

"You're just like my grandmother."

"Ouch. You really know how to insult a guy."

"I meant that you're one of those people who always come up smelling of roses, just like her. Whereas I always come up smelling of dung."

"I've warned you before about buying that cheap knockoff perfume from the market."

I'd just finished my cup of tea when Kathy rang.

"Jill, I'm sorry to be a pest."

"Since when?"

"Funny. I was just wondering if you've had chance to come up with a plan to sort out my—err—problem?"

"Your ghost, you mean?"

"Have you?" She still couldn't bring herself to admit she believed in ghosts.

"Yes, but I'll need to spend some time in the shop alone."

"You can go there any night after we've closed."

"I need to do it during the daytime."

"Why?"

"Because I do. Do you want me to help or not?"

"Yes."

"Then let me do my thing."

"I can't just close the shop."

"Just for an hour or two you can. You can put up a notice on the door saying power cut or something."

"Okay. When?"

"Err, I'll need to get back to you on that."

"Alright, call me."

As soon as I'd finished on the call to Kathy, I sent a text to Lizzie. I didn't ring her because I figured she'd probably be in class. I was wrong because she called me within minutes.

"How did you manage to persuade Mum to close the shop?"

"I've always been able to wrap your mum around my little finger."

"I wish I could."

"When would work for you?"

"I have two consecutive study periods on Friday at two o'clock."

"Great. I'll tell your mother that I want her to close the shop at two-thirty. That'll give me time to make sure she's nowhere around. I'll send you a message when the coast is clear. Is that okay?"

"What happens if the ghost isn't there?"

"I'm hoping that between the two of us we'll be able to reach out to her."

"Okay."

"Great, I'll see you on Friday."

Despite Kathy's protests that Fridays were one of her busiest days, I got her to agree to close the shop between two and three thirty.

"Are you still feeling okay?" I asked Mrs V when she came through to collect my cup.

"Yes, thank you, dear."

"I have to ask. When Armi was here yesterday morning, I couldn't help but notice that he had a plaster on his nose—was that err—?"

"The clippers? Yes, I'm afraid so. He was feeling bad about our argument too, so after I'd left for work, he gave them a try. Most of his birthday cards are covered in blood."

"Oh dear." I really did try not to laugh, but I failed miserably.

Just then, Mr Brown walked into the outer office, with a manila folder under his arm.

"I hope it's okay to drop this off without an appointment." He handed me the folder.

"That was quick."

"I figured the sooner I got it to you, the sooner you'd be able to start. Nothing is more important in my life right now."

"Okay, thanks. I'll work my way through this and if any questions arise, I'll give you a call."

"Thanks, Jill."

I took the folder through to my office and opened it on my desk. Mr Brown may have been quick to respond to my request, but he hadn't skimped in the amount of information he'd included. I could have written a biography of his son based on the contents of the file. At the very top were numerous photographs of Max, starting when he was a child of five or six, and ending with one taken yesterday, according to the scribbled note on the reverse. I compared that final photo to one taken a year ago, and it was like looking at two different people. Max had been a fresh-faced, healthy-looking young man whose smile lit up the photograph. The pale, gaunt man staring into space in the final photo looked—*sad* didn't really do justice to it. Defeated was perhaps a better description.

An hour later, I'd barely managed to read half of the documents, and I was beginning to flag, so I decided to take a break and pay a visit to Cuppy C. One of the assistants was behind the counter; the twins were seated at a table at the far end of the tea room. They were too engrossed in something to notice my arrival.

"Hi, Jenny. The twins look busy."

"They've been at it on and off all day. I don't mind, though, I like working the counter. Caramel latte and a blueberry muffin?"

"I was just going to have a coffee but seeing as you're twisting my arm. Any idea what they're up to?"

"Not a clue." She grinned. "It's top secret, apparently. They said I wasn't to bother them unless it was an emergency."

"In that case, I probably should leave them in peace." Once I had my drink and cake, I walked over to where the twins were seated. "Good morning, girls. Room for a small one?" I took a seat opposite them, but before I could see what they were working on, Pearl had grabbed the paperwork and placed it on her lap. "What are you two up to?"

"Nothing." She shrugged.

"Let me see."

"No," Amber said.

"I knew it wouldn't last." I inhaled the blueberry deliciousness.

"Knew what wouldn't last?" Pearl demanded.

"It's only a few days since you said you'd done with madcap schemes. What was it you said? Oh yes, I remember: you were going to focus on your core business."

"This is about our core business," Pearl protested.

"Pearl!" Amber shot her sister a look. "Don't forget what we agreed."

"Sorry. She just winds me up."

"Look, if you don't want to tell me, that's cool, but don't blame me when your new crazy scheme backfires again."

"This is not a crazy scheme!" Amber snapped.

"Amber!" It was Pearl's turn to do the glaring.

"I'm sorry, but you know what she's like. She's not going to let it go until we tell her."

"Fine." Pearl laid out the paperwork on the table for me to see.

It was not what I'd expected.

Chapter 6

"Is this what I think it is?" I said. "Are you planning to revamp this place?"

"Yeah. A total makeover."

"Look at this." Amber opened a brochure and handed it to me.

"You're having new furniture too?"

"Yeah. New counter, new furniture and redecorated throughout." Pearl placed another sheet of paper on the table; it was an artist's impression of what the revamped Cuppy C would look like.

"I'm impressed, but it's going to be expensive."

"We believe it will pay for itself in the long run. And besides, the business that doesn't reinvent itself soon becomes extinct."

"Where did you read that?"

"It's true," Amber insisted.

"It's definitely better to spend money on this than on your more madcap schemes."

"You haven't seen the best part yet," Pearl said.

"There's more?"

Pearl had been holding back one large sheet of paper, which she now placed on the table. It appeared to be another artist's impression. "What do you think?"

"I don't understand. Is this from another angle? Where's the counter?"

"It isn't a different view," Amber said. "It's a different floor."

"Hang on. Are you telling me that you're going to extend the tea room upstairs?"

"Yeah, by our calculations, we'll double the number of

covers by doing that."

"Hold on, what about Bobby? You're not going to send him to Dragon Rescue, are you?"

"Of course not," Amber said. "We'd never do that."

"We had a long talk with him," Pearl said. "He's agreed that we can try and find him a new home through the Dragon Adoption Program. We'll miss him like crazy, obviously, but it would be better if he had a home where the people can spend more time with him than we're able to do."

"But I thought he was bringing in the punters?"

"That was true at first, but people are fickle, and the novelty has worn off. On average, he only gets a handful of people visiting him each week."

"As long as he's okay with it, I guess it's alright to find him a loving home," I said.

"We asked Mum," Pearl laughed. "But she said she already had enough on her plate with your two dogs and a tortoise."

"Converting upstairs too is going to cost a small fortune. How can you afford it?"

"We can't. That's why we have a meeting with our bank manager next week."

"You're going to take out a loan?"

"Not for the full amount, but yes."

"Do you think you'll get it?"

"When he sees our business plan, yes. It's not like we're launching a new business. We have a good track record."

"I don't know what to say."

The idea of them taking on a loan was a little scary, but if the added space increased takings, that shouldn't be an issue. I was actually jealous if I'm honest. My little business was pretty much the same now as when I'd taken over from my father. There was a time when I'd dreamed of growing the business and having offices throughout the country, but I was realistic enough to know that was never going to happen now.

"*You* don't know what to say? That's a first," Amber said and they both laughed.

"Seriously, though, girls, I admire your courage. It's a risk, but it's a calculated risk. I hope your meeting goes well."

"Thanks, Jill." Pearl beamed.

I'd finished my cake and coffee and was just thinking of leaving when Amber said, "What's all this about you getting a medal?"

"It was nothing."

"Yeah, that's pretty much what we heard," Amber chuckled.

"Okay, if you must know, I was given a medal for exceptional valour."

"Impressive," Pearl said whilst looking not the least bit impressed.

"Who was it who gave you the medal?" Amber asked.

"The king of the gnomes."

"*Gnomes*, eh?"

"What's funny about that?"

"Nothing. It must have been a big ceremony if the king himself presented it."

"It was amazing. No expense spared."

"And yet, I've not seen anything about it in the Candlefield press," Pearl said. "Have you, Amber?"

"Not a thing."

"The king said he'd rather there wasn't any publicity for

this kind of event."

"That's rather disappointing. Still, I can't wait to see the medal," Amber said.

"Me too." Pearl nodded. "When can we see it?"

"Unfortunately, the gnomes don't allow their medals to be taken out of the palace. They're kept in a display case there."

The twins exchanged a look and then broke into laughter.

"You're so full of it, Jill. Was there even a medal?"

"Of course there was. Why would I lie about something like that?"

"Is it really small?"

"I have to get back." I stood up.

"I bet it's so tiny you can hardly see it."

"Goodbye, girls."

I was beginning to wish I'd never been awarded that stupid medal. I had hoped it would boost my standing in the Candlefield community, but so far it had only succeeded in making me a laughing stock. I blamed the king of the gnomes. If he hadn't been so lazy and disorganised, I would have had a proper medal that I could have shown my doubters. As it was, all I had was a medal that had been intended for gnome scouts.

I was still chuntering away when I magicked myself back to the office.

"What's up with you?" Winky said.

"Nothing," I snapped.

"It doesn't sound like it. Come and look at this." He headed to the window and pointed across the road.

"I've already seen them working on the helipad."

"Not that. Look at the sign they've put up."

I walked over to the window and took a look. "Fun Rat? What's that?"

"Do you really not know?"

"No. Should I?"

"It's the newest and biggest social media company on the planet."

"Never heard of it. If it's such a big deal, why are they here in Washbridge? It's hardly the centre of the universe, is it?"

"They have offices everywhere. It does explain the helipad, though. Those tech people are absolutely minted."

I spent the rest of the afternoon studying the information that Charles Brown had provided, and by the time I'd finished, I felt like I had a good handle on his son, Max. A straight A student, he'd excelled in all his subjects at school, and had followed that by gaining a very respectable degree from one of the top universities. He was an all-round sportsman who had a large circle of friends. After university, he had chosen to return to Washbridge where he had taken a position at one of the top accountancy firms in the area. In summary, he was the kind of son any parent would have been proud of. What could have caused such a sudden and dramatic change in him? I already had my suspicions, but I hoped they proved to be wrong.

***

"What's up? Jack asked when I walked into the house.

"Nothing."

"Something is."

"I'm just being silly."

"Go and sit in the lounge, I'll make us both a cup of tea, and you can tell me all about it."

"A cup of tea would be nice. Where's Florence?"

"Upstairs, playing with her dragon egg."

"How did she get on at CASS?"

"Okay, I think, but all she could talk about was the dragon egg. Let me go and make the tea."

Over our drink, I told Jack all about the twins' plans to extend Cuppy C, and how that had made me realise that my own business had become stagnant.

"You have to be realistic, Jill. Most private investigators are one-man bands like yours."

"You're right, I know, but it would be nice to build a big business that I could pass on to Florence one day."

"Even if you did, she probably wouldn't be interested. Not many kids want to take over the family business like you did."

"I sometimes wonder what I would have ended up doing if I hadn't taken over the agency. I could have been a highflying lawyer, a brain surgeon or a venture capitalist."

"Do you even know what a venture capitalist is?"

"No, but I know they make tons of money."

"Money isn't everything."

"I know. Take no notice of me. It's just been one of those days. What's for dinner?"

"Steak and kidney pudding. Talking of which, I'd better make a start on it."

"Did you hear her, Mabel?" Wanda said. "Feeling sorry for herself again."

"I did, dear." Mabel tutted. "Pathetic."

"You two do realise I can hear you, don't you?"

"You need to get a grip, woman. You've got a lovely house, a husband who adores you, and a beautiful daughter. So what if your business isn't the most exciting thing in the world? I can guarantee you it's a lot more exciting than swimming around and around in a tank full of water all day."

"Yeah, we'd swap with you in a heartbeat."

"You're right, ladies." I stood up. "Sorry for being such a downer."

"I thought you were going to stay in the—" Before Jack could finish his sentence, I put my arms around him and gave him a kiss.

"I love you, Jack Maxwell. I'm sorry for being such a grouch."

"That's okay. I'm glad the cuppa did the trick."

"It wasn't the tea. It was the pep talk from the goldfish."

The three of us were at the kitchen table, eating dinner.

"Do you like my dragon's egg, Mummy?" The object in question had been given pride of place in the centre of the table.

"Err, yeah, it's very nice. What does it do?"

"It doesn't do anything, silly, it's just an egg."

"Right?"

Despite my criticism of the Wiz-A-Boo, it did at least do something, even if that something was just spinning around and making a booing sound. As far as I could make out the so-called dragon's egg was just an egg-shaped piece of—err—I wasn't actually sure what it was made of. Some kind of weird plastic that felt warm to the touch.

"I'm the only one who has a red one," Florence said, proudly. "Mandy said she wished hers was red."

"Did you do anything nice at CASS today?" I asked.

"Yeah, I got the dragon's egg."

"I meant apart from getting the dragon's egg?"

"We practised the doopcake spell some more. Mr Tomdrum said I'd made too many doopcakes."

"How many doop—err—duplicates did you make?"

"Tons. The classroom was full of Florences." She giggled.

Jack laughed too until I shot him a look. To be fair, I was having a tough time not laughing too. I could just picture the poor teacher when he was confronted with a room full of Florences.

"Did you do anything else?"

"Just boring stuff."

"Like?"

"We had to look at a book that had pictures of famous witches and wizards in it."

"I bet that was interesting."

"Nah, they were all old people. You were in there."

"Really?"

"I've finished my dinner. Can I go upstairs now?"

"Yes, you can."

She grabbed her dragon's egg and shot upstairs.

"Did you hear that, Jack. I'm in a book of famous witches and wizards?"

"The book full of old people, you mean?"

Once Florence was in bed, I decided to treat myself to a nice warm bath. It was the least I deserved after the hard day I'd had. And, as everyone knows, no warm bath is complete without chocolate and a small glass of wine. As soon as the water enveloped me, I could feel all the tensions of the day drifting away.

"Hi there," someone said.

I was so shocked I slid under the water. When I re-emerged, I saw the lubble at the far end of the bath.

"Simon?"

"Who's Simon? I'm Kevin. How come you can see me?"

"I wish I knew. What are you doing in my bath?"

"What's a bath?"

"Never mind. I assume you got here through the DLS thingy?"

"You mean LDS."

"Whatever. Will you leave, please?"

"How rude. I've got as much right to be here as you have. More, probably."

"We'll see about that." I grabbed the chain and pulled out the plug. "Bye, Kevin."

What do you mean that was *cruel*? It's me, not him, you should be feeling sorry for because my bath time had been ruined. Why, after all these years, had I suddenly started seeing lubbles?

As soon as I was dressed, I called Grandma.

"What do you want?" she snapped.

"You really should work on your telephone manner."

"I'm busy. What do you want?"

"Have you ever heard of lubbles?"

"Yes, why?"

"I've started to see them."

"What do you want? Another medal?"

"I was just wondering why it's suddenly started

happening?"

"It'll be the swooping cough."

"That can't be right. The first time I saw them was before I had swooping cough."

"Yes, but you probably already had the virus in your system."

"But I'm better now, so why am I still seeing them?"

"It's a permanent aftereffect of having the swooping cough."

"Are you telling me I'm always going to see them from now on?"

"Yes."

"But I—err—that's—"

"I have to go. My chiropodist is due any minute."

That was just dandy. If Grandma was right, every time I saw a body of water from now on, I'd have to put up with a load of lubbles. I would never be able to go swimming again. Or relax in a hot tub.

What? I know I hate hot tubs, but that's not the point.

"That was quick," Jack said when I joined him in the lounge. "I thought you were going to have a long, leisurely soak?"

"I had intended to but there were too many lubbles for my liking."

"You always put too much bubble bath in."

"Not *bubbles*. Lubbles."

"How much of that wine have you drunk?"

"Hardly any. Lubbles are weird little sups that live in water. The one in my bath just now was called Kevin. There were probably others too; they usually hang around in groups."

"Are you sure you're okay, Jill?"

"I'm fine. There were some in the flotation tank too. They're everywhere."

"How come you've never mentioned them before?"

"Because I couldn't see them until I contracted swooping cough."

"But I thought you were over that?"

"I am, but according to Grandma, this is a permanent aftereffect. I may never have a bath again."

Chapter 7

The next morning, I'd just stepped out of our bedroom when Florence came charging out of hers. Without so much as a word to me, she rushed downstairs like a bat out of hell. Jack was seated at the kitchen table, looking just as confused as I was.

"What's she up to?" he said.

"No idea. I thought you might know. She just came running through here and headed towards the lounge."

"I smell a rat."

We both set off for the lounge. At first glance, I didn't think she was in there, but then her head appeared above the sofa.

"Florence Maxwell, what are you doing?"

"Nothing, Mummy." She treated me to her best *butter wouldn't melt* smile.

"I don't think that's true, is it? Why did you come running downstairs and in here?"

"To see the fish."

"I don't think so. What are you really doing?"

"Looking for Digs."

"Who's Digs?"

"My baby dragon."

"Did you use magic on the toy dragon egg?"

"No."

"Florence!"

"I promise, Mummy. When I woke up this morning, the egg was cracking, then Digs popped out."

"How do you know his name is Digs?" Jack asked. My husband had a knack for asking the most irrelevant questions.

"He told me," Florence said.

"He can talk?"

"Yeah."

"Where did you last see him?" I asked.

"He was on my bed. He promised to stay there while I went to the toilet, but he was gone when I got back."

"Great. Okay, let's split up. Jack, you and Florence search down here, and I'll check upstairs."

"What do we do if we find him?" Jack said.

"Offer him a cup of tea and some toast."

"Really?"

"No, not really! Put him in a box and make sure he can't escape. Come on, we're wasting time. Let's go."

I hurried upstairs and started with Florence's bedroom.

"Here, dragon. Nice dragon. I've got some yummy dragon food for you."

Nothing.

Next, I tried our bedroom, looking underneath the bed, behind the bedside cabinets and even in the wardrobes.

Still nothing.

If he was in the spare bedroom, it would take hours to find him, so I decided to check the bathroom first, but before I could, Jack yelled from downstairs. I took the stairs two at a time, a little apprehensive about what would be waiting for me.

"What's he doing?" I said.

"Eating your Strawberrycandy Pops."

"I can see that, but why?"

"He didn't like the muesli."

"Understandable, but not the point. Why isn't he in a box?"

"Look at him, Jill," Jack said. "He's only a baby."

"Yes, a baby *dragon*."

"These are yummy," the dragon said.

"Isn't he cute, Mummy?" Florence was clearly taken with him.

"He's a dragon! Dragons aren't cute."

"He kind of is," Jack said.

"Where can we keep him?" Florence asked.

"*We* can't keep him anywhere. He has to go back to CASS."

"But he's mine. I bought him with my pocket money."

"I know that, but dragons can't live here."

"Why not?" the dragon asked.

"How come you can talk when you're just a baby?"

"We dragons have big brains." He looked around. "Where am I, anyway?"

"In the old watermill," Florence said. "It's our house."

"Cool, I like the food here."

"Don't get used to it because you aren't staying," I said.

"Why not? I'm no trouble. You won't even know I'm here."

"There are no dragons here in the human world."

"Cool, I'll be a celebrity."

"I'm afraid that's not going to happen because you're going back to the sup world."

"I think we should take a vote," Digs said.

"Hold on. You don't get to—"

"All those in favour of letting me stay here, raise their hand."

Unsurprisingly, Florence raised her hand. The dragon raised one of his front feet.

"All those against?"

My hand flew up.

"Can I abstain?" Jack said, but one look at me told him that wasn't an option, so he raised his hand.

"Deadlock," Digs said. "Guess that means I stay."

"Yay!" Florence whooped.

"No, it doesn't. And, anyway, the vote is irrelevant. You're going back and that's all there is to it."

"But where will I live? I don't have any family. I can't survive alone."

"He has a point," said Jack, the bleeding heart.

"Okay. You can stay, but only until I find you a family to live with. Agreed?"

"Deal." Digs nodded.

"Cool," Florence said. "Can I take him to school?"

"No, you can't. He isn't allowed to leave the house under any circumstances. Any questions?"

"Can I have some more of this stuff?" Digs had eaten all of the cereal.

"Sure," Jack poured him another bowl full. "It's not like we don't have plenty."

Once the dragon had eaten his second helping of cereal, Florence took him upstairs to her bedroom.

"Do you believe Florence?" Jack said. "Do you think the dragon really did hatch naturally?"

"I'm not sure, but I intend to find out. I'm going to pay another visit to CASS later today."

"How are you going to find somewhere for him to live? You're not going to ask your Aunt Lucy again, are you?"

"No, she's already made it clear that she won't be adopting any dragons."

***

"Are you still feeling okay, Mrs V?" I said.

"Never better, dear, which is more than I can say for that cat of yours."

"Winky? What's wrong with him?"

"When I came in this morning, I heard the most awful noise coming from your office. I thought he must be dying, but he was just snoring. I've never heard anything like it." Just then, an awful noise came from next door. "See what I mean?"

"I'd better check on him."

Winky was flat out on the sofa. I'd heard him snore before, but nothing like this, so I gave him a nudge.

"Winky, wake up!"

"What?" He didn't even open his eye.

"Wake up." I shook him again. "What's the matter with you?"

That did the trick because he jumped to his feet. "What? Where's the fire?"

"You were making the most awful noise."

"My head hurts."

"Are you poorly?"

"Nah, just a heavy night."

"Have you got a hangover?"

"No, but my head is pounding, and my mouth feels like a cockroach just crawled in there and died."

"That's pretty much the definition of a hangover. What were you doing last night?"

"I went out with Socks."

"Where?"

"Where didn't we go, that would be the question."

"What time did you get back?"

"What time is it now?"

"Eight-thirty."

"About an hour ago."

"You were out all night?"

"Yeah." He managed to get down from the sofa, and then crawled underneath it. "Please don't disturb me again until the new year."

I knew it. Whenever that brother of his was around, there was trouble.

My recent experience of visiting royalty had left a bad taste in my mouth, so it was with some trepidation that I prepared to pay a visit to meet Stella, princess of the Yellas. Before magicking myself to the palace, I used the 'shrink' spell to make myself a similar size to Ralph.

Just like the Yellas themselves, the palace was also red. I'd visited a few royal residents in Candlefield, but this was undoubtedly the most impressive. The red walls were encrusted with red jewels, which surely couldn't be real rubies, could they? The huge doors to the palace were a contrasting, lighter shade of red. Ralph had said he would meet me there but there was no sign of him. I couldn't see a doorbell, so I was just about to knock when one of the two doors started to open.

"I'm so sorry that I wasn't here to greet you." Ralph beckoned me inside. "I was delayed by Anton—he's the royal family's chef, and between you and me, a real pain in the bum."

"That's okay. I'd only just arrived when you opened the door." I took a moment to take in the enormous entrance hall. "This place is amazing. I never realised there were so many different shades of red."

"The queen designed it herself. Princess Stella is waiting

for you in the royal family's private suite if you'd like to follow me."

He led the way up the imperial staircase and down a corridor that was so long, I could barely see the other end. When we were about a third of the way down, I became aware of a sort of rumbling noise that grew gradually louder. The palace had otherwise been almost silent, and I assumed there must be some kind of construction work taking place.

Ralph stopped outside a pair of double doors, knocked, but didn't wait for a response before leading the way inside. The room was actually a large office with (unsurprisingly) red sofas on either side, and a large desk facing the door.

"You must be Jill Maxwell." The pretty Yella stood up, came around the desk and offered her hand.

"I'm very pleased to meet you, Your Majesty."

"Please, none of that *Your Majesty* rubbish." She shook her head. "Call me Stella."

"Right. I was just commenting to Ralph what a beautiful home you have here."

"It's certainly a beautiful building, but it isn't my home. I normally live in an apartment across town, but I moved back here when my mother—err—I assume Ralph explained her predicament?"

"He said that she's been asleep for several weeks and no one can wake her."

"That's correct as far as it goes, but it isn't a natural sleep."

"You suspect foul play?"

"I do, which is why you're here. I'm hoping you'll be able to find out what happened to cause this, and who is behind it."

"I'll certainly do my best."

"Excellent. It might be best if we start by paying a visit to my mother, so you can see her for yourself."

"Okay."

"Just one moment." She went back behind the desk, opened one of the drawers and took something out. "Here, you'll need these." She handed me a pair of ear defenders, which I thought a little strange until I remembered the construction work that I'd heard outside in the corridor.

Before putting her ear defenders on, she told Ralph he could leave us. I followed Stella out of the office, and we continued down the corridor. Even with the ear defenders, I could still hear a low rumbling sound that got progressively louder the further we went. I figured that the construction work, whatever it was, must be a major undertaking to make so much noise. If the queen could sleep through that racket, she really must have a serious problem.

I was about to ask Stella what the construction work was when she stopped outside a door near the end of the corridor.

"Mother is in here," she mouthed and then led the way inside.

Once inside the luxurious bed chamber my question about the construction work became redundant because I could now see that the source of the ear-piercing noise was the woman lying beneath red satin sheets in the huge bed.

Stella gestured for me to stand on one side of the bed while she stood on the opposite side. The queen looked perfectly healthy; there was nothing to suggest that she had been asleep for weeks. I had several questions, but holding a conversation, with or without the ear defenders, would have been impossible. We stood there for a couple of minutes before Stella gestured that we should take our leave. Once we were back in her office, we both removed the ear defenders.

"Why don't I get us a drink and then we can talk," she said. "We have tea and coffee, or you could try yellberry juice."

"Err—" I hesitated.

"I promise you'll like yellberry juice; it's amazing."

"Sure, why not? I'll give it a try."

Stella made a call, then we made small talk for the couple of minutes that it took for the drinks to arrive. The yellberry juice was wonderfully refreshing and like nothing I'd ever tasted before.

"This is fantastic."

"I'll have Ralph send you a crate of it."

"That's very kind. Thanks."

"So, we probably should get down to business. What do you think, Jill?"

"If I hadn't known, I would have thought your mother was just enjoying a normal sleep. She looks like she could wake up at any moment."

"I know. And for the first couple of days, I thought she would."

"She looks healthy enough."

"She is. Her physicians check on her every day. All her vital signs are fine."

I decided it was time to address the elephant in the room. "Does your mother usually snore so loud?"

Stella smiled. "Goodness no. I'm not sure I've ever heard her snore at all before this happened."

"I've never heard anything quite like it. Is it like that all the time?"

"More or less. Occasionally, it stops, but it's only for a few seconds, and then it starts up again."

"Strange. Can you tell me more about the period leading up to when this first started?"

"What do you mean? What exactly do you want to know?"

"Had your mother been acting strangely at all?"

"No. We had lunch together on the Thursday and she was her usual happy self. When her handmaid came to see me the next morning, to tell me she couldn't wake my mother, I knew something was wrong because my mother is usually a light sleeper and an early riser."

"Were there any other issues that had been troubling her?"

"She's the queen. There are always things for her to deal with in the kingdom, as I've found out over the last few weeks. But she took it all in her stride."

"Do you have any siblings?"

Her eyeroll said more than her answer. "I have a brother called Michael."

"Who is next in line to the throne?"

"I am. Michael is three years younger than me."

"Will I be able to speak to him?"

"You can try. He rarely visits the palace except when he needs money."

"I get the impression that you and he aren't close?"

"That would be an understatement."

"If I'm to carry out this investigation, I'll require access to all areas and to be able to speak to anyone I choose. Will that be a problem?"

"Absolutely not. I've already issued instructions along those lines. Unfortunately, because of the demands upon my time, I may not always be available, so I have asked Ralph to be your point of contact. Anything you need, ask him. If something really important crops up that requires my attention, I will of course make myself available. How does that sound?"

"Perfect."

"Great." She picked up the phone. "Ralph, can you come to my office, please?" Less than a minute later, he appeared. "I've told Jill that you will be her first point of contact."

"Yes, Your Highness."

"Anything she needs, make sure she gets it."

"I will."

"If that's everything, Jill, I have a meeting in ten minutes."

"Yes, that's fine. Thanks for your time."

Ralph led the way out of her office, down the corridor and back down the stairs.

"Is there anything you need me to do right now?" he asked.

"Can you arrange for me to meet with the queen's private physician and with Stella's brother."

"I'll try." He seemed unsure.

"Is there a problem?"

"Arranging a meeting with the physician is no problem. Prince Michael, though—"

"What?"

"We barely know where he is most of the time, and

even if I manage to find him, there's nothing to say he'll cooperate. He can be—err—"

"Awkward?"

"I was going to say a pain in the backside. I'll give you a call when I've managed to set something up."

"Great, thanks, Ralph."

Chapter 8

According to Florence, the toy egg she'd purchased from the shop at CASS had hatched of its own accord, but I still had a sneaking suspicion that she might have used magic. Either way, I wasn't okay with her having a baby dragon as a pet.

After leaving the Yella palace, I magicked myself over to CASS.

"Hello, Jill." The receptionist greeted me with a smile. "I was hoping you might pop over some time."

"Oh?"

"My niece, Mandy, is a big fan of yours, and she asked me if I could get your autograph." She opened one of her drawers and took out a photo of me seated on a dragon. "I hope you don't mind."

"Not at all."

"If you could just write 'To Mandy'."

"Sure." I signed the photo and handed it back to her.

"Thanks. I'll be her favourite auntie now. What can I do for you?"

"I'd like to see the headmistress if she's free."

"I'll just check." She made a call and then confirmed I could go straight to the headmistress' office.

"It's lovely to see you again, Jill." Hildegard Bogart was at the top of a ladder, which ran back and forth along the bookcase that took up half of her office. "Do take a seat. I won't be a minute. I'm trying to find Frogs and Their Place in the History of Magic by Candida Justso. Have you read it?"

"I can't say I have."

"A fascinating read. Total nonsense of course, but

riveting, nonetheless." She ran her fingers along the spines of the books on the top shelf. "No, it's not here. Someone must have borrowed it." Instead of walking down the steps, she slid down the ladder and took a seat behind her desk. "Now, to what do I owe this pleasure?"

"I promise I won't keep you long. I just wanted to ask you a question."

"Fire away."

"Florence bought a—"

"I hear wonderful things about that daughter of yours."

"She seems to be enjoying it so far."

"And doing remarkable things, by all accounts. Sorry, Jill, I interrupted you."

"I was saying that she bought a toy dragon's egg from the shop here at CASS."

"The new shop seems to be quite a hit with the pupils, and it has certainly provided a much needed boost to our fundraising efforts."

"That's good. Anyway, the thing is that last night, the dragon's egg hatched."

"I thought you said it was a toy?"

"It was supposed to be, but I now have a baby dragon, which is running around my house."

"That's unfortunate. Those creatures are practically impossible to house train."

Great. I was probably going to go home to a house smelling of dragon poo.

"I wanted to speak to you, to see if you knew anything about this."

"Specifically?"

"Is the school deliberately selling real dragon's eggs?"

"Definitely not. At least, not to the best of my

knowledge, but I'll investigate. We can't have baby dragons roaming the dormitories."

"Thank you. In the meantime, do you have any suggestions as to what I can do with the baby dragon that's running around my house?"

"Have you tried Dragon Rescue?"

"That was my first thought, but they don't accept baby dragons, and they don't know anyone who does."

"Sorry, Jill, I don't have any other bright ideas, but I will check with the school shop to see if I can find out what's going on."

"And you'll let me know?"

"Of course."

***

"Penny for them," Winky said.

"I'm trying to think who might want to adopt a baby dragon."

"As you do. How come you have a baby dragon?"

"Florence brought a toy dragon egg home from school, but it turned out to be real, so I now have a little dragon pooing all over my house."

"Can't you just dump it somewhere?"

"*Dump it*?"

"Yeah. Just drive out into the country and kick it out of the car. No one will ever trace it back to you."

"I'm not doing that, and I can't believe you could be so heartless."

"It was a joke. Sheesh. I can remember when you used to have a sense of humour."

"I'm under a lot of pressure at the moment. Haven't you

got something you should be doing?"

"Socks and I are going out again tonight, so I'll probably get my head down for a couple of hours."

"That brother of yours will be the death of you."

Mrs V came through to my office and closed the door behind her. "You spend too much time talking to that cat, Jill."

"You're not wrong."

"I have a Mr Albert Bert outside."

"Albert Bert?"

She handed me his card:

Albert Bert - Partner

Bert, Hurt and Pert - Solicitors

"Did he say what it was about?"

"He just said he represented Harmony Fashion."

Oh bum!

"Ask him what he'd like to drink and then show him in, please."

"Do you want a drink too?"

"Only if he has one."

She disappeared out of the office and then returned followed by a diminutive man, wearing a grey suit.

"Mr Bert? I'm Jill Maxwell. Won't you have a seat?"

"Thank you."

"Is my receptionist getting you a drink?"

"I declined her offer. I'd prefer to get straight down to business."

"Of course. How can I help you?"

"You need to read this." He took an envelope out of his briefcase and handed it to me.

I ripped it open and skimmed the first page.

"Harmony are suing me?"

"That is correct."

"Why?"

"I suggest you read the whole of the document."

"That will take me all afternoon. Can't you give me the Cliff notes version?"

"In short, you are being sued for the damage you did to my client's brand and reputation. Additionally, for obtaining a dress free of charge under false pretences."

"But, but—err—it was all a misunderstanding. Nothing more than that."

"In which case, I suggest you brief your own solicitor accordingly. You do have a solicitor, I assume?"

"Err, yes, of course."

"Excellent." He stood up. "I will look forward to hearing from them soon. Good day, Mrs Maxwell."

"Err, goodbye."

Oh bum! Times one thousand. This could not be happening.

"Everything okay, Jill?" Mrs V said.

"Not really. I need a good lawyer. Do you think Armi might be able to help?"

"He's retired."

"He's still registered as a lawyer, though, isn't he?"

"Yes, but he hasn't—"

"I'm really desperate, Mrs V. Will you at least ask him?"

"Alright, but don't go getting your hopes up."

***

Jack didn't look very happy.

"What's up?" I said.

"Do you have any idea how many times a baby dragon

does poopoo?"

"*Poopoo*?"

"Every hour, that's how often. And he doesn't much care where he does it. I've spent most of the day cleaning up after him. Please tell me you've found a home for him."

"I'm afraid not."

"Jill!"

"I've been trying. And, anyway, you're not the only one who's had a bad day."

"Why? What's happened?"

"I'm being sued."

"Who by? What for?"

"Harmony Fashion."

"I knew it. You can't blame them."

"You're supposed to be on my side."

"You made them look like idiots. What are you going to do?"

"It's okay. Armi is going to represent me. He's bound to get the case thrown out."

"I thought he'd retired?"

"He has, but he's going to come out of retirement to help me."

"Has he said he'll represent you?"

"Not yet. Where's Florence?"

"Outside. I made her take Digs out there before he does more poopoo inside."

"Please stop saying *poopoo*."

"What would you have me call it?"

"Anything but that."

I found Florence at the far end of the garden, on her hands and knees, looking under a bush.

"What are you doing, darling?"

"Digs won't come out. He's been in there for ages."

"Here, let me try." I crouched down and peered under the bush. "I don't see him."

"That's where he was."

"How long has he been under there?"

She shrugged.

I got down on my hands and knees so I could get a closer look, but there was still no sign of the baby dragon.

"Where's he gone, Mummy?" Florence began to well up.

"He can't be far away. Don't worry." I headed back inside. "Jack, when was the last time you saw the dragon?"

"I'm not sure. About half an hour ago, I think. Why?"

"Florence thought he was under the bush at the far end of the garden, but there's no sign of him."

"He must be somewhere in the garden." He hesitated. "Unless—"

"Unless *what*?"

"Can baby dragons climb?"

Oh bum!

"I don't know."

"Digs does have really sharp claws." Jack noted. "Maybe he—"

"Go out there and look for him." I headed past him towards the front door.

"Where are you going?"

"To check if our baby dragon is running amok in the village. If you find him in the garden, message me. Okay?"

"Okay."

This day was going from bad to badder.

And before you lot ask, I don't care what the dictionary police say—badder is definitely a real word.

Where to start? That was the question. Come on, Jill, think! If Florence was right that Digs had been in the bush, then he would most likely have scaled the fence at the far side of the house, so I started there.

Claw marks!

The little monster must have scrambled up the fence behind the bush and then slid down this side.

"What are you doing?"

I spun around to find Grandma eyeing me quizzically.

"Have you seen a dragon?"

"What kind of question is that? I've seen hundreds of them."

"No, I mean have you seen one just now. A baby one."

"What would a dragon be doing in Middle Tweaking?"

I told her that Florence had brought home what was supposedly a toy dragon's egg from CASS, and that Digs had hatched from it.

"*Digs*? What kind of name is that for a dragon?"

"His name isn't important. I have to find him before someone else sees him. Will you help me look for him?"

"Me? Why should I help?"

"Because I'm your granddaughter."

"Nah, that's not a good enough reason."

"Please."

"If I do, you'll owe me a favour."

"I'm not putting cream on your bunions."

"You don't get to choose what favours you have to do in return. Agreed?"

"Okay, but we have to find that dragon quickly."

"This one?" She took a tiny dragon from her pocket and held it out to me. It was definitely Digs, but she must have shrunk him because he was no bigger than my thumb.

"Where did you find him?"

"It's lucky for you that I was the one walking down the street when he came over the fence. Just think what might have happened if he'd attacked a human."

"Why didn't you tell me you had him straight away?"

"Because that way, you wouldn't have been in my debt."

"You can't expect me to honour that."

"I most certainly do. You said if I found the dragon that you'd do me a favour in return. And I found the dragon."

"But I—you—"

"I'm afraid I don't have time to hang around and shoot the breeze with you. I have a hotel to run." And with that, she left.

I put Digs in my pocket and went back inside the house.

"He's not in the garden," Jack said. "What are we going to do?"

"Relax, I've got him in my pocket." I took the miniature dragon out, making sure to keep a firm grip of his legs.

"Where was he?"

"Grandma was passing by, and she caught him."

"That was lucky."

"Not for me."

"What do you mean?"

"Nevermind. We have to find a home for this guy."

"Florence won't be happy."

"I don't care. There's no way we can have a dragon here in the village."

"Who will take him in?"

"I might have an idea, but first I need a small box."

"What for?"

"To put this guy in."

"Hang on." Jack went to the cupboard, took out my box of Strawberrycandy Pops, and poured them into a Tupperware bowl. "Put him in here."

The smell of the Strawberrycandy Pops meant Digs didn't need any cajoling to get inside.

"Okay, I'll be back in a second. Wish me luck."

"Good luck."

I magicked myself to Everything Reptile from where I'd purchased Rhymes some years ago. Just as on my previous visit, the shop was deserted.

"Hello? Anyone in?" I shouted.

"Just a minute." Moments later, a man appeared behind the counter. "Hello again."

"You remember me?"

"Of course. I never forget a customer. How is your tortoise?"

"Rhymes is doing really well, thank you. It's Truman, isn't it?"

"That's right. Truman Turtle at your service."

"I was hoping you might be interested in taking something off my hands."

"Oh? What's that?"

I opened one of the flaps of the box and gently extracted the baby dragon. "This is Digs."

"Gosh!" Truman stared at the creature in disbelief. "I've never seen a dragon as tiny as that."

"He's not really that small. I had to shrink him to make sure he didn't do a runner. I can reverse the 'shrink' spell if you like."

"That won't be necessary. I'm afraid I can't buy him from you."

"I wouldn't want any payment. You can have him free of charge."

"It's not the money. Dragons aren't really my thing."

"They're reptiles, surely."

"That's open to debate, but either way, I don't deal in them. You need Everything Dragons."

"I had no idea there was such a shop. Where is it?"

"Out of town. It's run by another one of my cousins, Elsie Wyvern."

"Could you give me directions?"

"Of course, and I can give her a call to tell her that you're on your way if you like?"

"That would be great. Thanks."

After putting Digs back in the cereal box, I made my way out of town, following the directions that Truman had provided. Everything Dragon was well and truly in the back of beyond. The shops at either side of it were boarded up and looked like they'd been that way for several years. From the outside, there was nothing to tell what the shop was. The sign above the window simply read E.D., and the window was empty. The door creaked as I stepped inside. Unlike the other 'Everything' shops I'd visited, there were no animals on display. In fact, the shop was empty other than the counter, behind which stood an elderly witch.

"Are you Elsie?"

"I am." She glanced at the cereal box under my arm. "Truman said you were coming over."

"I'm Jill. Did he tell you what I wanted?"

"He did. Can I see him?"

"Of course." Once again, I took Digs out of the box. "I used magic to shrink him."

"Do you think you could reverse the spell, please?"

"No problem, but you'll have to watch he doesn't do a runner."

"Don't worry." She took the baby dragon in her hand. "I'm used to handling these little minxes."

As soon as I'd reversed the spell, Digs tried to make a break for it, but he had met his match in Elsie.

"He's a handsome guy," she said. "Can I ask where you got him?"

I explained that Florence had bought a dragon's egg, thinking it was a toy, but then Digs had hatched from it.

"Makes sense." She nodded.

"Not to me. Would you care to explain?"

"You may or may not be aware that it's illegal to buy or sell dragon's eggs."

"I didn't know that."

"That doesn't mean it doesn't happen. It just means the traders have had to become more inventive. One of the ways they get around the law is to hide real dragon's eggs in batches of toy eggs. The toys are so realistic nowadays that it's practically impossible to tell the difference. They will usually put one or two real eggs in a batch of up to a thousand toy eggs. Once the toy eggs are in the shops, they purchase the real ones before anyone else can."

"How do they know which ones are the real ones?"

"Although they look identical, the seasoned trader can spot the real ones. You said your daughter got hers from CASS?"

"That's right."

"They clearly hadn't expected the eggs to be sent there.

They're used to retrieving the eggs from shops in and around Candlefield. They can do that without attracting any attention. They couldn't just walk into CASS."

"Do you think there might be others in the CASS shop?"

"It's possible."

"I assume you'd be able to recognise them?"

"Of course."

"If I cleared it with the headmistress, would you be willing to go over there and take a look?"

"Absolutely. I've heard lots of stories about CASS. I'd love to see it for myself."

"Excellent. And what about this guy? Can you take him off my hands?"

"Willingly. I'll find him a good home."

I glanced around the empty shop. "Where do you keep your—err—stock?"

"I don't keep any dragons here on the premises. Their location is kept a secret."

"Oh?"

"As I mentioned before, it's illegal to buy or sell dragon's eggs. It's also illegal to buy or sell dragons except to registered individuals or organisations. Obtaining a licence to keep a dragon is quite an onerous procedure."

"But you still think you'll be able to find a home for Digs?"

"Yes, you don't need to worry about that. In fact, I already have someone in mind."

"That's great. I'll give you a call after I've spoken to the headmistress at CASS."

"I'll look forward to hearing from you."

"No luck?" Jack was looking at the cereal box in my hand.

"Mission accomplished." I turned the box upside down to show it was empty. "Digs has a new home."

"Brilliant. Well done you. Now, how are we going to tell Florence?"

"How are *you* going to tell her, you mean. I've done my bit by rehoming the dragon."

Chapter 9

Unsurprisingly, Florence hadn't reacted well to the news that Digs had been rehomed, but by the next morning, she seemed to have got over it. Mainly because we had refunded her pocket money, which meant she could now buy the Bluebottle Girl book. While Jack had been breaking the news about Digs to Florence, I had spoken to the headmistress at CASS and explained what Elsie Wyvern had told me about the real dragon eggs being smuggled in amongst the toy ones. She was horrified and said she would take the remaining ones off sale until they had been examined and given the all-clear by Elsie. She also asked me to refund Florence's payment. I'd given Florence the option to use the refund to buy another toy dragon's egg, once they had been checked and cleared, but she was already over that particular craze and was adamant that she would prefer the book.

"Please stop buzzing, Florence," I said.

She'd been buzzing ever since she'd joined us for breakfast.

"I'm Bluebottle Girl."

"I'm sure even she doesn't buzz while she's eating her breakfast."

"When can I get my book?"

"We can all go into Washbridge after you've been to dancing tomorrow," Jack said.

"I'm afraid I can't." I sighed. "I've got a meeting with Jack Maxwell, remember."

Florence gave me a puzzled look.

"I don't mean your daddy. It's another man with the same name."

“Not to worry, pumpkin,” Jack said. “You and I will go and get the book, then we can get lunch at Big Burger.”

“Can I have the Kid’s box?”

“Sure.”

“Yay!”

As soon as Florence had finished her toast, she jumped down from the table and buzzed her way upstairs.

“It’s a pity you can’t come with us tomorrow,” Jack said.

“There’s not much I can do about it, I’m afraid. Have you got any plans for today?”

“There’s a careers fair in West Chipping in the community rooms. I thought I might take a drive over there and see if there’s anything of interest. What about you?”

“I’m ghost hunting with Lizzie this afternoon.”

“Your days always sound much more exciting than mine.”

***

“You have to do something about that cat,” Mrs V said. “He’s been meowing like that ever since I arrived. It’s giving me a headache.”

What sounded like meowing to Mrs V was actually Winky singing.

“I’ll sort him out. Did you ask Armi about my case?”

“I did, but he isn’t very keen. Not because he doesn’t want to help you; he does. It’s just not really his area of expertise.”

“Did he say no, though?”

“No, he said he would do it if you’re desperate, but he

highly recommends that you hire someone more qualified."

"I'm desperate. I'm definitely desperate. Will you ask him when would be a good time to discuss the matter? I can come to your place if that's easiest."

"Okay, dear, I'll ask him. Now, can you please shut that cat up or I'll have to go home."

"I'm on it."

Winky was singing the same few lyrics on loop: *I'm in the money, I'm in the money.* He was dancing too. If you could call it that.

"Winky! Stop!"

"Good morning, Jill. Isn't it a wonderful day?"

"What's going on?"

"There's no better way to start the day than with song and dance. Would you care to join in?"

"No, and I don't want to hear any more from you. That awful racket you're making is giving Mrs V a headache."

"The old bag lady wouldn't know a good tune if it hit her in the face with one of her knitting needles."

"And why are you so happy?"

"Because, as the song goes, I'm in the money."

"How come?"

"Socks and I won big at the casino. Well, to be precise, Socks won, but we agreed beforehand that we'd share all our winnings."

"How much did you win?"

"Ten big ones."

"Ten thousand?"

"Yep, five grand each."

"What did you win it on?"

"The golden wheel."

"Roulette?"

"Yeah. Socks had an amazing lucky streak. Whatever he bet on came up trumps."

"Where's the cash, then?"

"Socks took it home with him. We're going to divvy it up later."

"You trusted him with your share of the money?"

"Why wouldn't I? We're family."

Winky was supposed to be smart, but he definitely had a blind spot when it came to his brother. I hoped he didn't live to regret the trust he had placed in him.

I'd read and reread the file that Mr Brown had prepared on his son, Max, but there was only so much you could glean from reading. I wanted to meet his son face-to-face, so I gave Charles Brown a call.

"Max is still in bed." He sighed. "As usual. He rarely surfaces during the daytime these days."

"Okay. Do you think you could make yourself scarce so he's alone in the house when I call around?"

"I can, but I can't guarantee he'll drag himself out of bed to answer the door."

"It's worth a try."

"Okay. I'll get changed and then drive into town. How long will you need, do you think?"

"Not long. An hour should be plenty of time."

"No more singing while I'm gone," I warned Winky on my way out. "Mrs V, I'm going to see Mr Brown's son and this afternoon, I'll be at Kathy's shop. I'm going to help out for a couple of hours while she has to go out."

"Oh?" She looked surprised. "Did your sister ask you to step in?"

"Yes. Why?"

"Nothing. It's just that I've never pictured you working in retail, but I'm sure you'll do fine."

With that overwhelming vote of confidence still ringing in my ears, I took my leave.

Charles Brown lived in a modest sized house on a leafy street in Underwash. I'd tried the doorbell a couple of times without any luck, so I hammered on the door. That too met with no response. I knew Max Brown was at home, so either he was ignoring me, or he was asleep. Either way, I had no intention of giving up, so I made my way around the back of the house. There was a fence that bordered the rear garden, which meant I didn't have to worry about the neighbours seeing me. There was no sign of life through the rear windows or patio doors, so rather than wasting any more time, I magicked myself inside. A quick check around the rooms on the ground floor confirmed Max wasn't there, so I made my way upstairs. I found him in the second room I tried. Lying on his back on the bed, fast asleep, he was dressed in shorts and a black t-shirt. He looked even worse than in the latest photograph his father had given me. His pale complexion emphasised the dark circles around his eyes; his lips were cracked and dry.

"Max!"

No response.

"Max, wake up!"

When he still didn't stir, I began to think he might be under the influence of something, so I looked around the room, but there was no sign of a needle, powder or pills. His chest of drawers was full of nothing more than clothes. If he was using, he didn't appear to be keeping the gear in his room.

I tried again to wake him, but he was as dead to the world as Queen Bella. Just because there was no drug paraphernalia, didn't mean he wasn't high. Maybe I'd find evidence on his body, so I checked his arms and legs, but there were no track marks. I was just about to try one last time to wake him when I noticed something on the side of his neck. There were two faint puncture wounds, but not the kind that would have been inflicted by a needle.

Oh bum!

Somewhat stunned, I magicked myself outside. The puncture wounds on Max's neck were undoubtedly the result of a vampire attack. No wonder the poor boy's personality had changed out of all recognition.

Suddenly, the nature of this case had changed completely. Charles Brown had hired me to find out what had caused the dramatic change in his son. I now knew the answer to that question, but there was no way I could tell him the truth. In the unlikely event that he believed me, what good would it do? At best, he would be forever frustrated that he was unable to help his son. At worst, it would drive a wedge between father and son forever.

I had to find out how it had happened. Turning a human was one of the most serious crimes a vampire could commit. I wanted to know who had done it, and make sure they faced the full force of the law in Candlefield. More importantly, though, I had to find a way for father and son to live together in harmony. That was not going to be easy.

I considered going back to the office, but I couldn't bear the thought of Winky bragging about his casino winnings, so after picking up a healthy snack for lunch (hotdog), I made my way to Kathy's bridal shop. I'd told Lizzie to be somewhere close by, and that I would call her once her mother had left the shop.

"I'm really not happy about this, Jill," Kathy said. "Closing down the shop on a Friday afternoon is a terrible idea. I don't know why I let you talk me into it."

"You were the one who contacted me in the first place, remember?"

"I know, but maybe I was a bit hasty. I haven't seen—err—that thing since I came to see you."

"That thing is called a ghost."

"There's no such thing."

"It's up to you. I've got tons of work on at the moment, so I can leave now if you like. One thing, though, if the ghost does come back, don't come running to me. This is your one and only chance. So, what's it to be?"

She glanced back at the stockroom. "Okay, I suppose I could put a notice on the door saying I'll be back at four o'clock."

"Good plan."

It took her four attempts before she was happy with the wording for the notice, but eventually she stuck it on the door, and left me alone in the shop. I wasn't totally convinced that Kathy wouldn't change her mind and come running back, so I gave it ten minutes before I called Lizzie.

"I was beginning to think Mum had changed her mind," Lizzie said when she came through the door.

"She nearly did." I locked the door and the two of us

headed for the stockroom. "Are you sure she won't find out you've skipped school? She'll have my guts for garters if she knows I've involved you in this."

"I'm sure. She'll never find out."

"Good. Well, this is your show. Can you sense Hilda's presence?"

"*Hilda*?" Lizzie shot me a puzzled look.

"I find it easier to deal with ghosts if I give them a name."

"O—kay. I'm not picking up any vibes yet. I'll try down the other end." She made her way to the far side of the room and closed her eyes.

Several minutes had passed during which time Lizzie hadn't moved or spoken, but then she said, "She's here, and her name isn't Hilda. It's Gillian."

"Okay." I still couldn't see the ghost. "Where is she?"

Lizzie opened her eyes. "Behind you."

I spun around and then stumbled backwards.

"Sorry," said the ghost. "I didn't mean to make you jump."

"You didn't," I lied. "I just tripped."

"I'm Gillian."

"I'm Jill, and this is my niece, Lizzie."

Lizzie came forward to stand beside me and said, "Hi."

"This is a new experience for me. I've never been able to communicate with the living before. Do you both live here?"

"No, this is my sister's shop. That's Lizzie's mother."

"Is she here too?" Gillian looked around.

"No. Kathy, that's her name, isn't able to communicate with ghosts, but she did see you a few days ago."

"I think I remember the lady in question. I'm afraid I

may have scared her."

"She doesn't really believe in ghosts—at least that's what she says, but she asked me to check out this stockroom, to find out what was happening."

"I'm sorry. I didn't mean to upset anyone."

"Don't worry about it. There's just one thing that I don't understand: Kathy's had this shop for several years now and she's never seen you before."

"I can explain that. I normally live in the adjacent property."

"Jeff's Pizzas?"

"I think she means the shop on the other side," Lizzie said.

"That shop has been empty for ages."

"Your niece is correct. I've lived there for almost a hundred years now, and I've seen it change hands numerous times. Fortunately, I've always had the basement to myself."

"You've lived there for a hundred years?"

"That's right. I used to run a small bookshop in the property next door until the accident."

"*Accident*?"

"I was standing on the top rung of the ladder, dusting the books on the top shelf, when someone came through the door. In my hurry to get down, I tripped and—err—it was such a silly way to go. Anyway, I've lived there ever since."

"In the basement?"

"I tried living on the main floor, but it always caused problems, similar to what happened with your sister. Until now, none of the occupants have ever bothered to use the basement, so I've stayed down there."

"What's changed?"

"New owners recently bought the property, and they're making major alterations to the building, including the basement. They obviously intend to utilise all the floors. While the worst of the construction work was being carried out, I sought refuge in here."

"What will you do when the new business opens next door? You obviously won't be able to remain in the basement."

"I honestly don't know. I guess I'll have to find a new home, but I don't know where to start."

"What about GT?" I asked.

"What's that?" Gillian said.

I could have bitten my tongue off. Although Lizzie was able to see ghosts, she had no idea that Ghost Town existed, and I didn't want to risk blowing her mind by enlightening her.

"Lizzie, can you go through to the shop, in case your mother comes back early, please."

"What shall I do if she does?"

"Just come and warn me."

"Okay."

Once she had left the stockroom, I addressed Gillian. "You must have heard of GT?"

"No, I don't think so."

"It's sort of another world where ghosts live. GT stands for Ghost Town. You should have been given the option of going there when you had your accident."

"Oh? Maybe I was. I really don't recall. But I wouldn't have wanted to leave my little shop. Ever."

"What about now? Now that you know the basement is going to be occupied?"

"I don't know."

"It's surely worth considering?"

"I suppose so, but how would I do it?"

"Would you like me to make enquiries for you?"

"Can you do that?"

"Yes, but you mustn't mention this to my niece. She doesn't know about GT, and I'd prefer to keep it that way."

"Okay."

"It might take me a day or two, but I'll get back to you. In the meantime, though, I need you to promise that you won't return to this stockroom."

"That's fine, but how will you contact me?"

"I'll find you next door."

"I really do appreciate this, Jill."

"My pleasure. I'd better be making tracks now." I went to join Lizzie in the main shop.

"What's happening, Auntie Jill?"

"Gillian has promised not to return to the stockroom."

"But where will she live now that she can't stay in the basement?"

"I'm going to ask Mad to find her a suitable new home. You'd better get going because your mother is bound to come back early."

"Before I do, what did you mean by GT?"

"Gin and tonic. I wanted to make sure the stress hadn't made Gillian turn to drink."

"Oh, okay."

"Thanks for your help, Lizzie."

"No worries. I enjoyed meeting Gillian."

Twenty minutes before she should have returned, Kathy came through the door.

"You're back early."

"I couldn't stay away another minute. What happened?"

"You can relax. The ghost won't be returning."

"You mean I really did see a ghost?"

"Yeah. Her name is Gillian."

"You're making this up."

"I promise you."

"You're winding me up as usual, aren't you? I bet you and Jack have had a good laugh about this."

"If you weren't going to believe me, why did you ask me to help?"

"She's really gone?"

"Definitely. You'll have no more scares, I promise."

"I wasn't scared."

"Okay, if you say so. Before I go, where shall I send it?"

"Send what?"

"My bill of course."

Chapter 10

I had thought the previous morning's buzzathon had been bad, but this morning, Florence had managed to take it to another level.

"Florence! Enough!" I snapped. "I need you to stop buzzing, right now."

"But, Mummy, I'm—"

"I know who you are, but I'd like you to be a silent version of Bluebottle Girl for the rest of the morning. If you aren't, there'll be no Bluebottle Girl book for you."

She drew a zip across her lips.

"Do you think you'll be able to join us for lunch?" Jack said.

"I've no idea, but I'll try my best. I'll send you a message to let you know either way."

The 'other' Jack Maxwell had asked me to meet him at West Chipping Castle at ten o'clock, so I was the first one to leave the house. I was just about to get into the car when Mr Ivers called my name.

"I can't stop, Mr Ivers. I'm meeting a client in West Chipping at ten."

"Really? I'm on my way to West Chipping too. I was going to get the bus. I don't suppose there's any way—?"

He left the question hanging in the air. I couldn't think of anything I wanted to do less than share a car journey with him, but how could I refuse? I still felt a twinge of guilt about his shoulder that was still strapped up.

"Sure, get in."

"Sorry if I'm a little slow. Everything's more difficult with my shoulder."

Now he was just laying it on thick.

"No problem. Take your time."

When we set off, he said, "Do you know of anyone who has a room to rent in the village, Jill?"

"Err, not offhand. I thought you'd settled in above the store."

"I have. I love it there, but I'm a little concerned about what might happen when it changes hands, so I'd like to keep my options open."

"The store?"

"Didn't you know? The sisters have decided to put it on the market."

"I had no idea. They've only just added the newspaper and magazine section."

"I know. Ironically, I think that may have been the straw that broke the camel's back. Neither of them likes the earlier start that that requires."

"Is that definite, then? They're selling up?"

"That's what they told me last night."

"Wow!"

Incredibly, I'd actually learned something of interest from Mr Ivers. Even though the Stock sisters were pretty hopeless, I would kind of miss them.

"You'll never guess where I'm going this morning, Jill."

"I assumed you were going shopping."

"No, it's the quarterly meeting of West Chipping Toppers."

"Oh."

"They're much more active than the Washbridge branch."

"Really?" Yawn city.

"Oh yes. There are some very knowledgeable toppers in

this group. None as knowledgeable as myself, obviously."

"Obviously."

I contemplated throwing him out of the moving car, but I figured, after the stepladder incident, no one would believe it was an accident.

What? Of course I was joking. Sheesh, do you think I'm some kind of psychopath? Don't answer that.

He fell silent for a couple of minutes, and I thought maybe he'd noticed my eyes had glazed over.

Who was I trying to kid?

"I don't think I've told you about my recent bottle top acquisitions, have I, Jill?"

Oh bum! This was going to be one extremely long journey.

By the time I finally dropped off Mr Ivers, I knew way more about his bottle top collection than was healthy. I arrived at the castle fifteen minutes early, so I decided to give Jack a call to tell him about the Stock sisters' decision to sell the store.

"Jill? Is everything okay?"

"Yeah, I'm running early so I thought I'd give you a call."

"Did I see Mr Ivers get in the car with you?"

"Yeah, I've just dropped him off at a meeting of West Chipping Toppers."

"West Chipping *what*?"

"Don't you remember his obsession with bottle tops?"

"Oh yeah. I'd forgotten about that. Did he bore you to death with his tales of bottle tops all the way there?"

"For the most part, but he did tell me something of interest."

"That reminds me. Guess what I've just heard? The Stock sisters are selling the store."

"That's what I was going to say. Mr Ivers told me, but I wasn't sure whether to believe him."

"It's true. I've just heard it direct from the horse's mouth. I went over there to buy some toothpaste, seeing as how you'd used the last of it."

"There was plenty left in that tube. You just need to know how to squeeze it properly."

"Anyway, Marjorie told me that they put the store on the market yesterday."

"I'm surprised. I thought those two would be there until they were carried out feet first."

"Me too, but she said it was one of the first things they'd agreed upon for ages. They're going to buy a small cottage on the coast, apparently."

"Oh no, I've just had a horrible thought."

"What?"

"You know what Grandma is like. She can't get enough businesses. I hope she doesn't buy it."

"I wish we had the money to buy it," Jack sighed.

"Us?"

"I've been saying how I'd like a totally new career. I really like the idea of running a village store."

"The hours are crazy, and I doubt it makes much money."

"It's incidental, anyway. We don't have that kind of money."

"I'd better go. Your namesake will be here in a few minutes."

"Okay, be careful. See you later."

Jack had taken me by surprise when he'd said that he

would have liked to buy the store. It's not something that would ever have crossed my mind. To do that we would have to sell the old watermill, and there was no way we were ever going to do that because, as far as I was concerned, that was our forever home.

West Chipping castle wasn't really a castle; all that was left of it were a few crumbling walls. Every time Jack and I drove past it, I remarked that it was time they cleared away the crumbling walls to make way for something more useful, like a new cinema. My saying that, drove Jack crazy because, according to him, I had no appreciation for our heritage. That wasn't true, but give me a blockbuster movie any day.

We'd had several days of rain, so the castle grounds were sodden and muddy. The only path up to the castle was made up of uneven stones—I really should have given more thought to my footwear. Although I'd been talking on the phone, I'd kept an eye open in case I spotted Jack Two (to avoid confusion, I will refer to the other Jack Maxwell as Jack Two from now on), but there had been no sign of him. As far as I could tell there was no one else up there, which was hardly surprising, given the horrible weather (and the fact that no one is interested in a few crumbling walls).

When I eventually reached the castle, I turned around so that I could look back down the path to the road. That way I'd be sure of spotting Jack Two when he arrived.

"Jill." I spun around to see him peering out from behind the tallest of the two walls. He must have arrived before me. "Sorry. I didn't mean to make you jump."

"That's okay. I'm not really sure why you wanted to meet here, though."

"Because no one ever comes here."

"That's true." *Unlike a multiplex.* "Who are you worried about? Your probation officer?"

"Nah, that lot couldn't find their own backsides."

"Who then?"

"I just spent what should have been the best years of my life behind bars for a crime I didn't commit. I can never get those years back, but with your help, I'm determined to prove that I didn't murder Joseph Deer."

"I understand that, but—"

"The real murderer was my half-brother, Keith. The only way to clear my name is for you to prove he is the guilty one, but I'm afraid he'll find out that I've hired you and try to stop me. That's why I asked you to meet me here."

"I see. I did some research into your case in the newspaper archives, but I'd like to hear what happened in your own words."

"It's very simple, really. Joseph, Keith and I were partners in a small business called Trentmore Construction. The first few years were pretty tough but eventually we began to land larger, more profitable contracts. We weren't the cheapest, but we'd built our reputation on the quality of our work. Then, one day, quite by chance, I discovered that the wrong materials had been used in the construction of a small office block where we'd been the lead contractor."

"What were the implications of that?"

"If it had come out, it would have been the end of our business. At first, I assumed that it was the result of some kind of freak error, but when I checked back through the paperwork, I discovered that the original specs had been deliberately changed. By Keith."

"Your brother?"

"Half-brother."

"Why would he do something like that?"

"Money. When I investigated further, I found out that the client had paid the full price for the materials even though the inferior stuff was substantially cheaper."

"And you think your half-brother pocketed the difference?"

"I know he did."

"Did you confront him?"

"Of course, but he looked me straight in the eyes and denied it. I had the evidence, though, and I told him that I was going to tell Joseph what I'd discovered, and that he was finished in the company. Joseph and I would vote him out."

"How did he react?"

"He just laughed. I don't think he believed I would do it."

"But you did?"

"I didn't get the chance. In the early hours of the next morning, I was dragged out of bed and arrested for the murder of Joseph."

"There has to be more to it than you're telling me. How did you become the prime suspect? How did they secure a conviction? They must have had evidence."

"They did."

He took a brown envelope out of his jacket's inside pocket and handed it to me. Inside were two black and white photographs. The quality of the images wasn't great, but they were clear enough to see Jack Two entering and then exiting the same building. The photographs were obviously still images taken from a CCTV recording, complete with date and time stamps.

"What are these?"

"Those images are what got me convicted; they were taken from the cameras inside and outside of Joseph's apartment block. The prosecution used those to prove that I was the only person who entered that building during the hours that he was killed."

"So, you were there that night?"

"No, that's just it. I never left my own apartment, and I certainly never went to Joseph's."

I looked again at the photos. "But I don't—"

"Understand? Neither do I, but I promise on my life, that isn't me in those images." I said nothing for the longest moment, and he must have sensed my rising doubts. "You promised you would help."

"I know and I will, but this is going to be even more difficult than I thought."

"But you'll try?" For the first time, I sensed a touch of desperation in his voice.

"I said I would."

He glanced around. "I have to go. Keith has eyes everywhere."

Before I could respond, he hurried down the uneven path, jumped into a car, and drove away.

Our meeting had left me with more questions than answers. Cold cases were, by their nature, always difficult, but this one had suddenly become much more so. The images that Jack Two had shown me were extremely worrying. If the murder had been committed within the last year or two, I might have suspected deep fake technology had been used to create the images, but the murder had happened almost two decades earlier when such technology was the thing of science fiction.

***

"Buzz, buzz, buzz." Florence had her head in her book, but still managed to buzz while reading.

Because my meeting with Jack Two had been so brief, I'd been able to meet up with Jack and Florence in time to get lunch at Big Burger. Florence clearly wasn't the only kid obsessed with Bluebottle Girl because the restaurant was full of buzzing.

"What do they see in this stupid Bluebottle Girl?" I asked Jack.

"She's amazing," Jack gushed. "You should read Florence's book."

"Don't tell me you're a fan too?"

"I definitely would be if I were Florence's age. Are you really going to eat all of that thing?"

"I didn't have any breakfast."

"Yes, you did. You had a bowl of that awful cereal."

"Did I? Well, I'm still starving."

"There must be a week's worth of calories in that burger."

"Don't exaggerate. And anyway, it was on special offer."

Big Burger had just launched the Supermax burger, and they were selling it at half-price for the first week, so it would have been criminal not to take advantage of the offer.

"How did your meeting with my namesake go?"

"Not great. He showed me photos, taken from CCTV

images, that were the main evidence against him. It shows him entering and then leaving the apartment block of the deceased at around the time the murder took place."

"That's not good. How does he explain that away?"

"He doesn't. He just insists he didn't go there that night."

"That's it?"

"Yeah."

"And he expects you to prove he was wrongly convicted?"

"Yeah. According to Jack Two, his half-brother was the one who killed their partner."

"Jack *Two*?"

"Yeah, sorry, I've taken to thinking of him as that, so I don't get the two of you mixed up."

"Mixed up? In case you forget which one is your husband?"

"You know what I mean."

"So, what's your plan?"

"I don't have one, but that's nothing new."

Florence looked up from her book for the first time since we'd taken our seats. "Bluebottle Girl is the bestest."

"Best."

"She killed Maggot Man with her laser blaster."

"Lovely."

"There's a maggot in your burger, Mummy. Don't worry, I'll zap it. Zap! Zap! Zap!"

I put what was left of the burger in the wrapper and placed it on the tray.

"Aren't you eating that?" Jack said. "I thought you said you were starving."

"I've suddenly lost my appetite."

Chapter 11

It was Monday morning. I'd worked some of Saturday, but Sunday had been a long, lazy, rainy day at home. Jack and I had originally toyed with the idea of the three of us taking a run out into the countryside for a picnic, but the weather had put paid to that. Instead, we'd had to settle for a picnic in the lounge, but at least we didn't have to contend with wasps and flies.

Unless of course you count Bluebottle Girl, who spent all day buzzing around the house, zapping imaginary (I hope) maggots.

"It's a wonder Florence still has any voice left," Jack commented over breakfast. "All that buzzing must take a toll on her vocal chords."

"It's taking a toll on my eardrums."

As soon as she finished breakfast, she started buzzing again, so I insisted she took it upstairs to her bedroom. There was only so much I could stand.

"Are you doing anything exciting this week?" Jack asked while chomping on a slice of burnt toast (I'd forgotten to reset the control on the toaster, and it was the last slice of bread—whoops!)

"I'm going to try and find a new home for a ghost, and hopefully I'll find out how my client's son was turned into a vampire. I also have to try and work out why the queen of the Yellas has been asleep for several weeks."

"Just another boring week, then?" He grinned.

"And, of course, I have to somehow prove that Jack Two was wrongly convicted. How's your week looking?"

"I'm going to follow up on something I saw at the careers fair."

"I'd forgotten all about that. How was it?"

"Pretty useless for the most part. There were only about a dozen stands there altogether."

"What's the thing you're following up on?"

"I'm not saying."

"Why not?"

"Because you'll only take the mickey."

"What? I'd never do that."

"Yes, you would. You do it all the time."

"Come on, Jack. I'm really intrigued now."

"No. I'll tell you if anything comes of it."

"It doesn't have anything to do with sewers, does it?"

"I'm not telling you anything."

"It better not have. I don't want you coming home smelling of poopoo every day."

"Buzz, buzz, buzz." Our own little Bluebottle Girl came buzzing downstairs. "Who's done poopoo?"

"No one has," Jack said. "Mummy is just being silly.

"Are you looking forward to CASS today," I asked, mainly to take her mind off buzzing.

"Yeah, Miss Downscope said we're going to do kill work."

"Do what?"

"Make pots and stuff. I'm going to make a Bluebottle Girl bowl."

"You mean *kiln* work, darling."

At least I hoped she did.

***

When I arrived at the office, Armi was seated in front of Mrs V's desk; the two of them were enjoying a cup of tea.

"Good morning, both of you. Armi, this is a pleasant surprise."

"I had to come into town today, anyway, so I thought I'd pop in, to see if you had time to discuss your—err—little problem."

"I have a few things on, but nothing that can't wait. I really can't thank you enough for offering your services."

"I'd still prefer it if you instructed someone with more relevant experience, but Annabel seems to think that isn't an option."

"I can't afford to, and besides, I have every faith that you'll be able to sort out this little misunderstanding. Shall we go through to my office?"

"Would you like a drink, Jill?" Mrs V asked.

"Yes, please."

There was no sign of Winky, so I figured he was probably with his brother.

"Take a seat, Armi. How much has Mrs V told you?"

"She's given me the gist of it. From what I understand, you obtained an outfit free of charge from Harmony Fashion, under false pretences."

"It sounds terrible when you say it like that. That's not really what happened."

"In that case, why don't you tell me what did actually happen, and we can take it from there."

"Sure. It's quite simple, really. I needed a new outfit for a special occasion, so I paid a visit to that store."

"Harmony Fashion?"

"Correct. I asked the assistant for advice on what I should buy, and she called her manageress over. It was she who recommended the coat dress. I wasn't sure at first, but in the end, I decided to take her recommendation. They asked if they could take a photo of me, which I assumed they would use for their marketing. By way of thanks, they allowed me to have the garment free of charge. The next thing I knew, I was being sued by them."

"Right." Armi finished the last of his tea. "I feel as though a part of the story is missing."

"How do you mean?"

"Annabel showed me the advertisement that Harmony Fashion ran."

"She did?"

"Yes. The whole thrust of the piece was that they had provided the garment free of charge because you intended to wear it when you were awarded a medal by the king."

"Ah, I see what you mean."

"Well?"

"Would you like another cup of tea, Armi?"

"No, thanks. One is plenty."

"Right. What about a coffee?"

"I'd rather we cracked on."

"Absolutely."

"So? Why did Harmony Fashion run an advertisement saying that you were going to get a medal from the king?"

"It must have been a misunderstanding on their part. That's it. Just a simple misunderstanding."

"Okay, and how do you think that came to be? What exactly did you tell them you wanted the outfit for?"

"I—err—"

"If I'm going to represent you, Jill, I'm going to need you to tell me the truth."

"Right."

When I didn't follow up, he pressed, "So? Were you

really being given a medal?"

"Yes."

"Really?"

"Yes, in fact I have it here." I went over to my desk and, after several minutes of searching through the drawers, I retrieved the medal and handed it to Armi.

I can't adequately describe his expression, but I can safely say he wasn't overly impressed.

"It's rather small. And why does it say scout on it?"

"It was awarded to the Washbridge scouts. I accepted it on their behalf."

"And you left it in your desk drawer?"

"I—err—"

"What about the business with the king? Did he really present you with the medal?"

"Not exactly."

"What does that mean, Jill?" I hadn't seen Armi look quite so exasperated before.

"The medals are issued on behalf of the king to scout packs around the country."

"So, he didn't present it to you in person?"

"No, of course not."

"Then why did you need the new outfit?"

I had no idea Armi could be like this. He had always seemed so mild mannered.

When it became clear that I had no answer, he said, "I'm sorry, Jill, I can't represent you."

"But why?"

"Because it's obvious you have no defence. If you want my advice, you'll try to reach a settlement with Harmony because if this goes to court, the financial implications could be disastrous."

"But Armi, I—"

"Sorry, Jill." He left without another word.

"That went well." Winky jumped in through the window.

"I don't suppose you'd like to donate some of your winnings to my legal costs, would you?"

"No chance. From what I just heard, you have zero chance of winning, anyway."

Why was life so unfair to me? It's not as though I lied to the woman at Harmony Fashion, but if I stood up in court and told the truth, that the medal had been presented to me by the king of the gnomes, not only would I lose the case, but I'd probably be taken away by men in white coats.

To take my mind off things, I gave Mad a call.

"Hey, Jill, I was going to phone you later to see how you and Lizzie got on last week."

"That's why I'm calling. Is there any chance you can spare me a few minutes today?"

"Sure, but you'll have to come to the record store. I had a bit of an accident on the course last week."

"Nothing serious, I hope."

"You'll see when you get here. When do you want to come?"

"I'm free now if you are."

"Sure, come on over."

I ignored Mrs V's disapproving look on the way out. Vinyl Alley was busier than I'd ever seen it, but then from what I'd read, vinyl records were making a big comeback. Brad spotted me, and he gestured that I should go upstairs to their flat.

Mad must have heard me coming up the creaky stairs because she came out of the small kitchen; one of her legs was in a plaster cast and she was on crutches.

"Looks like the course went well," I said.

"I didn't want to go on it in the first place."

"What happened?"

"Harry Brentwood happened."

"Huh?"

"I'd just reached the top of the wall on the assault course when he came up behind me and caught my back. I lost my balance and—" She pointed to her leg.

"Did he do it on purpose?"

"No, the man is just a first-class klutz. It couldn't have come at a worse time. Brad just about managed to struggle by alone while I was on the course. Now, I'm going to have to take at least another week off, probably longer."

"It was very busy in the shop when I came through just now."

"It's been like that for some time, which would normally be good news, except for my stupid leg. I've told Brad we'll have to set someone on, but he's not keen."

"How come?"

"He's worried that business might not stay at this level, and he'd have to let them go again. Ideally, we could just do with someone for a few weeks, to see how things go, but no one is going to be interested on that basis."

"I might know someone who would be interested."

"Who?"

"Jack."

"*Your* Jack?"

"Yeah, he's fed up of working from home and he's been

looking for something else."

"Would he want to work in a record shop?"

"I don't know, but I think he might. Do you want me to ask him?"

"Yes, please. So, how did it go last Friday at Kathy's shop?"

"Pretty good, all things considered. Lizzie sensed the ghost within a few minutes of us arriving there. Her name is Gillian and, apparently, she used to run a bookshop in the property next door. She's been living in the basement there ever since she passed away, but the new owners are going to be using that space, so she's looking for a new home. That's why she was in the stockroom."

"I take it she hasn't had any luck yet?"

"No, and get this: she doesn't have a clue what GT is."

"What? How can that be?"

"That was pretty much my reaction. She said she didn't remember ever being offered a chance to live in Ghost Town, but then the bookshop was the only place she ever wanted to be."

"I take it that's no longer an option?"

"It seems not. I think she might be amenable to the idea of moving to GT, but after all this time, she understandably finds the prospect terrifying. I was wondering if you might know of anyone who can help her."

"It's an unusual situation, but I can make a few phone calls."

"That would be great. Thanks, Mad."

Chapter 12

On my way back to the office, I received the call I'd been dreading.

"Jill? It's Charles Brown. I realise you haven't had long, and I'm sorry to pester you, but I was wondering how you got on when you went to see Max?"

"I'm afraid I didn't manage to see him. He wouldn't answer the door."

"I was afraid of that."

"You mentioned that Max rarely goes out?"

"That's right. Not during the daytime, anyway. Although, he has been going out at night more often. I've tried asking where he goes, but he won't tell me."

"The next time he goes out at night, I want you to call me straight away. Can you do that, please?"

"What are you going to do?"

"Follow him and see if I can find out what has caused the change in him. Will you call me?"

"Yes of course."

I'd no sooner finished talking to Charles Brown than my phone rang again.

"Jill, it's Ralph. I've managed to arrange those meetings you requested."

"Both of them?"

"Yes. Doctor Grovemore was quite amenable, as I expected. Prince Michael was a different matter. At first, he refused point blank, but the princess put some pressure on him, and he relented. Even so, I'm not one hundred percent certain he'll show up."

"You've done all you can, Ralph. When are the meetings?"

"Both of them are tomorrow. I realise that's short notice. I hope it fits in with your schedule."

"That's fine. What time?"

"You're meeting the doctor at eleven o'clock, and then you'll see the prince at midday."

"Shall I meet you at the palace doors like last time?"

"Yes, please."

"Great, I'll see you tomorrow."

"Any calls, Mrs V?"

"No, dear." She still had that disapproving look on her face.

"I take it Armi told you what happened?"

"He did."

"It's not as bad as it might sound."

"Really?"

"Okay, it probably is, but I'm going to sort it out."

"I do hope so, Jill. I'd hate to see you go bankrupt because of a silly lie."

"It won't come to that," I said with as much confidence as I could muster.

Winky was sitting on my desk, looking very pleased with himself.

"Get off my desk!" I snapped.

He jumped down and then onto the sofa. "Just because you're going down, there's no need to take it out on me."

"No one's going down."

"I'll remind you of that when you're homeless and penniless."

"I can't believe you're twisting the knife after everything I've done for you."

"It's because I can't bear to see you feeling sorry for

yourself like this. Instead of holding a pity party, why don't you fight back?"

"And how am I supposed to do that? Armi said I don't stand a chance if it goes to court. My only defence is that the medal was given to me by the king of the gnomes. They'd laugh me out of court."

"So, you have to make sure that it doesn't go to court."

"By grovelling to Harmony Fashion and begging them to drop the case? If I thought it would do any good, I'd probably do it, but I don't believe for one minute that it would."

"There are other ways."

"Such as?"

"Everyone has at least one dirty little secret that they don't want anyone to know. You have to find out what Harmony's is and use it against them."

Much as I hated to admit it, sometimes that cat of mine came up with a brilliant idea.

"I suppose it might work, but how would I find out what their dirty little secret is?"

He rolled his eye. "Remind me again what you do for a living."

"Oh yeah, right. Sure, I can do that."

"*Thank you, Winky.*" He said, trying to imitate my voice. "*You are a genius who deserves extra salmon for the rest of the week.*"

"That sounded nothing like me."

"It was spot on. So, do I get the extra salmon?"

"Yes, but only if this idea of yours works."

"Red not pink."

"Obviously."

Although Winky's suggestion was a longshot, I felt a little better, just knowing that there was something I could do. If Harmony Fashion did have any dirty little secrets, I would find them, and hopefully I'd be able to use them as leverage.

I'd still had no word from Martin, which I assumed meant he hadn't yet managed to track down Braxmore. Once he had managed to locate him, I would be able to face my nemesis at long last. My family had lived under his shadow for far too long already.

For now, though, I needed to focus on my open cases. I'd been giving a lot of thought to Jack Two's case, which all hinged on the CCTV images presented in court. Unless I could find some way of discrediting them, I didn't see how I'd be able to prove his innocence. I'd already done some research into the murder that Jack Two had been convicted of. Joseph Deer had been stabbed to death in his bed. His body had been discovered by his wife, a nurse, when she'd returned to their apartment after working a nightshift at the local hospital. His time of death had been put at some time between one and three o'clock in the morning. The murderer had left no fingerprints or DNA, and the weapon, thought to be a short-bladed knife, had never been found. Essentially, the only evidence that the police had been able to find was the CCTV from the apartment block, which showed only one person entering the building between the hours of one o'clock and three o'clock in the morning. That person was Jack Two. The only other evidence against him was the testimony of the secretary, a Mrs Jean Longton, who worked for the three men. She testified that there had been a violent argument between Jack and Joseph on the day before the murder.

According to her, the two men had almost come to blows, but she didn't know what the argument was about because she was in the next room. Jack hadn't mentioned the argument when we talked at the castle, but then he'd been desperate to get away as quickly as possible. I made a mental note to ask him about it the next time we spoke.

Next, I focussed on Trentmore Construction. During the years that Jack Two had been incarcerated, it had grown at an exponential rate, and was now a multi-national concern with a turnover running into the tens of millions. The CEO and majority shareholder was Keith Maxwell, Jack Two's half-brother. Judging by the profile of him that had appeared in a lifestyle magazine a couple of years earlier, the man was incredibly wealthy. I had hoped I might find some dirt on Keith or the company, but I'd come up emptyhanded. Either both he and the company were squeaky clean, or his PR people were doing an excellent job of keeping any indiscretions out of the press. If the most recent photo of Keith Maxwell was anything to go by, he liked the finer things in life. Leaning against the bonnet of a Ferrari, his suit probably cost more than I made in a month. I could get only so much from reading articles. In order to get a real feel for the man, I would need to meet him face-to-face.

"Mrs V, I'm calling it a day. You should do the same."

"I'm meeting Armi in thirty minutes. He's taking me to dinner."

"Nice. What's the occasion?"

"There isn't one. He suggested it out of the blue when he came to see you."

"Very nice. Tomorrow morning, I'd like you to try and arrange for me to have a meeting with this man." I handed her one of the articles I'd printed out. "I don't want him to know who I am, so I'll need you to pretend that I want to do a feature on him for a magazine."

"Which magazine?"

"I'll leave that to you. Any of the major glossies should do the trick."

"I'll do my best."

Jack was in the lounge when I arrived home.

"Why don't you ever surprise me with a dinner date?" I said.

"What prompted that?"

"Armi is taking Mrs V out for dinner tonight."

"It's probably a special occasion."

"No, I asked her that. She said it was just a spontaneous decision."

"Anyway, I did take you out for a meal on Saturday."

"Big Burger doesn't count. Where's Florence?"

"In her bedroom, rereading her Bluebottle Girl book for the hundredth time."

"She's really into that, isn't she?"

"You're not kidding. She's talked about nothing else since she got home. Speaking of Armi, how did your meeting with him go? Is he optimistic he can help?"

"I wouldn't say *optimistic,* exactly."

"But he's going to try?"

"Actually, no. He said he wouldn't be able to represent me."

"How come?"

"Who knows? He probably feels rusty after being out of the game for a while."

"Why do I get the feeling you aren't telling me

everything. What did he say?"

"He—err—"

"And don't lie."

"Okay, he basically said I didn't have a leg to stand on, and that I should grovel to Harmony Fashion to try and get them to take pity on me and drop their action."

"That's not good, but if that's what it takes, I guess you'll just have to swallow your pride and do it."

"No chance."

"You have to, Jill. This is no time to be stubborn. If they proceed with the case, you could end up bankrupt."

"It won't come to that because I have a plan."

"What kind of plan?"

"A cunning one."

"You're going to have to give me more than that."

"Okay, it was Winky's idea, actually."

"That doesn't exactly fill me with confidence."

"Hear me out. He said the best way to get Harmony to drop their action is to dig up one of their own dirty secrets."

"What if they don't have any?"

"Everyone has a dirty secret that they don't want anyone to know."

"I don't." Jack insisted.

"Okay, everyone except you has one."

"What's yours, then?"

"I don't have any."

"So, in conclusion: one hundred percent of people in this room don't have a dirty little secret. That isn't looking very promising for your cunning plan."

"Enough of the negativity. A business like Harmony is bound to have something they don't want anyone to know, and I intend to find it."

"I hope you're right."

"How did the career fair thingy that you were going to follow up on go?"

"It was a complete waste of time."

"Sorry to hear that. How would you feel about working in a record shop?"

"I didn't think there were any left. Doesn't everyone stream music these days?"

"I'm talking about Mad and Brad's vinyl record shop."

"I love vinyl records. That's when music really was music."

"Mad broke her leg on the outward-bound course last week, so Brad is really struggling. It would only be a temporary thing."

"Yeah, I'd definitely be up for that. What about the hours, though?"

"Mad knows you'd have to work around Florence, and she's cool with that. Shall I call her and say yes?"

"Definitely. When would I start?"

"I'll ask her, but I suspect they'd like you to start straight away. Would tomorrow be okay?"

"Absolutely. Let's go through to the kitchen. I haven't started dinner yet."

I followed Jack into the kitchen, but then stopped dead in my tracks.

"What on earth is that thing?" I pointed to a green and yellow lump of something on the kitchen table.

Before he could respond, I heard buzzing and the sound of feet on the stairs.

"Mummy!" She threw herself into my arms and gave me a kiss. "Do you like my Bluebottle Girl bowl?"

"Where is it?"

"It's there, silly!" She pointed at the green and yellow object on the table.

"It's brilliant," Jack said. "Isn't it, Mummy?"

"Err, it's fantastic, darling."

"You can have your cereal in it tomorrow." She beamed.

"Great!"

Chapter 13

"Why won't you use my bowl?" Florence demanded to know at breakfast.

"I tried, darling, but the milk won't stay in it."

"You don't like it, do you?"

"Of course I do. It's a beautiful bowl, but it's just not any good for cereal."

"I have an idea," Jack said. "Why don't you put it on the windowsill in the lounge, so that everyone who visits us will see it?"

I shot him a look.

Florence thought about it for a moment. "Okay." She jumped off the chair, picked up the green and yellow blob, and headed for the lounge.

"Why did you tell her to do that?" I said.

"She was upset, and besides, I don't think it's all that bad."

"It's—"

"I've put it next to the fish tank," Florence said.

"That's a good idea." Jack nodded his approval. "I bet the fish will love it too."

I seriously doubted that, so after I'd finished my breakfast, I went through to check on them. I fully expected those prima donnas to show their displeasure by filling their tank full of bubbles. To my surprise, the water was still, and the two fish were just staring at the green and yellow monstrosity. So transfixed were they, that neither of them seemed to notice my approach.

"Ladies, I can only apologise for—err—that thing, but don't worry, I'll remove it in a few days."

"No," said Wanda.

"No?"

"It's an amazing piece, isn't it, Mabel?"

"Magnificent. It must have cost a small fortune. Who is the artist?"

If it hadn't been for their earnest tone and the fact that neither of them could tear their gaze away from the blob, I would have thought they were trying to wind me up.

"Florence made it at school."

"Your daughter?"

"Yeah."

"What a prodigy," Wanda said.

"You must nurture her talent," Mabel chipped in.

"Nurture it?"

"Absolutely."

"Right."

It was on days like this that I began to wonder if I was the crazy one.

There was no sign of Jack when I returned to the kitchen, so I went upstairs and found him in our bedroom, standing in front of the wardrobe mirror. He had changed into jeans and a t-shirt.

"What do you think?" he said.

"About what?"

"This outfit. Does it say hip and cool to you?"

"The clothes have not yet been invented that could make you *hip and cool*."

"You know what I mean. Is this outfit okay for working in the record store?"

"Yeah, it's fine. Whenever I've been in there, Brad is always wearing jeans and a t-shirt."

"Great. What were you doing in the lounge? You haven't moved Florence's bowl, have you?"

"No, the fish wouldn't let me."

"The fish?"

"Yeah, they're big fans of the bowl. They reckon Florence is some kind of prodigy."

"See, what did I say?"

"Where is the budding Michelangelo?"

"She was buzzing around the garden when I came upstairs."

"I'd better be making tracks. I'll give her a kiss on my way out. Good luck with the new job."

"Thanks. I can't wait. It's going to be groovy."

Oh boy!

***

"How was your meal last night, Mrs V?"

"Delicious. I highly recommend The Horse and Cart the next time you and Jack have a meal out."

"That'll be never."

"The food was amazing and the service first class. They couldn't do enough for us."

"That's great. Have you remembered I want you to try and arrange for me to interview Keith Maxwell?"

"I have, dear. I'll get straight on it at nine o'clock."

"Let me know how you get on."

I expected Winky to still be gloating about his win at the casino, but he was on the phone, and looked very unhappy about something.

"Who took it Bro? Okay, okay I understand. I'll get over there as quick as I can." He ended the call.

"What's wrong?" I asked.

"That was Socks. He was robbed last night. They took

all the winnings from our casino win."

"Who did?"

"He doesn't know. They must have got in during the night when Socks was asleep."

"Hmm."

"What does that mean?"

"Nothing."

"Come on. You've obviously got something on your mind. Spit it out."

"Are you sure it was a robbery? You only have Socks' word for what happened."

"Do you honestly think my own brother would fake a robbery, just to cheat me out of my share? I'd trust Socks with my life. There's no way he'd do something like that."

"If you say so. What are you going to do?"

"You have to find out who stole the money and get it back."

"*Me*?"

"You're a PI, aren't you?"

"Yeah, but—"

"I wouldn't expect you to do it for free. You can have ten percent of everything you recover."

"Okay, but I'll need to ask you and Socks some questions."

"Fine, but that will have to wait until later. I need to go and check on my brother first."

It was almost eleven o'clock, and I was about to ask Mrs V if she'd made any progress with arranging the interview with Keith Maxwell, when she came through to my office.

"Any joy, Mrs V?"

"None at all, dear. I can't get past his personal

secretary's personal secretary."

"His personal secretary has a personal secretary?"

"It appears so. She said that Mr Maxwell only does one or two interviews a year, and that we could write in and express an interest in being considered for one of those if we wished, but even if he was to agree, it would not be for at least nine months."

"That's a blow."

"Sorry, dear, I did my best."

"Don't worry about it. I'll just have to come up with another cunning plan."

"Oh dear." She frowned.

"What?"

"Nothing, dear. I have every confidence in you."

Damned with faint praise.

My plan was actually a very simple one: get Edna, the surveillance fairy, on the job. One call, and a few seconds later, she was standing on my shoulder.

"Before we start," she said. "I should tell you that—"

"You can't possibly have increased your rates again. Every time I hire you, they've gone up again."

"If you had let me finish, I would have said that I am going on holiday on Sunday, so I'll only be able to work for you for a few days."

"That's okay. That should be more than enough. I need you to follow this man." I showed her some of the clippings I had of Keith Maxwell.

"Okay. What has he done?"

"He may or may not have been involved in a murder several years ago."

"A murderer, eh? That will require payment of an additional danger premium."

"I might have known. Can you do it?"

"Of course. What specifically do you want to know about him?"

"I need to know what his daily routine is because it's important I find a way to talk to the man. All my efforts to reach him so far have failed."

"No problem. As soon as I have your initial payment, I'll get straight onto it."

"Fine." I took three packets of custard creams out of my drawer. "Will that do?"

"That's fine. I'll report back to you on Saturday before I go on holiday."

***

This time, when I arrived at the Yellas' palace, Ralph was already waiting outside the doors.

"Good morning, Jill."

"Hi. Everything still okay for my meetings?"

"Doctor Grovemore is waiting for us in the surgery he has here in the palace. I should warn you that he is a bit of a fanboy of yours."

"Really?"

"Apparently, he loves to watch videos of you in tournaments."

"Right. What about Prince Michael?"

"That's an entirely different matter." Ralph sighed. "I haven't been able to track him down yet today."

"But he did agree to talk to me?"

"He did, but what he says and what he does are very often quite different things. While you're with the doctor, I'll do my best to find him."

"Thanks, Ralph."

The surgery was on the ground floor of the palace. Ralph showed me in.

"Doctor, would you give me a call when you and Jill are all done, please?"

The doctor, a Yella who looked much older than the others I'd met so far, didn't respond. He was too busy staring at me, which I found a little unnerving.

"Doctor?" Ralph prompted.

"Sorry, Ralph, yes I'll call you when we're done." After Ralph had left us alone, the doctor said to me, "May I call you Jill?"

"Of course, Doctor."

"Please call me Grover."

"Is that a nickname?"

"No, it's my first name."

Grover Grovemore? Seriously?

"I imagine Ralph told you I'm something of a fan of yours?"

"Yes, he did mention it."

"I've watched your tournament videos hundreds of times. Thousands probably. Is it true you've retired from them?"

"That's right."

"That's so sad. I do hope you'll reconsider someday."

"I don't think that's very likely. Now, maybe if we could—"

"Before we get down to business, do you think you could possibly let me have your autograph?"

"Sure."

He went behind his desk, and picked up a cardboard box, which he placed on the desktop.

"The thing is, Jill, I'm the president of the Yella Jill Maxwell Appreciation Society."

"You're joking?"

"Certainly not. We have forty-six members now. Forty-seven if you count Smythe."

"What's the issue with Smythe?"

"He's also a member of the Ma Chivers' Appreciation Society. My feeling is that no one should be able to be a member of both societies, but I'm still awaiting a ruling on that."

"I see. Out of curiosity, are there many Yellas in the other society?"

"Very few. Less than ten, I believe."

Call me petty, but that gave me a warm feeling inside.

"If you could see your way to signing these posters. There's one for every member of the society." He took a pile of them out of the box and dropped them onto the desk. "Not for Smythe, though, obviously."

"Obviously."

It took me almost thirty minutes to sign all of the posters, during which time the doctor was telling me about his favourite tournament moments. Eventually, after I'd signed the final poster, I said, "Can we discuss the queen now, Doctor?"

"Grover, please."

"Sorry. Have you seen anything like this before?"

"Never, and neither has anyone else. In my efforts to get to the bottom of this I've been in touch with physicians throughout Candlefield: Witches, Wizards, Vampires, Werewolves, Nymphs, Elves—you name it, I've spoken to them."

"Everyone is convinced she's asleep. Do you agree with

that, or do you think she could be in some kind of coma?"

"Her vital signs and brain activity are what I'd expect to see in someone who is sleeping."

"What about the snoring?"

"That's really something, isn't it? I've never heard anything like it, but then I've never known anyone to sleep for weeks either."

"The princess is hoping if I can find out what or who caused this to happen, that might lead to a cure."

"I don't envy you your task."

"Before this all started, how was the queen's health?"

"Absolutely fine. All of the royal family have a full medical check-up once every three months. The queen's last check-up was only a couple of weeks before this started, and she got a clean bill of health."

"I take it from that that she wasn't taking any medicine?"

"None."

"I realise this is an unfair question to ask you, Grover, but do you think this was caused by some freak of nature or do you think it's the result of a malicious act?"

"I simply don't know, but if I was forced to guess, I'd say the former, but only because it would be practically impossible for anyone to poison the queen, if that's what you're suggesting."

"Why? Because you would have found traces of the poison?"

"No, that's not it. There are definitely poisons that leave no trace. I was thinking about the practicalities of doing it. The queen has security personnel with her at all times. She has food-tasters who check everything she eats or drinks before it is served to her. I just don't see how anyone could bypass those measures."

"What if the person in question was a member of the royal family?"

"You surely can't be suggesting that—?"

"I'm not suggesting anything. Just asking the question."

"It's true that the prince and princess have unrestricted access to the queen."

"Thank you for your time, Grover. Could you contact Ralph to let him know we're done?"

"Certainly, and thanks again for the posters. The members will be so excited."

Chapter 14

Ralph didn't have to say a word; I could tell by his expression that things hadn't gone to plan.

"No Prince Michael?" I said.

"That man will be the death of me. I knew he'd do this."

"I take it you couldn't find him?"

"No, he's nowhere in the palace. I've searched everywhere."

"That's a pity. It's really important that I speak with him."

"There is one place you could try, but I have to warn you, it could be dangerous."

"Danger is my middle name."

"He often frequents a tavern called The Last Breath."

"Sounds nice."

"It's even worse than the name suggests. It attracts most of Yellaville's lowlifes."

"Why would the prince want to go somewhere like that?"

"I honestly have no idea. I think maybe he gets some kind of weird buzz from mixing with people so different to those he spends most of his life with at the palace."

"Isn't it dangerous, though?"

"From what I've heard, whenever he visits there, he is always incognito."

"And you think I might find him there today?"

"I think there's a strong possibility. He clearly wasn't keen to speak to you, and he probably thinks that's one place you'll never visit."

"He got that wrong, then."

"Are you sure about this, Jill? I mean no disrespect, but

it really is a dangerous place."

"I'll be fine. You said he may be incognito, but is there anything that will help me identify him?"

"The prince has a birthmark in the shape of a lemon on the back of his neck."

"A *lemon*?"

"Yeah. Maybe that's why he's such a sour faced individual."

The Last Breath was on the opposite side of town, a twenty-minute walk from the palace. The closer I got to the tavern, the more rundown my surroundings became. Most of the buildings were in a state of disrepair and the few Yellas that were on the street eyed me suspiciously. I assumed they didn't see many shrunken witches around these parts. I was finding it more and more difficult to believe that the prince would frequent a tavern in this area of town, but Ralph had been adamant that it was one of his regular haunts.

Ignoring all the strange looks that I was attracting, I continued on my way, but then stopped dead in my tracks when I came across the tavern. A sorry looking sign swung precariously above the door, and looked as though it might plunge to the ground at any moment. If it hadn't been for the fact that I could hear voices inside, I would have thought the building was deserted.

As soon as I stepped inside, the room fell silent. I'd expected the interior to be dark and poorly lit, but quite the opposite was true. It was so bright inside that it took a few seconds for my eyes to adjust to the light. When they did, I realised that everyone in there was staring at me. Considering it wasn't yet midday, the place was doing brisk business. A quick glance around confirmed that I was the only non-Yella in there, and I silently cursed myself for not changing my appearance.

The Yella behind the bar had a long grey beard. He had been in the process of pouring ale from a flagon into a glass when I'd walked in. Distracted by my appearance, he had overfilled the glass and the ale was now spilling onto the wooden countertop. After passing the glass of ale to his customer, he wiped it and then turned his attention to me.

"Can I help you?" He glared at me.

"Do you have anything—err—non-alcoholic?"

He said nothing for the longest moment, but then burst into laughter. "Non-alcoholic? Did you hear that, everyone? The tiny witch wants something non-alcoholic."

That caused an uproar as everyone laughed and banged their glasses on the tables.

"Where do you think you are?" Someone shouted. "In a tea room?"

"What are you doing in here, anyway?" A Yella at the table nearest to me stood up. "Have you been sent to spy on us?"

"What? No, I just came in for a drink."

Another Yella stood up. "And you just happened to be passing by, did you?"

The atmosphere had quickly changed from one filled with laughter to something much more intimidating. I had thought that I'd be able to get a drink and mix with the customers, in the hope of spotting the prince by his birthmark. Now, my only concern was getting out of there in one piece.

"Come with me." A female Yella took my arm in hers, and she started to head for the door.

"What are you doing, Rosy?" Someone called after her. "We should teach the witch a lesson."

"Sit down and drink your ale," Rosy said without looking back.

I was relieved to get back outside, but Rosy kept hold of my arm and continued walking.

"Where are you taking me?"

"To safety. Don't look back." I did as she said and allowed her to lead me back the way I'd come. Only when we had reached a more salubrious area of the kingdom, did she release my arm. "You should be okay here."

"Thanks for coming to my rescue. I'm Jill, by the way."

"No problem." She turned to walk away.

"Wait. What happened back there? Why did everyone turn on me?"

"Do you really not know?"

"I have no idea. I just popped in there for a drink."

"Yeah, right." She sneered. "Just because I helped you, doesn't mean you can take me for a fool."

"I don't. Honestly."

"Then tell me why you were really there. Do you work for Candlefield law enforcement?"

"What? No."

"I didn't think so. That lot are pretty incompetent, but even they aren't stupid enough to send a teeny-tiny witch into the lion's den."

"Why would Candlefield law enforcement be interested in what happens in the Yella kingdom? Don't Yellas have their own law enforcement?"

"Of course, but all of the independent kingdoms still

have to report back to Candlefield, ultimately."

"I didn't know that, but I guess it makes sense."

"If you're not the law, what were you doing there?"

I hesitated, unsure if I should reveal the real reason for my visit to the tavern, but Rosy seemed like a reasonable person, so I decided to risk it.

"I was looking for Prince Michael."

"Yeah, right." She rolled her eyes. "Look, if you don't want to tell me, that's fine, but there's no need to lie."

"I'm telling you the truth, I promise."

"You're being serious, aren't you?"

"Deadly."

She burst into laughter. "This gets better and better. And why on earth would you think the prince would be in The Last Breath?"

"I have it on good authority that it's one of his favourite haunts."

"You saw the reception you received. Yellas in the Jedmond district hate two things: non-Yellas and the Yella royalty, but not necessarily in that order."

"Why?"

"Because Jedmond is the most deprived district in the kingdom. Those who live there feel abandoned by Candlefield and our own royalty. Do you know how many non-Yellas visit The Last Breath, on average, during the course of a month?"

"I've no idea."

"None. That's why you got the reception you got. And we see even less of the royals."

"Is it possible that the prince could be in there in disguise?"

"Impossible. The whole idea is laughable. He could

wear any disguise he liked, but he'd still stand out like a sore thumb. What do you want with the prince, anyway?"

I explained who I was and that I'd been hired by the princess to find out why her mother, the queen, was in a sleep from which she couldn't be woken.

"I had no idea that the queen was ill, but then we're always the last to hear the news."

"I really appreciate you helping me out back there, but I have to ask, why did you?"

"Because I hate to see anyone being bullied, no matter who they are."

"Thanks, I suppose I should get going."

"Jill, wait."

"Yes?"

"Have you heard of the brewmaidens? No one knows more about potions than them."

"I can't say I have. Do you think they might be able to throw some light on what happened to the queen?"

"Let's put it this way, if they can't, I'm not sure anyone else will be able to."

"Where can I find them?"

"I have no idea. I've never had the need of one."

"Okay, well thanks for the advice and for getting me out of there."

"No problem. I hope you're able to help the queen."

As I watched Rosy walk away, I was still trying to make sense of what had just transpired. Ralph had been so sure that Prince Michael was a regular visitor to The Last Breath, but that now seemed unlikely. I still needed to talk to the prince, and I was keen to have it out with Ralph, but I'd had enough of the Yella kingdom for one day.

***

Winky was back in the office, looking only slightly better than he had earlier.

"How's your brother?"

"Livid. Those toerags got away with every penny, but he cheered up a little when I told him that you were going to recover our money."

"I hope you told him I couldn't guarantee to get the money back."

"Of course you will. You're the best PI in the country—I've always said so."

"Hmm. Right, well you'd better tell me all about this casino."

"It's called Winskers. It's a combination of *win* and *whiskers*."

"That's a rubbish name."

"Can I continue?"

"Yeah, sorry."

"Do you know the tripe shop on West Street?"

"I didn't know there was a tripe shop in Washbridge. Is that all they sell?"

"Yeah, it's called What A Load Of."

"You're making this up."

"Why would I make it up? Will you please let me finish?"

"Sorry, go on."

"The casino is in the basement below the tripe shop. It opened about a year ago."

"Had you been there before?"

"No, it was Socks' idea."

"I might have known."

"Do you mind?"

"Sorry. Is it just for cats?"

"No, it's open to all animals. Anyway, we started off on the slots, but our luck wasn't in. We both lost half of our stake money on those things. They're rigged if you ask me. After that experience, I was all for cutting our losses and leaving, but then this sexy little minx came over and asked if we'd ever considered playing the roulette."

"*Sexy little minx*? Really?"

"That's what they call the hostesses who work there: Sexy Little Minxes."

"That's awful."

"Anyway, she told us they were offering new members fifty pounds worth of free bets on the roulette, so me and Socks were over there like bullets out of a gun. Neither of us really knew what we were doing, so we just put the free chips on the first number that popped into our head. And guess what?"

"You won?"

"No, I lost it all in double-quick time, but Socks could do no wrong. He just kept on winning."

"While you were there, did you notice anyone watching you?"

"Are you kidding? The buzz soon got around that Socks was on a hot streak and, before long, the crowd around the table was ten deep. Practically everyone in the place was watching him."

"What about when you left? How did you get home?"

"We walked on air."

"Don't tell me you carried all that cash home?"

"Yeah, we did. The people at the casino gave Socks a briefcase, which I thought was pretty neat of them."

"Hmm?"

"What's that mean?"

"It can't be a coincidence that someone just happened to rob Socks a few days after he'd had a big win at the casino, which means whoever did it must have known about the winnings. I think I need to start by paying a visit to the casino."

"Good idea. I'll come with you."

"No, you won't."

"Why not?"

"Because as soon as they spot you, they'll be on their guard. Much better if I go alone."

"They're open twenty-four seven, but it only starts to get busy after nine o'clock."

"Okay, I'll try and get there in the next few days."

"Why not tonight?"

"Because I need time to formulate a plan first."

"Will it be a cunning one?"

"Obviously."

"Heaven help us."

Chapter 15

"You two look ridiculous," I said in between mouthfuls of Strawberrycandy Pops.

"We don't think so, do we, pumpkin?" Jack countered.

"Why don't you put yours on, Mummy?" Florence said.

"Because I refuse to eat my breakfast while wearing a pink wig."

"They're purple," Jack corrected me. "It's only three days until the Purple Festival."

"Whoop-de-doo." I sighed. "Anyway, won't you have to work on Saturday?"

In contrast to my awful day, yesterday, Jack had apparently had a ball, working at Vinyl Alley. After Florence had gone to bed, he had talked about nothing else. Don't get me wrong, I was pleased he'd found a job he liked, even if it was only temporary, but there was only so much talk about vinyl records that I could take. Things had got so bad that I'd almost resorted to asking him about the latest ten-pin news, just to change the subject.

"No, Brad was very understanding when I told him that I'd already arranged to take the family to the festival. He said he'd be able to cope by himself."

"I could stand in for you on Saturday."

"You?"

"Yeah, why not?"

"You looked bored when I was talking to you about the job last night."

"Ridiculous. I was fascinated."

"Anyway, you can't work in the shop because Florence and I want you to come with us, don't we, pumpkin?"

"Yeah, you have to come, Mummy. Everyone at my

school is going."

"Okay."

As soon as Florence had finished her muesli, she reverted to Bluebottle Girl, and buzzed her way upstairs.

"Grandma must be making an absolute fortune on this purple nonsense," I said. "How come that woman always comes up smelling of roses?"

"I know you don't like to admit it, but despite all her faults, your grandmother is an astute businesswoman."

"And what faults would they be, Jim?" said Grandma who was standing in the kitchen doorway.

"How did you get in?" I demanded.

"I—err—think I'll go and check on Florence." Jack exited stairs left at the speed of light.

"Why does that human of yours always take off whenever I'm around? I'm beginning to think he doesn't like me."

"Maybe if you tried calling him by his proper name he wouldn't. You haven't answered my question. Why didn't you knock at the door instead of magicking yourself inside?"

"We're family. I shouldn't have to waste time knocking on doors."

"Listen up. The next time you do that will be the last. I'll ban you from coming to this house forever."

"Whatever, anyway the reason I'm here is to tell you that I'm going to need your help on Saturday."

"You're hilarious."

"I've been let down by the caterers that I'd hired, so I'll need you to lend a hand."

"*Catering*? Why on earth would you come to me? I can barely boil an egg."

"I'm not completely insane. I'm not asking you to provide the food. The twins are going to do that. I just need you to man the counter."

"Why can't you do it?"

"Because I have to oversee the whole event."

"If I agree to help, I'm not spending the whole day on the counter. I want to spend some time with Florence and Jack."

"Florence and *who*?" She cackled. "Just kidding. You won't be by yourself on the counter. The twins are going to be there too."

"Okay, I suppose."

"Great. Make sure you're there at seven."

"Seven? I didn't think it started until nine?"

"It doesn't, but you'll need to help set things up. By the way, did you hear the sisters are selling the store?"

"Please don't tell me you're thinking of buying it."

"Me? No, there's no money to be made in small village stores. Unless I bought it and converted it into something that would make real money."

"Like what?"

"A betting shop perhaps."

"You can't turn the village store into a betting shop!"

"Relax, I'm just winding you up. Right, I'm off."

"Before you go. Do you know where I can find a brewmaiden?"

"A what?"

"A brewmaiden. They are experts in potions and the like, apparently."

"Says who?"

"A Yella named Rosy."

"A Yella?" She sneered. "The next time one of those

creatures tells the truth will be the first. She probably made it up."

"She seemed genuine enough."

"Only to someone as gullible as you. I'm going. Bye."

A few minutes later, Jack came creeping down the stairs.

"Has she gone?"

"Yeah, you can come down, Jim."

"She does that on purpose. The name thing," he said.

"You think?"

"When I was working at the hotel, she never once forgot my name. She just does it to wind me up."

"That's where you're wrong. She does it to wind *me* up."

"What did she want?"

"She reckons her caterers have let her down, so she's asked me to step in."

"You do the catering?" He laughed.

"The twins are providing the food. I just have to man the stall for part of the day. You don't mind, do you?"

"Of course not. At least this way, I know you'll turn up. I was fully expecting you to come up with some lame excuse not to go at all."

My phone rang and caller ID showed it to be Charles Brown.

"Jill, you said to give you a call the next time Max went out at night-time."

"Err, yeah, but it's seven-thirty in the morning?"

"I know. He went out last night without my realising. I don't know how he managed it. I only realised when he came back this morning."

"What time did he get back?"

"About an hour ago. It was still dark."

No surprises there.

"Did you ask where he'd been?"

"I did, but he just blew me off. He did say that he'd be out again tonight, though. That's why I'm calling you."

"Okay. I'll try and follow him and find out where he's going."

"And you'll keep me updated?"

"Of course."

"Who was that?" Jack asked when I'd finished on the call.

"A client. Charles Brown."

"Does he want you to do some *snoop*ing for him?" Jack laughed. "Get it? Charlie Brown, *Snoop*—"

"You're almost as funny as Grandma."

"Ouch. Hey, I only have to work a half-day tomorrow, so I think I'll get my hair cut in time for the festival."

"Yeah, that makes sense, seeing as you'll be wearing a wig, and no one will be able to see your hair."

"It's ready for a cut, anyway. I thought I might make an appointment at Julian's new place."

"Who? Oh, you mean Zeus. Are you insane? I wouldn't trust him or his wife anywhere near me with a pair of scissors."

"I worry about you sometimes, Jill."

"You should be the one who's worried. Don't come crying to me when Sweeney Todd slices your throat open. I didn't even realise they'd opened for business yet."

"They opened last weekend. Guess what the shop is called."

"Abandon Hope All Ye Who Enter Here?"

"Catchy, but no. It's actually called A & J Hair."

"They should have used Zeus's *real* initial, then they could have called it The A to Z of Hair."

"And you said *I* wasn't funny."

***

"Armi said I should ask you what's happening with that lawsuit," Mrs V said when I walked through the door on Monday morning.

"Tell him not to worry. I've got it all in hand."

"Really?"

"Absolutely. There's nothing to worry about."

"Have you?" Winky asked.

"Have I *what*?"

"Got the lawsuit sorted? Did you dig up any dirty little secrets on Harmony Fashion like I told you to?"

"I haven't had the chance, and I'm so busy I don't know when I'll find the time."

"I have a suggestion."

"This should be good."

"Instead of taking ten percent of our winnings when you recover them, how about I dig up the dirt you need on Harmony?"

"And how are you going to do that?"

"By using my network of feline sleuths of course."

"*Feline sleuths*?"

"No one gives us felines a second glance. That's why we're able to listen in on two-leggeds conversations without raising suspicions. If you agree to my proposal, I'll contact the felines who live in and around Harmony's place, and if there are any dirty little secrets to be found, they'll find them. What do you say?"

"I'm not sure."

"Would you rather face bankruptcy? Because from what I heard Armi say, that's pretty much a given."

"Okay, it's a deal, but your friends had better come up with the goods."

"Excellent decision. You won't regret it."

No sooner had we reached an agreement than Winky was out of the window. He seemed confident that his feline sleuths would come up with the goods. For my sake, I hoped he was right. Before I did anything else, I decided to have a quick recap on the various cases that I was trying to juggle, so I jotted them all down:

Charles Brown: I needed to find out where Charles' son, Max, was getting his supply of blood. Hopefully, he wasn't attacking humans on his nightly excursions. I should know more after following him that night.

Jack Maxwell (AKA Jack Two): I desperately needed to speak to his brother, Keith. My idea to get him to agree to an interview with a magazine had failed miserably, so I would have to take a different approach.

Queen Stella: I still wanted to talk to Prince Michael, but I suspected tracking him down wasn't going to be easy. I also needed to find a brewmaiden, but I didn't have a clue where to start looking. I just hoped Grandma wasn't right about Rosy being a liar. She had seemed genuine enough to me.

Winky/Socks: I still wasn't totally convinced that Socks had been robbed, but Winky clearly believed his brother. It wouldn't do any harm to pay a visit to the casino to see if that revealed anything of interest.

My workload wouldn't have been quite so bad if Jack

was still working with me, instead of poncing around in that record shop. Speaking of record shops, my phone rang with a call from Mad.

"Have you called to tell me you're sacking that husband of mine?"

"What? No, of course not. Brad reckons Jack is a natural. He's very good with the customers. I'm calling about Gillian, your sister's ghost."

"Oh, right. Did you manage to come up with anything that might help her transition to GT?"

"Yes, I think so. When I was asking around, an old colleague of mine overheard my conversation, and told me something that I think might be of interest. There's a small bookshop on the outskirts of GT, and the owner is looking for an assistant because it's getting too much for her to run by herself. Ideally, she would like someone who has experience of working in a bookshop."

"That does sound interesting, although it's quite a while since Gillian actually worked in a book shop."

"I spoke to the book shop owner, Patricia, and she said she'd definitely like to speak to Gillian."

"That's brilliant."

"It gets even better. The job comes with a small flat above the shop."

"That would solve all Gillian's problems in one fell swoop. I'd better go and let her have the good news. I'm pretty sure she'll jump at the opportunity."

"Okay. If she does like the sound of it, let me know and I'll set up a meeting with Patricia."

I felt sure that Gillian would be thrilled when she heard about the job in the bookstore in GT. The sooner I let her know, the sooner Mad could get the ball rolling, so I headed straight out to Kathy's shop.

I had hoped it would be bustling with customers, so that I could sneak into the stockroom without Kathy noticing me, but I was out of luck because she was behind the counter, looking at something on her phone. I waited until the street was deserted, then made myself invisible, and magicked myself straight into the stockroom. Once in there, I reversed the 'invisible' spell, and then peered out into the shop, to make sure Kathy was still seated at the counter. She was, and from this angle, I could see she was flicking through stupid short video clips.

The last time I'd been in the stockroom, I had relied on Lizzie to summon Gillian, but this time I'd have to try and do it myself. But how was I going to do that without attracting Kathy's attention? For once, luck was on my side because I heard the main door to the shop opening, followed by voices.

"Alison, how lovely to see you again," Kathy said. "Are you excited?"

"I am. I can't wait to see it."

A young woman, accompanied by another woman who I took to be her mother, was talking to Kathy. Based on what I'd heard, the young woman had come for the final fitting of her wedding dress. The three of them were soon deep in conversation about the upcoming nuptials, which gave me the opportunity I needed.

After making my way to the far side of the stockroom, I called in a low voice, "Gillian, are you there?"

I waited but there was no response, so I tried again, a little louder this time.

"Gillian, are you—?"

"Here I am." She appeared a few feet in front of me.

"Do you have your young friend with you again?"

"Not today. Lizzie is at school. Look, I'll have to make this quick while my sister is occupied in the shop."

I explained what Mad had told me about the job in the bookshop and I could tell by the way her face lit up that she was thrilled.

"I can't believe it, Jill. That's way better than I could ever have hoped for. And accommodation too."

"You'll have to have an interview with the owner, but I think it's just a formality. Would you like me to tell her to go ahead and arrange that?"

"Yes, please."

"When are you available?"

"Anytime. It's not like I have anything else going on."

"Okay, I'll get that set up."

"Jill? Is that you?" Kathy shouted.

Oh bum! She was on her way towards the stockroom.

"You'd better go," I told Gillian.

What to do? If I made myself invisible, Kathy would think the ghost had returned. I would just have to do what I did best. Lie.

"Hi, Kathy."

"What are you doing? How did you get in here?"

"You were busy with customers, so I came straight through."

"I didn't see you."

"Like I said, you were busy with those customers."

Still puzzled, she said, "Why are you here, though?"

"I just wanted to check Gillian had definitely left."

"The ghost?"

"Yeah, and I'm pleased to report that she has. Gone, that is." I made a point of checking my watch. "Is that the time? I have to get going."

"But I—err—what—err—?" She spluttered as I hurried past her and out of the shop.

Chapter 16

I was about to return to the office when I received a call from Aunt Lucy, asking if I could pop over. I asked if everything was okay and she assured me it was, but there was something in her voice that made me suspect she wasn't telling me the truth.

"I baked some cupcakes yesterday. Would you like one with your tea?"

"I probably shouldn't."

"Okay."

"Hold on. That wasn't a *no*."

"It sounded a lot like one."

"No, it was a guarded yes."

"O—kay." She rolled her eyes. "Why don't you go through to the lounge while I make the tea?"

Five minutes later, I took a bite of one of the most delicious cupcakes I'd ever eaten.

"This is amazing, Aunt Lucy. What flavour is it?"

"Waddle berry."

"*Waddle*?"

"They're only found in the forests that surround CASS. I was lucky to get hold of them. It's over twenty years since I last saw any on the market."

"Those forests are full of dragons and goodness knows what else. Who would risk their life to collect berries?"

"I have no idea but I'm jolly glad they did. I hear Grandma has recruited you to help with that festival of hers."

"I assume the twins told you?"

"Yeah, I don't imagine they're best pleased at having to supply the cakes for the festival."

"They're not, but they are looking forward to spending the day in Washbridge."

"I'm just surprised that Grandma allowed the catering company to renege on their commitment like that. She's usually such a tough cookie when it comes to business."

"Hmm." Aunt Lucy grinned.

"What?"

"Think about it for a second and you'll understand."

"There never was a catering company, was there? She always planned to get me and the twins to do it for free, didn't she?"

"That would be my guess."

"And I fell for it. Hook, line and sinker. Does that woman have no scruples?"

"If she does, she keeps them well hidden."

"Are these cupcakes smaller than usual?"

"Is that Jill-speak for *can I have another*?"

"Go on, then. If you insist."

After Aunt Lucy had handed me a second waddle berry cupcake, she said, "While you're here, do you think you could have a chat with Rhymes? He's not been himself lately."

"I knew something was wrong when you called."

"I'm sure it's nothing to worry about, but he won't open up to me. Maybe, you'll have more luck."

"Where are the other two rascals today?"

"They're at my friend, Geraldine's, house. She has two corgis who are good friends with the boys."

As soon as I'd finished the second cupcake, I went upstairs to see Rhymes, but there was no sign of him in the spare bedroom where he spent most of his time.

"Rhymes?"

"Under here." The tiny voice came from under the bed.

As he showed no sign of coming out, I got down on all fours and peered underneath.

"What are you doing under there? Are you okay?"

"I'm fine." He sighed.

"It doesn't sound like you are. Can you come out here, please?"

"Okay." He sighed and made his way out at a snail's (or should that be tortoise's) pace.

"Aunt Lucy is worried about you."

"She doesn't need to be. I'm fine."

"Clearly, you aren't. Why don't you tell me what's wrong?"

"I'm just being silly."

"Let me be the judge of that. What's the matter?"

"It's not that I don't like Buddy, but—" He hesitated.

"He's not been nasty to you, has he?"

"What? No. Nothing like that."

"What then?"

"Before he came to live here, Barry and I used to hang around together all of the time, but now those two spend all their time together."

"Don't they include you?"

"Sometimes, but mostly I can't do the sort of things they like to do. Can you picture me chasing after a ball?"

"I see what you mean. How about I have a word with the two of them and ask them to come up with stuff that you can join in with?"

"No, don't do that. They'll just resent me."

"I don't like to see you down like this."

"There is something you could do."

"What's that?"

"If I had a friend, it wouldn't matter that I didn't get to spend time with Barry and Buddy."

"Another tortoise, you mean?"

"Yeah."

"I'm not sure."

"Please, Jill, I'm so lonely. If it's the cost, I have some savings."

"It's not the money, and I think it's a good idea. It's just that—"

"What?"

"I don't know how Aunt Lucy would feel about having another pet in the house."

"Would you ask her? Please?"

"Yeah, I'll see what I can do."

"Thanks, Jill." He managed a weak smile that almost broke my heart.

"Did you find out what's wrong with him?" Aunt Lucy said when I got back downstairs.

"He's lonely."

"How can he be lonely when he's got Barry and Buddy for company?"

"That's just it. Those two tend to spend most of their time doing things together. I don't think they're being mean; it's just that dogs don't want to do the same things as tortoises."

"I see. Poor thing. I had no idea. I'm not sure what we can do about it, though. I doubt we can persuade the dogs to take an interest in poetry."

"He did have one suggestion, but I'm not sure you're going to like it."

"What's that?"

"He said he wished there was another tortoise in the

house who could be his friend, but I told him that you'd already said you don't want any more animals here."

"I said that when you were trying to get me to take in a dragon. Another tortoise wouldn't be a problem. It's not like they need taking out for walks."

"So, you'd be okay with it?"

"Yes, but you'll have to go and buy the new tortoise."

"No problem. I'll go and get one as soon as I leave here. Mind you—" I hesitated.

"What?"

"I'm going to need another one of those delicious cupcakes to sustain me on the walk over there."

"You're incorrigible. Go on, then."

"Thanks, Aunt Lucy. These really are delicious."

"How's work at the moment? Are you busy?"

"I am. Very. I'm working on several cases but I'm not making much progress on any of them. For instance, I've been hired by the Yella royal family to find out why their queen has been sleeping for several weeks."

"There are some days I feel like I could do that too. Sorry, that was rather flippant of me. Do you know what's causing it?"

"No, and the only lead I had has proved to be a dead end. I was told that I needed to make contact with a brewmaiden, but no one seems to know where I can find one."

"Have you looked in Candlefield Pages?"

"They aren't going to advertise in there." I scoffed.

"You never know." She went over to the sideboard and grabbed the directory. "Let's see. Breweries, Brewing Supplies, here it is: Brewmaidens."

"Really?"

"Yes, but there's only one listing under that category."

"Can I see?" I took the directory from her. "I can't believe it."

"Sometimes the simple way is the best."

"Thanks, I would never have thought of checking there." I made a note of the brewmaiden's name and phone number.

I had expected to find Truman Turtle behind the counter of Everything Reptile, but instead it was Bill Ratman, the owner of Everything Rodent, who greeted me.

"Hi, I wasn't expecting to find you here, Bill."

"Truman has had to go into hospital to have his appendix out. I said I'd look after this place while he's away. My wife is covering Everything Rodent while I'm here. What can I do for you?"

"I bought a tortoise from Truman some time ago, and I'd like another one to keep him company."

"I see. Did you want another male or a female?"

"I hadn't really thought about that. Probably best to make it another male."

"Okay, but I have to warn you that I'm not nearly as knowledgeable about reptiles as I am about Rodents, and it can be notoriously difficult to accurately sex young tortoises. Anyway, they're over this way." He led the way to the other side of the shop. "These are all we have at the moment."

I looked at the four tortoises in the glass tank, but they all looked the same to me. "Bill, do you think you could leave me to think about it for a few minutes?"

"No problem. Give me a shout when you've made your

mind up."

I turned my attention to the tortoises. "Okay, you guys, which of you are male?"

Two of them raised a paw (very slowly).

"I'm Harry," one of them said.

"And I'm Doodles."

"What about us?" said one of the females.

"Sorry, ladies. I'm looking for a male today."

"You'll regret it. These two are lazy slobs."

"That's not true," Harry defended himself.

The two females huffed and puffed a little more, but then turned around and started towards the other side of the tank, leaving me to address the two males.

"What do you two like to do?"

"Eat," they chorused.

"Apart from eating?"

"Sleep," Harry said.

"I like to draw," Doodles answered.

"Right, thanks." I walked back to the counter. "I've made my choice, Bill."

***

"Do you really have to go out tonight?" Jack asked when we'd finished dinner. "I thought we could watch TV together. There's a great new reality program starting today."

"There's no such thing as a *great* reality program. What's this one about?"

"It's called On Pins. It follows the ups and downs of the staff of a bowling alley."

"Unmissable as that sounds, I really do have to go out."

"What are you doing?"

"Following a vampire to find out where he's getting his supply of blood."

"I wish I hadn't asked." He pulled a face. "Don't you ever take on any *normal* investigations?"

"Very few, unfortunately."

I arrived at Charles Brown's house just before nightfall. I parked my car some distance from his house, but close enough that I would be able to see anyone leaving the property. Within only a few minutes of nightfall, the front door opened, and Max stepped out. Even from that distance, he looked pale and drawn. Dressed in a leather jacket and jeans, he set off in the opposite direction to where I was parked, so I set off after him on foot. To have survived this long, he must have been getting a supply of blood from somewhere. I just hoped he wasn't satisfying his thirst by attacking humans. When I'd visited Max's bedroom, he'd been dead to the world, which meant I could follow just a few yards behind, without the fear of him recognising me. If it looked as though he was about to attack someone, I would be able to intervene. We had walked about a mile when he stepped into a park. There were no streetlights in there, but fortunately the light from the full moon meant that I was still able to see Max's silhouette. He kept to the path and appeared to be headed towards the gate at the other side of the park. I was just beginning to think that he was simply taking a shortcut when he took a right off the path and headed towards a clump of bushes. Moments later, I heard voices coming from behind the bushes. I quickly made myself invisible and went to investigate.

"That's twice as much as you charged me last time!"

Max said.

The vampire, who had obviously been waiting for Max, shrugged. "That's the price. Take it or leave it."

Clearly unhappy, Max handed over the cash and snatched the bottle. He no sooner had it in his hand, than he unscrewed the cap, and took a huge swig.

"Don't drink that here," the older vampire scolded. "A human might see."

Max either wasn't listening or simply didn't care because he took a second drink. "When will you be back?"

"The day after tomorrow."

"Same time?"

"Yeah, and don't be late."

Although I was relieved that Max hadn't resorted to attacking humans, I was pretty sure that the blood he was drinking was real, not synthetic. That's why, instead of staying with Max, I followed the older vampire. He left through the gate on the opposite side of the park. Waiting just outside the gate was a car with the engine idling. Another vampire was seated in the driving seat. I needed to follow these guys and the best way to do that was to magic myself into the back seat of the car.

"How did it go?" the driver asked his colleague.

"Piece of cake."

"He paid the higher price?"

"Course he did. You know what these newbies are like; they're desperate."

"You've got to hand it to Lanzo. It was a brilliant plan of his."

"How many more drops have we got tonight?"

"Another six."

For the remainder of the night, I stayed with this pair of

reprobates, as they sold blood to several vampires across Washbridge. Their customers all had a number of things in common. They were all young, and they were all what the blood-pedlars referred to as newbies. And they were all desperate.

"Okay?" the driver enquired after the last drop.

"Yeah, she would have paid double to get her hands on it."

"Let's get back and report to Lanzo."

"And grab a beer."

"Of course."

I gathered from that exchange that the two of them were about to head back to Candlefield. As a witch, I was able to magic myself back and forth between the two worlds, so I sometimes forgot that other sups had to make the journey by more conventional means. The journey to Candlefield brought back a few memories, not least of which was my first attempt to drive there when I'd completely missed the turn-off.

The car eventually came to a halt outside a rundown pub—apparently it was my week to visit sleazy pubs. Outside the door were two doormen who waved my new friends inside. I was about to follow them when I happened to glance up and spotted the sign above the door. Then, instead of going inside, I called Daze.

"Hey, it's Jill."

"Hi."

"What's the name of that pub you and Blaze have been watching?"

"Bar Red. Why?"

Chapter 17

Florence had finished her breakfast and gone up to her bedroom to play with Jay before she had to go to school.

"Do you think she's okay?" Jack gestured to the stairs.

"Florence? Yeah. Why?"

"She hasn't buzzed once this morning."

"She hasn't, has she? Hopefully, that means she's come through the Bluebottle Girl phase."

I was just about to leave the table when Aunt Lucy called. She had promised to call me today, to let me know how Rhymes and his new companion were getting along. I hadn't expected her to contact me so early, and my first thought was that there had been some kind of problem.

"I hope I haven't called too early, Jill, I wasn't sure if you'd be up yet."

"It's fine. What's wrong?"

"Nothing. I just wanted to tell you that Rhymes and Doodles are getting on like a house on fire."

"That's great. I was worried they might not hit it off."

"You can stop worrying, then. They were up until the early hours of the morning chatting." She laughed. "Much to Buddy's annoyance."

"Oh dear."

"It's okay. He and Barry often do the same thing, so he can't complain. Have you seen any of Doodles' work?"

"No. He mentioned that he liked to draw, which is the main reason I chose him. With Rhymes being a poet, I thought he might appreciate someone with an interest in art."

"You were right. It's pretty much a mutual appreciation society. And the best thing is that Rhymes is back to his old self."

"That's fantastic. Thanks for letting me know."

"Good news, I take it," Jack said when I'd finished on the call.

"The best. Doodles and Rhymes have hit it off big time."

"That's great, but I still don't understand how a tortoise can draw."

"Who cares? Rhymes is happy. That's all that matters. By the way, have you made a Will?"

"What?" Jack looked stunned. "Where did that come from?"

"Just in case you don't make it back from Sweeney Todd's."

"Very funny. Joking apart, that's something we both should do. We're not getting any younger."

"Speak for yourself. I'm not the one with grey hairs."

"I don't have any grey hairs. You're just trying to wind me up, but it isn't working." He stood up and started for the stairs.

I would have bet a year's supply of custard creams that he was going to check his hair in the bathroom mirror. Tee-hee.

***

I'd no sooner got into the car when my phone rang again.

"It's Jack."

No, it wasn't my lazy husband who couldn't be bothered to come outside; it was the other Jack Maxwell in my life, AKA Jack Two.

"Hi. I was just wondering if you had any update for

me?"

"Not really. Your half-brother isn't the easiest person to get hold of. I do have a question for you, though."

"What's that?"

"How come you never mentioned the argument you had with Joseph on the day before the murder?"

"Because there wasn't one. I didn't even see Joseph that day."

"And yet, your secretary testified that she'd overheard the two of you arguing. She said it sounded like you almost came to blows."

"I know what she said, but it isn't true. I wasn't there."

"Are you saying she was lying?"

"I'm saying I wasn't there."

"What was your relationship like with Jean Longton?"

"We had a good relationship. At least, I thought we did."

"Why would she lie, then?"

"I've no idea. Sorry, Jill, I have to go."

I was rapidly losing confidence in anything Jack Two told me. He denied being at Joseph's flat at the time of the murder, despite CCTV evidence to the contrary. And now, he denied arguing with Joseph on the previous day, even though his secretary had testified that she had overheard them. Was he simply in denial? Ideally, I needed to speak to his half-brother, but so far that was proving difficult. Maybe I'd have more luck tracking down Jean Longton.

When I walked into the outer office, I thought at first it was deserted, but then I realised I was not alone.

"Mrs V? Why are you under your desk?"

"I can't find it."

"Find what? What have you lost?"

"One of my contact lenses."

"Since when did you wear contact lenses?"

"I got them yesterday."

"You never mentioned you were going to get contacts."

"I wanted to surprise you, but I dropped one of them."

"I'll help you." I got down on my hands and knees. "You take that side, and I'll take this side."

"Okay, thanks."

Ten minutes later, and I was beginning to think we weren't going to find it when Mrs V whooped, then yelled in pain. She was so excited at finding her contact lens that she'd banged her head on the underside of the desk.

"Are you okay?"

"I'm fine. I'd better go and clean this stupid thing before I put it back in."

"When you're sorted, will you pop into my office because I have a little job for you. Oh, and a cup of tea wouldn't go amiss."

"Will do, but I might be a while because I'm not very good at putting these things in."

"A fiver says it doesn't last until the end of the month," Winky said.

"What doesn't?"

"The old bag lady and her contact lenses. Care to take the bet?"

"What makes you think she won't make a go of them?"

"She's much too old."

"You're talking nonsense. Mrs V is more than capable of adapting to contact lenses."

Just then, the door opened, and Mrs V walked in carrying my cup of tea; she had one eye screwed tightly shut.

"Are you okay, Mrs V?"

"I'm still struggling to get it back in, so I thought I'd better bring you your tea before it went cold."

"Right, thanks."

"I'll pop back as soon as I've got the lens back in." She headed back to the outer office.

"I wouldn't hold your breath if I was you." Winky laughed. "She'll still be at it come lunchtime."

I didn't have to wait quite as long as Winky suggested, but it was almost forty-five minutes later when Mrs V returned.

"I'm sorry it took me so long, dear. That pesky thing didn't want to go back in."

"Is it okay now?"

"Oh yes. All sorted. I'm sure I'll get quicker at it. Now, what was it you wanted me to do?"

"You remember that you tried to make me an appointment with Keith Maxwell earlier in the week."

"I do and I'm afraid I failed miserably."

"Jean Longton was employed as a secretary by Trentmore Construction at the time Joseph Deer was murdered. I suppose it's possible that she still works there, but it's unlikely. Either way, I need you to track her down."

"Then what?"

"That's all. Once you've found her, I'll do the rest."

"Do you have any more information about her?"

"I'm afraid not."

"No problem." Her right eye began to blink rapidly. "I'll get straight on it."

"Are you okay?"

"I'm fine." She just managed to get her hand out in time to catch the contact lens. "Anything else, Jill?"

"No, that's it, thanks."

"Priceless." Winky was in hysterics. "I'm going to revise that wager. A fiver says she gives up on them by the end of the day."

Before I could respond, I got a phone call from Daze.

"Thanks for the tip off, Jill. We've been trying to close down Bar Red for some time, but we didn't have anything concrete to pin on them. We picked up your two friends on their way out of the bar. When we explained what we had on them, and how long they stood to face inside, they soon began to sing. In return for a reduced sentence, they've agreed to testify against Lanzo, the Mister Big of the operation. Shutting down Bar Red and taking that little scrote off the streets is a major win."

"That's brilliant news. I assume it was real human blood they were selling?"

"It was."

"Where were they getting it from?"

"Lanzo employed a gang of some of the most despicable vampires in Candlefield. They kidnapped innocent people from the human world and brought them back to Candlefield where they were drained of their blood."

"That's awful."

"They picked on people sleeping rough, in the hope that their disappearance would go unnoticed, and for the most part, that seems to have worked. Lanzo also employed small teams of vampires, like those two you saw last night, to sell the blood in the human world. They were told to target newly turned humans, but that was easier said than done. When they were unable to find enough newbies, some of the vampires took it upon themselves to create their own."

"Are you saying that they turned humans just to create customers?"

"That's exactly what I'm saying."

"There aren't words. I know you had to offer those guys a reduced sentence to get them to talk, but really the whole lot of them should spend the rest of their lives behind bars."

"I agree but it is what it is. Things happened so quickly last night that you didn't actually explain how you happened to stumble upon our two friends."

I told Daze how I'd been hired by Charles Brown to try and find out what was wrong with his son, Max, and that I'd realised he had been recently turned.

"I thought he might be attacking people to satisfy his bloodlust, so it was something of a relief when I discovered he was actually buying the blood from those two scumbags. I'm worried about what he'll do now that his supply has been cut off."

"I may be able to help there."

"Oh?"

"I have a contact in the synthetic blood industry. There's a network of synthetic blood outlets throughout the human world, specifically for people like Max. I'll have a word with him and find out where Max's nearest outlet is."

"That would be great. Now, all I have to do is to work out what I'm going to tell his father."

"I don't envy you that task. Good luck. I'll call you later."

"I should get some kind of compensation," Winky said.

"For what?"

"The trauma I suffer having to listen to you talk about vampires and blood. It turns my stomach."

"You'll not be wanting any salmon, then, I assume?"

"I wouldn't go that far. Seriously, though, don't you ever wish you did a normal job?"

"Like what?"

"I don't know. Something with fewer vampires and less blood would be a start."

"I've often thought I would have made a good barrister."

"Maybe, but those coffee machines can be pretty complicated."

"I said barrister *not* barista."

"You, a barrister? That's a joke."

"Okay, how about I become an influencer?"

"You don't even know what that is."

"Yes, I do. They make silly money just for making funny videos."

"But you're not funny. If anyone in this office could be a successful influencer, it's yours truly."

"What would you recommend I do, then?"

"Divorce Jack and find yourself a rich husband."

"Actually, that's not such a bad idea."

What? I was joking. Sheesh. I would never leave Jack for a millionaire. A billionaire, though, that's a different matter.

Chapter 18

I now had a contact number for the brewmaiden. When I made the call, I half expected an answerphone, but someone picked up on the first ring.

"Hello, this is Rebecca Rebel."

"Oh hi. I saw your listing in Candlefield Pages."

"Which one?"

"*Candlefield* Pages."

"No, I meant which listing? I have several."

"Oh? The one under brewmaidens."

"Ah, right. How can I help you?"

"It's rather complicated. Would it be possible to come and see you sometime within the next few days?"

"I'm afraid I'm going on holiday tomorrow for two weeks."

"Oh no."

"I could spare you a little time now if you can get over here in the next hour or so."

"No problem."

Once she had given me her address, I magicked myself straight over there. Rebecca Rebel lived in a rather unusual property. It was circular and resembled a very short lighthouse. The really strange thing was that there didn't appear to be a door at ground level. The only door I could see was on the upper floor of the property, so somewhat confused, I rang Rebecca.

"Hi, I'm outside your place."

"Gosh, that was quick."

"I'm not sure how to get inside. I can't see a door down here."

"Just a moment." The door opened and Rebecca peered

down at me. "Hang on, I'll lower the rope ladder."

"There's no need." I used the 'levitate' spell to float up to the door.

"Do come inside. Sorry, I didn't catch your name."

"It's Jill. Jill Maxwell."

"*The* Jill Maxwell?"

"I suppose so."

"Wait until I tell my mum you were here. I was just about to have a coffee. Would you like one?"

"Yes, please."

Once we had our drinks we took a seat in the lounge, which for such an unconventional property, was pretty conventional.

"This is a very unusual building."

"Its quirkiness is what attracted me to it. That and the price. It had been on the market for almost a year when I came across it. I still don't understand why no one else had snapped it up."

"Might it have been because of the door?"

"I don't think so. It's pretty solid; no trace of rot."

"I was thinking more about its position."

"Hmm, I hadn't considered that."

"Doesn't it make things a little awkward?"

"Not really. The rope ladder is perfectly safe."

"But what about when you come home? How do you get up here?"

"The door and rope ladder are all automated." She took a small gadget from her pocket. "I just press this button and the door opens and the ladder drops down. To rewind the rope and close the door, I press the other button. I love it."

"Right. I hope you don't think this a rude question,

Rebecca, but what kind of sup are you? You're not a witch, are you?"

"No, more's the pity. I'd love to possess just a quarter of your powers. I'm a brewmaiden, but I thought you knew that."

"I did, but I assumed that was just an occupation, like a chef or a mechanic. Sorry."

"No problem. You aren't the first person to make that mistake."

"You mentioned on the phone that you listed your services under a number of different categories?"

"I had to diversify because there simply isn't the demand for a brewmaiden's services these days. I do dog walking, house cleaning and origami tuition. Between them all, I just about manage to scrape by."

"That's quite a mix. It's a pity I didn't know about you a few weeks ago because I needed someone to teach my dog origami."

"Your dog?"

"That's a story for another time. The thing is, I've been hired to try and find out why the queen of the Yellas has been asleep for several weeks. All the physicians and scientists have drawn a blank, but someone suggested that a brewmaiden may be able to help. Hence why I'm here today. You're pretty much my last hope."

"How much do you know about brewmaidens?"

"If I'm being completely honest, nothing at all."

"Centuries ago, brewmaidens were in great demand. Sups of all kinds came to us for all manner of potions. More recently, though, witches and wizards have become more skilled in the art of potion making, which has resulted in fewer and fewer people needing our services.

These days, the only people who require a brewmaiden's services are those who need a potion for their pets."

"Does that mean you won't be able to help?"

"Not necessarily. I am occasionally asked for a potion to cure insomnia in dogs."

"I'm sorry, but I don't see how that helps me."

"The potion works like a charm on dogs, but it's known to have a few serious side-effects if taken by sups. Whenever anyone buys this particular potion, I always make a point of emphasising the need for care."

"What kind of side-effects?"

"One of them is that it can induce a permanent sleep state."

"That could be it. But how come none of the doctors or scientists identified the potion?"

"I wouldn't expect them to because all brewmaiden potions leave no trace once taken."

"Is there a way to reverse the effects of the potion you mentioned?"

"I'm afraid not."

"Is there nothing that can be done, then?"

"I didn't say that. There's another potion designed for dogs who, given half a chance, would spend all day asleep. It's just possible that may counteract the sleep potion."

"But you're not sure?"

"No, we're in uncharted territory here."

"But if we do nothing, will the queen wake up eventually?"

"No. Left alone, she'll sleep forever."

"Then, I guess we have nothing to lose. How long would it take to produce such a potion?"

"Normally, I'd say a couple of days, but because I'm going on holiday, I could start work on it immediately. If I do that, it should be ready by midnight. Would you be able to collect it then?"

"Absolutely, and I appreciate you doing this."

"Don't mention it."

"My second question is do you remember who purchased the sleeping draught from you?"

"I've sold probably half a dozen of these potions in the last year."

"How many of those did you sell to Yellas?"

"Only one."

"Could you describe the purchaser?"

"That's easy."

She proceeded to give me a detailed description of the Yella who had purchased the potion, and one particular thing she said rang a bell with me. I was now confident that I knew who was responsible for putting the queen in a deep sleep, so I made a call to Princess Stella.

"Jill? Do you have something for me?"

"Not yet, but I am starting to make progress. There's just one big stumbling block that is impeding my investigation, and I'm hoping you might be able to clear it away."

"Tell me what you need."

"It's essential that I speak to your brother."

"I thought Ralph had arranged for you to speak to Michael."

"He had, supposedly, but the Prince was a no-show. I was wondering if you might have more luck. I'm sorry to have to bother you with this because I know how busy you are."

"It's okay. Nothing is more important than my mother's health. Can you leave it with me?"

"Of course."

"I'll get back to you as soon as I've arranged something."

"Thanks."

***

When I arrived home, it was Florence who greeted me at the door.

"Daddy's got funny hair." She giggled.

I'd forgotten about Jack's hair appointment with Zeus. "Where is Daddy?"

"Upstairs."

Jack was in the bedroom, staring at himself in the wardrobe mirror. When he caught sight of my reflection, he turned around.

"Before you say anything, I like it," he insisted.

"Me too. It suits you."

"Why are you smirking?"

"I'm not. Whose idea were the highlights?"

"I told Julian what you'd said about my grey hairs, and he suggested highlights would be the best way to disguise them. You don't like it, do you?"

"I just need a while to get used to it. Five years ought to do it."

"I don't care what you think. I like it and it goes with my new image."

"I didn't realise you had one."

Just then, my phone rang. "I'd better take this. It's probably the nineties wanting their highlights back."

"Sorry?" Daze said.

"Nothing. My husband is just having a bad hair day."

"I've got the address for the synthetic blood centre closest to your client."

"Great. Can you text it over to me?"

"Will do. My contact did make the point that Max will need more than just a supplier of synthetic blood, though."

"What do you mean?"

"Think about it. One minute, he was a human, the next he's a sup."

"I kind of know that feeling."

"Not really. You were always a sup; you just didn't know it."

"That's true."

"This young man has been human all his life and now, suddenly, he's a vampire. He must be feeling terribly confused and lost."

"I guess so."

"He knows nothing about sups or about Candlefield for example."

"I guess that means I need to have a long talk to him."

"I think so. And don't forget to explain that once he starts to drink the synthetic blood, he'll be able to go out in the daylight."

"How does that work? I've never really given it much thought until now."

"Vampires who drink only human blood can only go out after dark in the human world. If they venture out in daylight—well, let's just say it's not a good idea. The synthetic blood contains a number of additives that allow a vampire to go out in the daylight. It might be a little uncomfortable at first, but it'll improve over time."

"Thanks, Daze, that's very helpful. I'll go and see him tonight."

"Good luck."

Jack was in the kitchen, making dinner.

"How was your day?" I asked.

"Okay until you started mocking my hair."

"Come here." I gave him a peck on the cheek. "I was only kidding. I think the highlights are kind of sexy."

"Really?"

"Absolutely. I'm not sure I'll be able to keep my hands off you tonight."

That got his attention. "Maybe we could have an early night, once Florence is in bed?"

"I'd love to, but I have an appointment with a vampire."

He shook his head. "Some wives would say they had a headache. My wife has a meeting with a vampire."

When it came time to put Florence to bed, I realised I hadn't heard her buzz once since I'd arrived home. Had she finally grown tired of Bluebottle Girl? I daren't raise the subject for fear of reminding her.

"Mummy, why am I a witch?"

The question took me aback. "Because I'm a witch."

"If you'd been a fairy, would I have been a fairy?"

"I suppose so."

She sighed. "I wish you had been a fairy."

"Witches are more powerful than fairies."

"But fairies' wings are super cool."

"Night, night." I gave her a kiss.

"I'm going to dream I'm a fairy."

"Okay. Goodnight."

***

The supply of blood that I'd witnessed Max purchase the previous night should have lasted him a couple of days, so I was hoping he'd be at home. I couldn't tell Charles that I intended to speak to his son because he would have wanted to know why.

By the time I left the house, Jack had said he'd forgiven me for the comments about his hair, and he'd asked me to hurry back as quickly as possible which, when translated, meant he was still feeling frisky. The only light on in the Brown house was in the room I knew to be Max's bedroom. Whichever way I did this, it was bound to startle the young man, so I just went for it and magicked myself into his bedroom. He was on his bed, but this time he was sitting up, eyes wide open. I had been worried that he would shout out and waken his father, but the young man was so shocked, he simply stared at me open-mouthed.

"Hi, Max."

"What? Who?" He spluttered.

"There's nothing to be scared of. I'm here to help you."

"Who are you?"

"My name is Jill Maxwell and I'm a witch."

"There's no such thing."

"I beg to differ. Just watch."

First, I shrank myself to a few inches tall. After reversing the 'shrink' spell, I made myself invisible. After a few seconds I reversed that spell, and then used the 'doppelganger' spell to change my appearance, so that I looked like Max.

"How? What?" He stared at me/himself.

"Do you believe me now?" I changed back into myself.

"I guess so, but what are you doing here?"

"I'm here to talk about what happened to you recently."

"I don't know what you mean," he said, defensively.

"It's okay to talk to me about it."

"About what?"

"The puncture marks on your neck for starters. And the blood you've been buying from that lowlife in the park."

What little fight had been left in him evaporated, and he sat there in silence for the longest moment, then eventually managed, "I don't know what happened. Well, I know what happened, but I don't understand it."

I wasn't sure that was entirely true; it was more likely he did know, but couldn't yet come to terms with it. Regardless, I played along.

"That's okay. I'll explain what happened and then you can ask me any questions you may have. Is that okay?"

He nodded.

"Is it okay if I take a seat?"

Another nod.

"The person who attacked you and made those puncture marks in your neck was a vampire."

"They're not real. They only exist in books and movies."

"They're real, trust me. The vampire who attacked you could have killed you, but instead they turned you."

"What does that mean?"

Once again, I was pretty sure he already knew the answer to that.

"It means that you are now a vampire, which is why you have had the uncontrollable desire to drink blood."

"It's disgusting. I hate myself for doing it."

"You mustn't be so hard on yourself. None of this is your fault."

"I don't want to be a vampire. Can you change me back to how I used to be?"

"That isn't possible."

"Please!" Tears began to well.

"If I could, I would, but I can't. I can do the next best thing, though."

"What's that?"

"I can show you how to get most of your old life back. You'll be able to go back to doing all the things you used to: socialising, sport, work."

"How can I when I can't even go out in the daytime? It's too painful."

"Before I get into that, I have one question for you: how did you know where to go to buy your supply of blood?"

"I don't remember much about the attack, but when I came around, I managed to make it back here. Halfway through the next day, I became incredibly hungry, but no amount of food satisfied my hunger. As the day went on, I began to feel more and more weak, so I decided to nip out to the local takeaway. I didn't make it very far because as soon as I stepped out into the daylight, the pain began. I came back inside and as I put my keys back into my pocket, I discovered a business card." He reached into the drawer of the bedside cabinet, took out the card and handed it to me.

The card contained a single word: **Hungry?** and then a phone number.

"I was so desperate that I called the number. The man I spoke to told me to meet him that night in the park. I was scared, but I was desperate for something to satisfy the hunger that seemed to be eating my insides. When I got there, he asked me for cash, and then handed me a bottle. I had no idea what it was at first, and when I took a sip, I almost threw up, but the hunger started to ease almost immediately. I hated myself for doing it, but I drank the lot."

"And you've been meeting with him regularly since then?"

"Yes. I try and go as long as I can without it, but after two or three days, I have no choice but to contact him again."

"Right. Now, I need you to listen to what I have to say, and I have to warn you that you might find some of it difficult to hear. Okay?"

"Okay."

"The vampire who attacked you is almost certainly the same person who now sells you the blood. By turning you, he created a customer for his contraband. I realise it will be little comfort to know that he and his colleagues have now been arrested and will be behind bars for a very long time."

"You're right. It isn't."

"In case you haven't already worked it out, the blood you have been drinking is human blood."

"Oh no." He shook his head. "I'd tried to convince myself it was animal blood. Are you sure?"

"Yes."

"Where does it come from?"

"It won't do any good for me to get into that. The important thing is that there are supplies of synthetic blood available, not too far from here."

"Will that satisfy my hunger in the same way?"

"Yes, and it has the added advantage of allowing you to go out in the daylight again."

"Really?" His face lit up for the first time. "Are you sure?"

"Yes, although you may have to ease yourself into it gradually."

He fell silent for a moment and then asked, "Are there others? Like me, I mean?"

"Most vampires who live here in the human world are—"

"What do you mean by the *human world*?"

"I'll get to that in a minute."

"Most of the vampires here in the human world were born as vampires. The others were once human but have been turned—just like you. It's actually illegal for vampires to turn humans, so it should never have happened."

"Are you saying I was just unlucky?"

"I'm afraid so. I realise you already have a lot to take in, but I need to explain something else. Vampires and witches are both sups, which is short for supernaturals. The majority of sups live in another world."

"What do you mean, *another world*?"

"Rather than try to explain, it will be easier to show you. Take my hand."

Somewhat reluctantly, he did as I said, and I magicked us both to the market place in Candlefield, which was still busy with sups visiting restaurants and bars.

"Welcome to Candlefield."

"How did you do that?"

"I'm able to magic myself back and forth between the

two worlds. Unfortunately, you won't be able to do that. You'll have to use your own transport or take the bus."

"This is wild. Who—err—what's that over there?"

"That's an elf. And the person behind him is a nymph. Once you start using the synthetic blood, I feel confident that you'll be able to live an almost normal life, but if you still find you can't cope, you always have the option of living here in Candlefield."

"This feels like a dream. I keep expecting to wake up."

"It's not a dream, I promise." I took his hand again. "We'd better get back."

I magicked us back to his bedroom where Max sat on the bed. Unsurprisingly, he looked a little shellshocked.

"Are you okay?" I asked.

"Yeah, it's just a lot to take in."

"I'm afraid there's still a little more I have to tell you."

"Okay?"

"I'm actually a private investigator here in Washbridge, and I was hired by your father."

"Dad? Why?"

"He's been worried about the way you've changed over recent months. He asked me to find out what had caused the change."

"Have you told him that I'm a—"

"No, he doesn't know any of this."

"Poor Dad. I've treated him terribly, but at least now I'll be able to explain why I've been acting so strangely."

"I'm afraid that won't be possible."

"You mean you don't think he'll believe it?"

"It's not that. It's illegal to tell humans that you are a sup."

"Not even my own father?"

"I'm afraid not. If you were to tell any human, the rogue retrievers would take you to Candlefield, and you'd be unable to leave there ever again."

"Rogue—?"

"Retrievers. They're kind of law enforcement."

"Won't Dad be expecting you to report back to him?"

"Yes, and I intend to, but I need to stall him for a week or so. If you start on the synthetic blood tomorrow, he'll hopefully see a change for the better in you by the time I report back."

"What will you tell him?"

"That I've drawn a blank. I think that's everything for now. Do you have any questions?"

"I don't think so."

I handed him my business card. "If you think of any or have any problems, just give me a call."

"Thanks, Jill, I appreciate everything you've done."

"No problem. Just do your best to build bridges with your father as soon as you start to feel better."

"I will. Don't worry."

I was really tired, but instead of going to bed, I had to magic myself over to Candlefield, to collect the potion from Rebecca Rebel.

"You're very prompt," she said, as she let me in.

"I can come back if I'm too early."

"No, it's fine. I finished the potion a few minutes ago. Wait here while I go and get it."

She returned a couple of minutes later and handed me a tiny bottle.

"Is this it? Will there be enough?"

"More than enough. Only a couple of drops are

required. You should place them on the patient's tongue."

"That's great, thanks."

"I hope it works."

"Just one more question before I go if I may?"

"Sure."

"Would the original potion, which caused the state of sleep, have been administered as drops too?"

"Yes, all brewmaiden potions are highly concentrated and administered as drops."

"Great. Thanks. Enjoy your holiday."

Chapter 19

The next morning, much to my chagrin, the buzzing was back.

"Florence, darling, what have I told you about buzzing when we're eating breakfast?"

"I'm not Florence."

Sigh.

"Bluebottle Girl, you have to stop buzzing while we eat breakfast."

"Okay."

"Thank you."

"Julie's mum has made her a Bluebottle Girl costume. She had it on at school yesterday. Will you make me one?"

"Your mummy isn't any good at sewing and stuff," Jack said.

What a cheek. "Yes, I am."

"Really?" Jack gave me a sceptical look.

"Just because I don't sew very often doesn't mean I can't."

"Fair enough. It looks like Mummy will be able to make you a Bluebottle Girl costume after all, pumpkin."

"Yay."

Florence had finished her muesli and jumped down from the table. As she walked by Jack, the two of them did a high-five, and unless I was very much mistaken, he winked at her.

"What was that about?" I said.

"What?"

"The high-five."

"Nothing."

"You winked at her."

"No, I didn't."

"I saw you." Suddenly it all became clear. "You two planned this, didn't you?"

"Planned what?" He shrugged, all innocent like.

"You knew I'd say no to making the costume, that's why you said I couldn't sew, isn't it? You knew I'd rise to the bait."

"I have no idea what you're talking about."

"Is this because I was late home last night?"

"Of course not, although I was a little disappointed. I'd been looking forward to sexy-time."

"It's not my fault you were fast asleep when I got home."

"You could have woken me."

"You were snoring."

"I never snore."

"Course you don't."

"How did it go last night, anyway?"

"A mix of good and bad."

"How so?"

"Good in the sense that the young man is probably going to be able to live a near normal life. Bad in the sense that I'm probably not going to get paid for that particular case."

"That sucks."

"Tell me about it."

***

Just when I thought there was nothing else Mrs V could do that would surprise me, she did.

"Good morning, Jill."

"Morning." I hesitated. "This may be a daft question, but why are you wearing a monocle?"

"It's the only way I can break in these contact lenses."

"Hang on. Are you telling me that you have a contact lens in the other eye?"

"Yes, I've not been able to keep both contact lenses in, so I decided to break one in at a time. As soon as I'm confident with this one, I'll swap the monocle to the other eye, and break in the second contact lens."

"You don't think it might be better to go back to the glasses?"

"Definitely not. Annabel Versailles doesn't give in that easily. I'm confident this approach will pay dividends."

"Fair enough."

I tried not to think about what my clients would make of my monocle-wearing receptionist.

"I managed to track down Mrs Longton, Jill."

"You did? Excellent."

"I've put a note with her current address on your desk."

"Thanks, Mrs V, you're a star."

"That woman has finally lost the plot," Winky said. "You need to get on the phone to those men in white coats."

"You know what they say, don't you? If you can't say anything nice, don't—"

"Wear a monocle?"

"I'll need you to be quiet this morning because I have a lot of work to do."

"Fair enough. You'll not want to know about Harmony Fashion, then."

"Have you dug up some dirt on them?"

"Might have." He grinned.

"Come on, then, tell me."

"Can't."

"What do you mean you can't?"

"The deal was that you find out who stole my money in return for me digging up some dirt on Harmony."

"I know that, but I haven't had the chance to get to the casino yet. I've spent the last two nights helping a young vampire."

"Not my problem." He shrugged.

"Why don't you tell me what you've found out and I'll go to the casino tonight?"

"I've got a better idea. Go to the casino tonight, and when you've recovered our money, I'll spill the beans on Harmony."

"I can't believe, after all the time you've known me, that you don't trust me."

"It's because of how long I've known you that I don't trust you."

Before I could respond, Mrs V came into my office. "The post has just arrived, Jill." She held out a brown envelope. "This is from Harmony's solicitors. Are you sure this is going to be alright?"

"Absolutely." I forced a smile. "There's nothing to worry about, honestly."

She didn't look convinced, but she didn't press the matter. After she'd left the office, I turned back to Winky who had a stupid grin on his face.

"Fine, I'll go to the casino tonight."

"Good decision."

Oh bum! Jack was going to be thrilled when I told him that sexy-time would have to be postponed again, especially when he discovered I was standing him up to help Winky.

***

As soon as I saw Jean Longton's address, I realised that she lived a few streets away from Kathy. I knew Kathy worked from home at least a couple of days a week, so I gave her a call on the off chance she was there, and for once, my luck was in.

"I didn't wake you, did I?" I said.

"Very funny. I've been hard at it for three hours."

"I'm going to be over in your neck of the woods shortly and I thought I could drop in for a quick chat."

"What do you want, Jill?"

"Why would you say that? Can't I just drop in to see my sister without there being some ulterior motive?"

"You could, but it's unlikely."

"I'm hurt."

"No, you're not. What time are you coming over?"

"I can be with you in thirty minutes if that's okay?"

"That's fine."

"See you soon."

I couldn't believe that Kathy thought I would only pay her a visit if I wanted something. I was genuinely hurt.

"Who's Bluebottle Girl?" Kathy said.

"She's some kind of weird superhero. All the kids, including Florence, are crazy about her."

"Can't you just buy her a costume?"

"I've already looked. There aren't any."

"I don't have time to make costumes. I'm snowed under with work."

"Come on, Kathy, you owe me for getting rid of your ghost."

"Hmm."

"And you're so good with a needle and thread. Please."

"When would you need it?"

"As soon as possible. How about Saturday?"

"That's tomorrow."

"Next Saturday, then?"

"Okay, but I'm doing it for Florence, not for you."

"You're the best sister in the world. You won't forget, will you?"

"Of course I won't."

"Do you have a diary?"

"Yeah."

"Write it in there."

"Sheesh, Jill, I said I won't forget."

"Please. Just humour me."

"Fine." She took out her diary, scribbled a note, and showed it to me:

BB superhero costume for Florence.

"Thanks."

"Were you really doing something in this neck of the woods, or did you just use that as an excuse to come over here, to ask me to make the costume?"

"No, I'm hoping to speak to a woman called Jean Longton. She lives on Westmoreland Road. Do you know her?"

"The name doesn't ring a bell. What has she done?"

"She hasn't done anything, but I'm hoping she might help me to prove my client, Jack Maxwell, is innocent of murder."

"Jack?" She looked horrified.

"Not *my* Jack Maxwell. Another one."

"That's a bit weird, isn't it? What are the chances of you having a client with the same name as your husband?"

"I call him Jack Two to avoid confusion. Anyway, enough about my work. How are the kids?"

"Okay. Lizzie is really devoting herself to her studies now. Mikey, not so much."

"Is he still into video games?"

"I'm afraid so. It's all he thinks about."

"How about Peter?"

"He's fine." She made a point of checking her watch. "I don't mean to be rude, but I've got a video conference call in fifteen minutes, and I need to prepare for it."

"No problem. I'll leave you to it. And you'll have that costume ready by next Saturday?"

"Yes, it'll be ready."

That's what I called a result. I hadn't just been flattering Kathy when I said she was an expert with needle and thread. Before she became a wealthy businesswoman, she often used to make clothes for herself and Lizzie. I could rest easy that the costume she made for Florence would be top notch.

I'd just left Kathy's house when I received a phone call from Princess Stella.

"Jill, I'm sorry it's taken a while to get back to you."

"That's okay."

"I've finally managed to pin my brother down. He's agreed to meet with you next Monday morning if that works for you?"

"That's fine. I'm glad you called because there's a couple of things that I need to ask of you."

"Shoot."

The princess was clearly surprised by what I had to say, but she agreed to go along with it, which would make Monday's meeting all the more interesting.

The properties on Westmoreland Road were much smaller than Maison Kathy. I had no idea how Jean Longton would react when I introduced myself, but as it turned out, I didn't get the chance.

"Oh?" said the slight, grey-haired woman who answered the door. "I wasn't expecting you for another twenty minutes." She had obviously mistaken me for someone else but before I could correct her, she had turned back into the house. "Come with me. It's in the kitchen."

I followed her into the kitchen at the rear of the house and looked out over a postcard perfect garden.

"What do you think?" She pointed to a foot spa.

The last time I'd seen one of those was when I'd bought one for Kathy and Peter's wedding anniversary. If I recall correctly, Kathy hadn't been too impressed.

"I think there may have been a mistake," I said.

"I don't see how. It's exactly the same as the photo I put online, and like I said in the listing, it's only been used once. It's practically brand new."

"I don't doubt it, but I'm not here about the foot spa."

"Oh? What do you want, then?"

"My name is Jill Maxwell." I handed her my card.

"A private investigator?"

"I've been hired by Jack Two."

"Who?"

"Sorry, I meant to say Jack Maxwell."

She glanced again at the card. "Are you related to

Jack?"

"No, that's just a coincidence."

"I thought he was still in prison?"

"He was recently released, and he's hired me to help prove he was never guilty of the murder of Joseph Deer."

"I think I'd better sit down." She pulled up the stool nearest to her. "This has all come as a bit of a shock."

"Are you willing to talk to me about what happened back then?"

"I guess so, but my memory isn't what it used to be."

"Thanks."

"Shall we have a cup of tea while we talk?" she offered.

"That would be lovely." So far this was going much better than I could have hoped.

Once we had our drinks, and were seated at the kitchen table, she said, "What do you want to know?"

"Could we start by you telling me what you remember of the three partners?"

"Okay. Of the three of them, I always liked Jack the best. He was always polite and kind towards me, not like the other two. That's why I found what happened so hard to believe. Joseph was okay, just very quiet. Then there was Keith." She shook her head. "I never liked him."

"Any particular reason?"

"He treated me like dirt, but to be fair, he did the same with everyone. And he could never accept responsibility. Whenever something went wrong, it was anyone's fault except his."

"How did the three of them get along together?"

"Jack and Joseph always seemed to get along alright. That's not to say they didn't have disagreements, but they always handled them in a civilised manner."

"And yet, from what I've read about the trial, you testified that you overheard Jack and Joseph having a blazing row."

"That's true. It was totally out of character for Jack. I'd never heard anything like it—not between those two at least. I honestly thought they were going to come to blows."

"You said at the time that you didn't know what the argument was about?"

"That's right. I couldn't hear what was being said."

"There's no doubt in your mind it was Jack who was arguing with Joseph?"

"None. I recognised his voice. And, anyway, I saw him when he stormed out a few minutes later."

"Did you speak to Joseph afterwards?"

Before she could answer my question, there was a knock at the door.

"Sorry, Jill, that must be the woman about the foot spa. Will you excuse me?"

"Of course."

A minute later, Jean returned, accompanied by a young woman wearing a tartan duffle coat and tartan high heels.

"This is it." Jean pointed to the foot spa.

The young woman's face lit up. "The Spa-man A245, excellent. I've been looking for one of these for ages."

"I only used it the once," Jean said. "But it was very relaxing."

"Oh, I won't be using it. I'm a collector."

"Of foot spas?" I blurted out without thinking.

"Are you here for the spa too?"

I was just about to say no when it occurred to me that I might be able to do Jean a favour, in return for the help she was giving me.

"Yes, I am," I said, confidently. "The A245 is such an iconic model, don't you think?"

"Whatever she has offered, I can beat it," the young woman said.

"Jean was just about to accept my offer of fifty pounds," I lied.

"I'll give you one hundred." She took five twenty-pound notes out of her pocket and held them out to Jean.

"Sold." Jean took the money and handed the woman the foot spa.

Clearly delighted with her purchase, the young woman hurried out of the house.

"I was only going to ask for a fiver." Jean grinned. "I had no idea that people actually collected those things."

"One thing I've learned over the last few years, is that people collect the weirdest things. Anyway, back to our conversation, I'd just asked if you spoke to Joseph after the argument."

"Yes, I remember he was kind of shellshocked by the whole thing. I asked him what had been going on, but he was adamant he had no idea what had sparked the row. According to him, Jack had gone into his office, looking for a fight, and he didn't seem to care what it was about."

"Did you get a chance to speak to Jack later?"

"No, because that night Joseph was killed, and Jack was arrested for his murder. The next time I saw him was in court when I was called to give evidence. I felt bad about doing it because I knew what I said would help to convict Jack, but I had to tell the truth, didn't I?"

"You had no other choice."

"Is there a chance that Jack is innocent?" she asked.

"I'm not sure. So far, I haven't been able to find any evidence that would overturn the verdict, but it's early days."

"Will you remember me to him the next time you see him?"

"Of course."

Although Jean hadn't told me anything that would help to prove Jack Two was innocent, she had clearly been shocked at the turn of events. Her description of Jack Two's character had been completely at odds with the way he had acted on the day of the murder.

Chapter 20

Shortly after I'd left Jean Longton's house, my phone rang.

"Hi, Aunt Lucy. Is everything okay? Is it Rhymes and Doodles?"

"No, they're still getting on like a house on fire. I just called to ask how you are?"

"Err, I'm fine. Why?"

"I just wanted to be sure. That's all."

"What's this about, Aunt Lucy?"

"You probably don't need to worry."

"Now, I'm really worried. What's wrong?"

"When I woke up this morning, I was covered in spots. Green ones."

"Oh dear. Do you feel alright?"

"Yes, I feel fine."

"What do you think caused it? Is there some kind of virus going around in Candlefield?"

"It isn't a virus."

"How do you know?"

"Because I went to see the doctor."

"What did he say?"

"He asked if I'd had anything different to eat over the last few days."

"The waddle berries?"

"It looks like it. I'm really sorry, Jill. I had no idea that they had this effect, or I wouldn't have used them."

"I don't have any spots and it's been a couple of days now."

"The doctor did say it doesn't affect everyone, so maybe you'll be okay."

"Yeah, I think I'd have got them by now if I was going to get them."

"Sorry again."

"Don't be daft. I hope your spots go soon."

Poor Aunt Lucy, and lucky for me that I'm not allergic to those berries.

When I got back to the office, Mrs V was wearing the monocle over the other eye.

"Any calls, Mrs V?"

"Just one, but I think it was another timewaster. I've put a note on your desk, anyway."

"Okay, thanks."

When I went through to my office, Winky and his brother were on the sofa. Normally, I would have told Socks to sling his hook, but he looked so despondent that I didn't have the heart to.

"I told Socks that you're going to the casino tonight, aren't you?" Winky said.

"Yes, seeing as you're blackmailing me."

"Blackmail is such an ugly word."

"Hmm." I turned to Socks. "Can you tell me exactly what happened the night the money went missing?"

"There's not much to tell. When I went to sleep the cash was next to my bed. When I woke up, it had gone."

"And you didn't hear a thing?"

"Nothing."

"I assume the money was still in the briefcase?"

"No, I had taken it out."

"You said the cash was next to your bed. Where was the briefcase?"

"Across the room. Under the table."

"Okay, that'll do for now. You can go."

Winky shot me a look which I ignored.

"Okay." Socks jumped off the sofa. "I'll catch up with you later, bro."

Winky waited until his brother had left and then turned on me. "Did you really have to be so sharp with Socks? He's feeling very vulnerable at the moment."

"Cry me a river."

"You can be such a hard person sometimes."

"I just have a good memory, that's all. I've given that brother of yours multiple chances and he's blown it every time. I can't think why you still give him the time of day."

"Because he's family." With that, Winky disappeared under the sofa.

Was he right? Had I been too hard on his brother? Was I really an uncaring, hard person?

Nah, course I wasn't.

I grabbed the note that Mrs V had left on my desk and was so shocked by what I read that I had to take a seat. It took me a couple of minutes to compose myself sufficiently to go and ask Mrs V about it.

"This note, Mrs V?"

"Another timewaster?"

"Err, yeah, probably. Is this all he said?"

"Yes. Are you okay, Jill? You look a little pale."

"I'm fine. Do you think you could rustle up a cup of tea, please?"

"I'll bring it through."

Back at my desk, I stared again at the note that read: **Mr Braxmore – Enquired if we sold compass stones.**

I waited until I had my tea and then I called Martin.

"Hey, Jill, I know why you're calling, but I still don't

have any news on Braxmore's whereabouts, I'm afraid."

"We might not know where he is, but he definitely knows where to find me."

"What do you mean?"

I told him about the phone message that Mrs V had taken and, judging by his silence, Martin was as shocked as I was.

"We have to find him, Martin."

"I know."

"Is there anything I can do to help?"

"I don't think so. I'm working my way through every contact I have."

"Let me talk to some of them."

"It's not that easy. Most of these people are paranoid. It's taken me years to gain their trust. They aren't going to speak to you."

"I know you're doing your best, but this is all so frustrating. After all the blood, sweat and tears it took to collect the compass stones, I never envisaged we'd be stalled like this."

"That makes two of us."

"Okay, let me know the minute you have a lead, no matter how tenuous it is."

"Will do."

I had intended catching up with some paperwork that afternoon, but Braxmore's message had completely thrown me, and I couldn't think about anything else.

"You can stop sulking and come out now, Winky, I'm going home."

He shuffled out from under the sofa. "You're still going to the casino tonight, aren't you?"

"I said I would, didn't I?"

Mrs V was now sans-monocle.

"What's happened to the monocle, Mrs V?"

"It started rubbing my cheek. I'm beginning to think I may have to revert to the glasses."

"I'm going to be working tonight, so I'm calling it a day now."

"Okay, dear, will you and the family be going to the Purple Festival tomorrow?"

"Unless I can come up with a good excuse between now and then."

"It's going to be amazing. Armi and I have been wearing our purple wigs every night this week to get into the mood."

Tragic.

"When will my Bluebottle Girl costume be ready?" Florence asked as soon as I walked through the door.

"It's going to take Mummy a while to make it."

"Tomorrow?"

"No, not that quick. Tomorrow is Saturday. The costume will be ready the Saturday after that."

"That's a long time."

"It'll soon be here," Jack said. "And you have the Purple Festival to look forward to tomorrow."

"Yay, I'm going to put my wig on." She buzzed away.

"You're back early." Jack gave me a peck on the lips.

"I've had a grueller, and I have to work tonight."

"Again? What is it this time?"

I'd been dreading him asking that, and I considered lying, but I knew it would only come back to haunt me if I did.

"I have to go to the casino where Winky's brother won

big time."

"There are casinos for cats?"

"No, it's open to all animals."

"Mind. Blown. Why do you have to go there?"

"A couple of days after Socks won, he was robbed of all his winnings. I'm going to try and find out who stole it, and hopefully get it back."

"Are you getting paid to do this?"

"Sort of."

"What does that mean?"

"Winky says he's managed to dig up some dirt on Harmony Fashion that I can use as leverage to get them to drop the case against me."

"That's good, isn't it?"

"Yeah, but he won't give me the details until I've done this for him. Can you believe he doesn't trust me?"

Jack hesitated a little too long for my liking, and when he did speak, he changed the subject. "Are you really going to be able to make Florence a Bluebottle Girl costume?"

"It's a bit late to be asking me that now, isn't it? You were the one who painted me into a corner so I had to agree to make it."

"Yeah, I feel a bit bad about that."

"How bad?"

"What do you mean?"

"It should be my turn to make dinner. Do you feel bad enough to make it instead?"

"Yeah, okay, but now you've promised that she'll have the costume by next Saturday, you have to deliver."

"Don't worry. I have it all in hand."

"You're way too relaxed about this. You're going to use

magic to make it, aren't you?"

"Oh yeah, because there's bound to be a spell to make a Bluebottle Girl costume. I shall be making it with my own fair hands."

He looked far from convinced but he let it go.

"What did Florence do at CASS today?" I asked.

"Your guess is as good as mine. I did ask her, but she just said *boring stuff*."

I waited until after Florence was in bed before setting off to the casino.

"What time will you be back?" Jack asked, as I was about to leave.

"I've honestly no idea. Don't wait up."

"Don't get carried away and start gambling."

"With my luck? You have no worries there."

A quick kiss, and I was on my way to Winskers. I drove into Washbridge and parked outside What A Load Of on West Street. I still couldn't get my head around the idea that there was enough demand for a shop that sold nothing but tripe. From the street, you would never have known there was a casino in the basement below that shop.

First job, once I was out of the car, was to turn myself into a cat; this time, I decided to be a cute white Persian, called Daisy. I took the steps down to a small door, which was just about tall enough for a small animal to get through. I tried the handle, but it was locked, so I pressed the doorbell. Moments later, a Ginger Tom opened the door.

"Hello, gorgeous."

"Hi."

"I haven't seen you before or I would have remembered."

"This is my first visit. Can I come in or is it members only?"

"No, everyone is welcome. Come in. I'm Billy, by the way."

"I'm Daisy. Nice to meet you."

He led the way to the main casino floor, which was busy with animals of all kinds, including cats, dogs, rabbits, squirrels and even a few bats. There was everything you'd expect to find in a casino for humans: card tables, roulette and hundreds of slot machines.

"What do you think?" Billy asked.

"Very impressive. It's much busier than I expected."

"It's like this most nights. Do you need any help deciding what to play?"

"No, thanks. I think I'd just like to take a look around."

"No problem. If you need anything, you'll find me at reception. Or you can ask one of the sexy little minxes. They're the ones wearing the orange t-shirts."

"Thanks, Billy."

According to Winky, Socks had won big on roulette, so I figured that was the best place to start. It turned out that there were two roulette tables, both doing brisk business. There were no free seats at one of the tables and I only just managed to nab the last one at the other table. Roulette seemed to be attracting many more punters than the various card tables—maybe word had got out about Socks' big win. I had a little cash with me, which I exchanged for a small pile of chips. I'd decided that I was going to bet on red every time, which meant I would win almost fifty percent of the time. That would allow me to stay at the table for the longest time. Everyone else around the table had eyes only for the roulette wheel as it spun around, but I was more interested in watching the punters and the croupier.

"Hey, lady." A rabbit nudged me. "Why don't you start to make some real bets or make way for someone who will?"

"What business is it of yours how much I bet or what I bet on?"

"I've been waiting for a seat at this table for nearly half an hour."

"That's not my problem. Now, will you please let me concentrate?"

"*Concentrate*?" He scoffed. "It must be really difficult to bet on red every time."

So rude.

All of a sudden, the volume level in the casino increased, and most of the noise seemed to be coming from the other roulette table, around which a crowd had started to gather. I wanted to find out what was going on, so I gave up my seat, which was immediately grabbed by the rude rabbit. The crowd around the other table was so deep, I couldn't see what was going on. I tried to subtly push my way closer to the front, but I was rebuked by one particularly nasty bulldog.

"What's going on?" I asked a friendlier hedgehog.

"Another cat is on a hot streak. I don't understand why it's always the cats that win big here. She's the third one this month. It's about time some of us other creatures got a look in. No offence."

"None taken."

If I was going to get a better view, a different approach

would be required, so I found a quiet corner of the casino, and quickly made myself invisible. After returning to the crowded roulette table, I levitated above the heads of the other punters, so that I had a bird's eye view. It soon became clear what all the commotion was about: a brown Burmese cat had accumulated several tall piles of chips. All eyes were on her as she placed half of the chips from one of the piles on number twenty-three. There were several gasps at such a high-risk wager, but she was clearly feeling confident. When the croupier launched the ball onto the wheel, the table fell silent as everyone held their breath. It felt like an eternity as the ball circled the wheel, but then it faulted and began to hop from one slot to the next before eventually coming to a halt. On number forty-seven.

Everyone groaned in disappointment. Everyone that was, except for the Burmese who smiled, shrugged, and said, "I guess that's a sign that my luck has run out." She stood up and then said to the croupier, "Could you cash these out for me?"

"Certainly, madam, if you'll make your way to the cash desk, they'll be glad to attend to you."

She left the table to a round of polite applause from the other punters who no doubt wished they had even half of her luck. Still invisible I followed the Burmese as she made her way to the cash desk. Billy, who had welcomed me to the casino, was waiting for her there. He led her into an office a couple of doors down from the cash desk. I was still trying to decide whether I should magic myself inside the room when Billy and the Burmese reappeared; she was carrying a briefcase.

"Are you sure I can't arrange transport home for you?"

Billy said to her. "It would be our pleasure."

"Thanks, but there's no need. I called my boyfriend and he's going to meet me outside."

"Okay, well congratulations again on your win."

The Burmese headed for the exit, with me just a couple of yards behind her. As soon as she stepped out of the casino, another Burmese cat came rushing down the steps and gave her a hug.

"I can't believe it," he said.

"Me neither. It's like a dream."

"How much did you end up winning?"

"Just over eleven thousand. It would have been more, but I made a stupid bet at the end."

"Eleven grand? That's unreal." He gave her a kiss. "Come on, let's get home."

The two of them set off down the road at a pace. Once again, I followed them. Ten minutes later, they stopped at a narrow townhouse. When they headed down the side of the house, I quickly reversed the 'invisible' spell before following them.

"How are we going to get it inside?" the female Burmese asked her companion.

They were both staring at the cat flap in the backdoor, which was clearly too small to accommodate the briefcase.

"Maybe I can help," I said.

The two of them almost jumped out of their skins.

"Who are you?" the male screamed at me.

"Relax, you don't have anything to fear, I promise."

"What do you want?"

"Let me help with that." I cast the 'shrink' spell to make the case small enough to go through the cat flap.

"What have you done to our money?" the female yelled.

"It's okay. I'll restore it to its normal size once we're inside." I grabbed the briefcase and jumped through the cat flap. By the time they had followed me inside, I had restored the briefcase and contents to full size.

"How did you do that?" the male asked.

"Who are you?" the female demanded.

I changed back to human form, which threw them into a total tailspin.

"What—err—who—how—?"

"My name is Jill. May I ask yours?"

"I'm Tulip," the female said.

"Robbie."

"I'm pleased to meet you both, and congratulations on your win tonight, Tulip."

"What do you want?"

"I'd like to take that briefcase."

"I knew it. You're after my winnings." Tulip clutched the briefcase for dear life.

"No, you misunderstand me. I don't want the cash, just the briefcase."

"Huh?"

"Please allow me to explain. Have either of you heard of a cat called Winky?"

"Everyone has heard of Winky," Robbie said.

"He's kind of dishy." Tulip grinned, but then saw the look on Robbie's face, and said, "Not as dishy as you, sweetie, obviously."

"Winky lives with me. Or to be more precise, he lives in my office. Oh, and by the way, I'm a witch."

"Is that why we can talk to you?"

"Yeah. I'm sorry if I gave you a start just now."

"That's okay," Tulip said. "But why do you want the

briefcase?"

I told them what had happened to Winky's brother after he'd had similar success at the casino.

"That's terrible." Robbie looked horrified.

"Do you think someone is going to come after our money too?" Tulip asked.

"Yeah, I think there's a very good chance they will. I'm pretty sure there's a tracking device in the briefcase. That's why I want to take it with me, so when they come after it, they'll find me waiting for them."

"Aren't you worried about what they might do to you?"

"I'm not the one who needs to worry. They are."

With their blessing, I took the briefcase and headed home.

Chapter 21

"Jill, wake up." Jack shook my shoulder.

I glanced over at the alarm clock. "It's only six o'clock. Let me go back to sleep."

"You need to see this."

"What's so urgent that you had to wake me up at this time on a Saturday morning?"

"That." The crazy man was pointing to the wardrobe.

"What are you talking about?"

"Look. In the mirror."

I shuffled forward a few inches until I caught my reflection. "Oh no!"

"Do you feel okay?"

"Apart from the fact I'm covered in green spots, you mean? Oh yeah, I feel great."

Florence came buzzing into the bedroom but stopped dead in her tracks when she saw me. "Why do you have green spots on your face, Mummy?"

"It's nothing to worry about." I reassured her. "Mummy just ate something she shouldn't have."

"What could have caused that?" Jack said.

"Waddle berries."

"*What* berries?"

"Aunt Lucy put them in the cupcakes she made. She called me yesterday to say she'd come out in green spots."

"You never said anything."

"I didn't think it was going to affect me."

"How long does it last?"

"I'm not sure. Not long, hopefully."

"Is it contagious?"

"No, of course not."

"Good, that means you can still go to the festival."

"You can't seriously expect me to go there looking like this."

"Can't you use some of that stuff you use to hide zits?"

"I'm not sure concealer is going to hide this lot. You'll have to call Grandma to tell her I can't make it."

"I'm not calling your grandmother. She'll find some way to blame me for your spots. You'll have to call her."

"Alright, I will. If you two will give me a little privacy, that is."

"Come on, Florence." Jack led her downstairs.

Yes, Grandma could be difficult at times, but I was confident that even she would sympathise with my predicament.

"What do you mean you can't do it," she yelled down the phone.

"I'm lying in bed, covered in green spots."

"And that's an excuse, why?" She was no longer on the phone. Instead, she was standing at the foot of the bed.

"Just look at me. Who is going to buy a cake from me, looking like this?"

She hesitated and then said, "You're right. One look at those spots would be enough to spoil anyone's appetite."

"Thank you for seeing reason."

"I'm nothing if not reasonable."

"I hope the festival goes well."

"Don't worry. It will."

"I'm just sorry I can't be a part of it. I was really looking forward to doing my bit."

"Don't worry. You can still do your bit."

"But what about the spots?"

"They won't matter for what I have in mind for you."

"What's that?"

"I'll be back to pick you up at eight o'clock. Make sure you're ready."

"But, Grandma, what—"

Too late. She'd gone.

Florence, Jack and I were at the breakfast table.

"What's wrong with your muesli?" I said to Jack.

"Nothing, I've just lost my appetite."

"They're only spots. They can't hurt you."

"I know. It's just—err—I'll probably get something later." He pushed the bowl away. "What do you reckon your grandmother has got lined up for you?"

"I dread to think. It's your fault. You should have called her like I asked you to."

"As if that would have made any difference. By the way, what's that briefcase doing in the lounge?"

"It's from the casino."

"Did you win?"

"No, I didn't, but another cat did. They gave her that case to take the cash home in."

"How come you have it, then?"

"Before I get into that, I'd like you and Florence to go and stay at Kathy's house tonight."

"Why?"

"Because if my hunch is correct, someone will be paying us a visit tonight, looking for the briefcase. It'll be better if you two aren't around."

"Will you be okay here by yourself?"

"Of course I will."

"What time did Kathy say we should get there?"

"She doesn't know you're going yet."

A few minutes later, I'd cleared it with Kathy. Obviously, I hadn't told her the real reason I wanted Jack and Florence to stay with her. Instead, I spun her a story about a leaking roof.

I'd done my best with concealer, but the spots were still visible. I don't imagine the manufacturers expected to have to deal with green spots.

"Lizzie says I can sleep in her room tonight, Mummy," Florence said.

"That will be fun, darling."

"Can I just make sure I've got the story right?" Jack said. "Our roof is supposed to be leaking, yeah?"

"That's right, and don't try to elaborate because you know what a useless liar you are."

Just then, there was a knock at the door.

"That'll be Grandma. I'll see you two later."

"Look at the state of you." Grandma cackled.

"I told you I should have stayed at home today. What have you got planned for me?"

"You'll find out soon enough." She took my hand and the next thing I knew she'd magicked us to Washbridge Park where the festival was being held. I assumed she had decided to put me to work backstage somewhere. Knowing my luck, I'd be on dishwashing duty again.

I was wrong about the dishwashing.

"I'm not wearing that thing."

"Stop complaining and put it on."

"What's it supposed to be, anyway?" I stared at the purple mascot costume.

"This is Purple Myrtle, the festival's mascot."

It looked like a cross between a rabbit and an elephant.

"It's ancient. Look at the state of it."

"Just get it on and stop complaining." She took my hand and helped me into the bottom half of the costume.

"It's way too big."

"Put the head on." She picked up the head, which had rabbit-like ears and a trunk.

"It smells in here."

"Hold your breath."

"I can't walk with this thing on."

"Of course you can. Follow me."

"I can't see you."

"You're supposed to look through the mouth."

"It's too low down."

"Stoop down a little."

With a bit of effort, I could just about see enough to know where I was going. Grandma led the way out of the tent and onto the showground where people were just starting to arrive.

"How long do I have to keep this thing on?"

"Until the festival ends."

"That's eight hours. I'll die from heat exhaustion."

"Why are you always so melodramatic? You can take a ten-minute break every hour."

"I'll need some lunch."

"Okay, thirty minutes for lunch, but while you're on show, you've got to make sure you fully embody the spirit of Purple Myrtle."

"What does that mean?"

"I expect you to be bubbly, bouncy and full of joie de vivre."

"That's not going to be easy."

"All the kids are bound to want to take selfies with you,

so make sure you show them a lot of love."

"Couldn't I just wash the dishes instead?"

"Off you go. There are some kids over there."

An hour later, and I was sweating in places I didn't realise it was possible to sweat. Not only that, but the costume was deceptively heavy, so the muscles in my legs were starting to cramp. As if all that wasn't bad enough, I had all the horrible kids to contend with. I didn't mind letting them take a selfie with me, but why did they want to pull my tail (oh yes, I forgot to mention that Myrtle also has a tail), or punch me?

I'd had enough, so I headed back to the tent, to take my break. Grandma had said I could have a ten-minute break every hour, but she could go whistle. It took me that long to get out of the costume. Once I was finally out of it, I hurried over to the refreshment stall where I should have been working. Pearl was out front.

"Hey, Pearl, can I get a Coke and one of those buns?"

"Jill? Are you okay?"

It was only when I saw the look on her face that I remembered the spots.

"These? Yeah, it's nothing."

"I don't mean the spots. Mum told us about the waddle berries."

She pointed to my hair, which was soaked in sweat, and plastered to my head.

"Oh, I—err—didn't get the chance to brush it this morning. Can you hurry with the drink and bun? I have to get back."

"Sure. What's Grandma got you doing?"

I didn't want anyone to know I was Purple Myrtle, especially not the twins. If they found out, I'd never hear the end of it.

"I—err—I'm helping out with the coconut shy."

"Right."

As soon as I had my drink and bun, I headed back to the tent.

"Where have you been?" Grandma said.

"I needed something to eat and drink."

"I said ten minutes."

"Look at the state of me. If I don't get a proper break, I'll die of heat exhaustion."

"Excuses, excuses. Hurry up and get back out there."

Somehow, I managed to make it through the rest of the morning. Much to Grandma's consternation, I took a full hour for my lunchbreak after which I was just about ready to face going back to that awful costume.

I'd not long been back on duty when I heard Florence's voice.

"Daddy, look over there! What's that funny purple thing?"

Oh bum! Florence was pointing straight at me. Whatever happened, I couldn't let them know I was inside the costume, or I'd never live it down.

"That's Purple Myrtle, pumpkin," Jack said.

"She's funny." Florence giggled. "What is she?"

"I'm not really sure. Why don't you go over and say hello to her?"

Oh no.

"She looks a bit scary." Florence hesitated.

Phew! Saved.

"She isn't scary," Jack reassured Florence. "I bet she'd like to say hello to you."

No, I wouldn't. I began to wave my arms around in an

effort to look scary.

It didn't work because Florence came running over to me.

"Hi, I'm Florence."

"Hello, Florence," I said in the deepest voice I could manage.

"What are you?" she asked, edging closer.

"I'm a—err—a Rabbiphant, darling."

"Jill?" Jack said.

Oh bum! And double bum!

"My name is Myrtle," I said.

"It's you, isn't it? Florence, that's Mummy in there."

"Mummy, why are you wearing that costume?"

The game was well and truly up, so there was no point in continuing the subterfuge.

"Your Great Grandma made me wear it."

"Kathy, Peter!" Jack shouted.

"Jack, don't!"

It was too late. They were already on their way over.

Kill me now.

"Jill is Purple Myrtle," Jack told them.

"Jill?" Kathy stooped down to look through the mouth of the costume.

"Hi." I sighed.

"You've found your vocation at last."

"Shut up, Kathy."

"Let's get a family snap." She collared a young man who was passing by. "Would you mind taking a photo of us all?"

The young man waited until everyone was lined up, with me centre stage, and then took a photo that I had no doubt would haunt me for the rest of my life.

Eventually, and not a moment too soon, the festival began to wind down. I couldn't wait to get out of that awful costume. Jack was waiting for me as I came out of the tent, all sweaty and exhausted.

"Are you okay?" he asked.

"I am now I'm out of that thing."

"We're heading off with Kathy and Peter now." He gave me a quick kiss. "Be careful tonight."

"I'll be fine. Give Florence a hug and a kiss from me."

"Will do. See you in the morning."

As soon as I got back home, I headed straight for the shower. Ten minutes later, I finally felt like I'd got rid of the terrible smell of the costume. I'd just stepped out of the shower when Edna appeared on my shoulder.

"Do you mind? I grabbed the towel to cover my modesty.

"Relax, you've not got anything I haven't seen before. Just much more of it. I hope those spots aren't contagious. I don't want to go down with the lurgy while I'm on holiday."

"Don't worry. It's just an allergic reaction to something I ate. Do you have anything for me?"

"Your Mr Maxwell is very security conscious. There are at least two bodyguards with him at all times. He is also a very boring and predictable man. He leaves his house for work at the same time every day, he drives the same route to work, and has one of his bodyguards collect a coffee from the same coffee shop en route. At one o'clock he goes to the same restaurant, accompanied by his bodyguards of course. He leaves the office at six o'clock on the dot and heads home."

"What about meetings?"

"He didn't attend any while I was watching him. He spends most of the time on the computer or the phone. The man leads a very boring life."

"That doesn't give me much to work with."

"I can't do much about that, I'm afraid."

"What's the name of the restaurant he goes to?"

"La Whistle. It's very expensive."

"Okay, Edna. Thanks for that. Have a great holiday."

"I think you've forgotten something."

"Oh yeah." By the time I'd paid her bill, I was left with only half a packet of custard creams.

***

It was just as well that Jack and Florence were staying the night at Kathy's because I'm not sure I could have handled the ridicule about Purple Myrtle that was inevitably headed my way. I never wanted to see another mascot costume for as long as I lived.

If my hunch was correct, I could expect a visit, that night, from whoever had stolen Socks' winnings. Given the day I'd had, and the mood I was in, whoever it was would be in for a nasty surprise. It was still light outside, and I didn't expect them to make a move until after dark, so I decided to relax with a small glass of wine and a box of chocolates. I'd just sat down on the sofa and was about to take a sip of wine when I was rudely interrupted.

"Hey, spotty, what gives?" Wanda shouted.

"How rude."

"Mabel, come and look at this one."

"Are those spots green?" Mabel said.

"I believe they are," Wanda confirmed. "Have you got the lurgy, Jill?"

"No, I don't have the lurgy. It's a reaction to a cupcake I ate a couple of days ago."

"That can't be right," Wanda laughed. "If you were allergic to cupcakes, you'd be permanently covered in spots."

The bowl began to fill with bubbles as the two fish laughed and laughed.

"Very funny. The spots were caused by waddle berries."

"Could you go and sit in another room? You're putting me off my food."

"Tough. I'm staying right here."

"So inconsiderate."

I must have been more tired than I'd thought because, when I woke up with a crick in my neck, I realised I'd slept right through the night. The briefcase was still where I'd left it on the armchair.

"Good morning, lazy bones," Wanda said.

"Did anyone come in here during the night?" I asked.

"Like who?"

"I don't know. Anyone. Did you see anyone checking out the briefcase?"

"The only person in here last night was you. How does Jack put up with your snoring?"

"I don't snore."

"If you say so. I see your spots have gone."

"Have they?"

I dashed into the hall to check the mirror. Wanda was right, the spots had completely faded. I had been totally convinced that the thieves would come looking for the briefcase during the night. It was beginning to look like my hunch had been wrong.

Kathy had said she would give Jack and Florence their breakfast, and then drive them home by mid-morning. I would be eating breakfast alone, so as a special treat, I decided to have a mix of Strawberrycandy Pops, Chococandy Pops, and ChocONut Pops. Mmm delicious; it doesn't get any better (or healthier) than that, trust me.

Jack and Florence arrived home a little earlier than I'd expected.

"Your spots have gone, Mummy."

"Yes, they have, darling. Thank goodness."

"If it isn't Purple Myrtle." Kathy followed them inside.

"I'm really not in the mood."

"Don't be such a misery guts, Jill. That performance was probably your finest hour."

Jack gave me a peck on the cheek. "Everything okay?"

"Everything is fine." I knew he was wondering what happened with the briefcase, but he'd have to wait until Kathy had left before I could get into that.

"How's the roof?" Kathy said.

"*Roof?*"

"The leak in our roof." Jack came to my rescue.

"Oh yeah, it's okay now. I managed to get someone out to do an emergency repair last night."

Chapter 22

It was Monday morning, and there were four of us at the breakfast table.

"What do you want for breakfast?" Florence asked Jay.

"What do you have?"

"Me and Daddy are having muesli. It's yummy and very good for you."

"Or there's Strawberrycandy Pops, Chococandy Pops or ChocONut Pops," I said.

"Ooh, they sound yummy. Can I have the strawberry ones, please?"

"Certainly." I grabbed the box and poured him a bowlful. "They're delicious and healthy too."

Jack shot me a look. "You shouldn't be encouraging people to eat that rubbish."

"Jay is old enough to choose his own breakfast cereal."

"How old are you, Jay?" Jack asked.

"Don't know," he said before putting a heaped spoonful of cereal into his mouth.

"Can I see my Bluebottle Girl costume, Mummy?"

"I told you it won't be ready until Saturday."

"Can't I see what you've done already?"

"No, it's bad luck to see it until it's finished. It's not long now until Saturday."

After Florence and Jay had finished their breakfast, they disappeared upstairs.

"How come Jay joined us for breakfast?" I asked Jack.

"He's still not very happy about the new colour of Florence's bedroom. She thought letting him have breakfast with us might cheer him up."

"He seemed to enjoy the Strawberrycandy Pops."

"Why don't you just tell Florence that Kathy is making the Bluebottle Girl costume?"

"I can't believe Kathy told you after I'd sworn her to silence."

"I don't think she did it on purpose. It just slipped out when we were chatting. Luckily, Florence wasn't around at the time."

"Are you going to snitch on me?"

"No, it's not my place to tell her. If you're okay with lying to your daughter, that's up to you."

"I don't really think of it as a lie."

"You don't think of any of your lies as lies. Anyway, that's up to you, what are you going to do about Socks' winnings now?"

"I was so sure that the thieves would come after the briefcase. I think I'm going to have to tell Winky that it's a bust."

"That'll go down well. He'll burst a blood vessel."

"No, he won't. Once he knows I've done everything I could, he'll be okay with it."

***

"What do you mean there's nothing else you can do?" Winky exploded. "I want our money back!"

"I went to the casino like I promised. I followed that night's big winner home, and I took the briefcase to my house. The thieves were a no-show. What else am I supposed to do?"

"What else? What else? How about you do some real investigating? We want that cash back!"

"I've already told you that I've done my best. You

getting in a flap isn't going to—hang on, that's it."

"What's *it*?"

"What I just said."

"You're giving me a migraine." He rubbed his head. "What are you talking about?"

"*Flap*. Don't you see?"

"I need to lie down." He jumped onto the sofa.

"When I was at the casino, a hedgehog complained that it was always the cats that had the big wins."

"What do you expect? All those hedgehogs do is complain."

"You're missing the point. If what he said is right, why is that? Why is it always cats that win big?"

"Because we're better at it?"

"No, it's because there's a very good chance there will be a cat *flap* where the winner lives. That's why no one came into my house last night."

"Because you don't have a cat flap?"

"Correct."

"If what you're suggesting is true, someone at the casino would have to fix it to ensure a particular cat wins. Is that even possible on a roulette wheel?"

"I'm not sure. I'll worry about that part once I've proven my theory about the cat flap is correct."

His migraine apparently forgotten, Winky now seemed much more engaged.

"What's the next step, then?" he asked.

"I need you to contact your feline friends and find someone whose owners will be away tonight, and who—"

"*Owners*?"

"Now is not the time for nit-picking, Winky, you know what I mean. I need somewhere that I can hang out tonight, to see if the thieves show up. Needless to say, the property must have a cat flap."

"There is another option."

"What's that?"

"You could have a cat flap installed at the old watermill. That way, I could visit."

"I'm going to stick with Plan A. Do you think you can find somewhere in time for tonight?"

"No problem. Leave it to me."

Once again, Ralph met me at the door to the palace.

"Welcome back, Jill, I believe the princess has managed to track down her brother."

"I hope so. I didn't have much luck finding him."

"I take it he wasn't at The Last Breath?"

"No, but I did meet a few interesting characters there."

Ralph led the way to the private suite where the princess and her elusive brother were already waiting for us.

"Jill Maxwell, Your Majesty." Ralph showed me into the room and was about to leave when the princess asked him to stay.

"Would you please take notes of this meeting, Ralph, so there can be no confusion later as to what was said."

"Of course, Your Majesty." He joined us around the large table.

"Thank you for coming here again today, Jill," Stella said.

"My pleasure."

"As you can see, my brother has deigned to join us today."

"So, I see." I turned my attention to the prince. "You're

a difficult man to tie down, Your Highness."

"You can call me Michael, and I apologise for my no-show the last time you were here, but something urgent came up."

"What was her name?" Stella snapped.

"Please ignore my sister, Jill, she judges everyone by her own low standards."

"How dare you, Michael!"

"Please," I interrupted. "Can you leave the bickering until after we've finished here because I have some important information relating to your mother, the queen."

"Sorry, Jill," the princess said. "Do carry on."

"I am pleased to report that I may have figured—"

I stopped midsentence because Stella suddenly slumped to one side, fast asleep. Moments later, her brother did the same thing.

"Your Majesty?" Ralph jumped off his chair and went over to the princess. "Wake up, Your Majesty." When he had no joy, he tried to awaken the prince, but with no more success. Finally, he turned to me. "What's going on, Jill? Shall I call the physician?"

"I don't think that will do any good."

"What do you mean?"

"I was actually here earlier, and I administered a few drops of this potion to all three of your glasses." I took a small bottle from my pocket.

"What is that?"

"I think you know the answer to that, Ralph. Are you starting to feel sleepy yet?"

He slumped onto the nearest chair. "What have you done? There's no remedy."

"It looks like you're in for a long sleep, then."

"No! No!"

He was in a state of full-blown panic now. So much so that he didn't immediately notice that the prince and princess were now sitting up.

"Whatever is the matter, Ralph?" Stella said.

Only then, did Ralph realise the two members of the royal family were wide awake.

"What's going on?" Ralph looked at me.

"Time to come clean, Ralph. Why did you do it?"

"I don't know what you're talking about."

The door to the suite opened, and in walked Queen Bella.

"Maybe I can jog your memory, Ralph," the queen said. "It was the day after I caught you with your hand in my jewellery box."

"That was all just a misunderstanding, Your Majesty."

"If that's true, why did you feel the need to poison me?"

"It wasn't poison. It was just a—" His face fell as he realised that he had incriminated himself.

The queen turned back to the door and called in two guards. "Please take this awful man away."

Thoroughly defeated, Ralph was led away.

"How are you feeling, mother?" Stella asked.

"Still a little woozy if I'm honest, but I'll be as right as rain in a few hours, I'm sure." She came to join us at the table. "And that is all down to you, Jill."

"I'm just pleased you're okay, Your Majesty."

"What she really means is that she's glad she doesn't have to put up with your awful snoring, Mother." Michael chuckled.

"I didn't get the chance to ask you earlier, Jill," Stella

said. "How did you work out what had caused mother to sleep for so long?"

"I wish I could tell you it was brilliant detective work, but mostly it was down to luck. When I was looking for Michael, Ralph sent me to The Last Breath tavern in Jedmond."

"Jedmond?" The prince looked horrified. "I would never go there."

"It's one of the most dangerous regions in the Yella kingdom," his sister added.

"Yes, I soon realised that. I assume that Ralph was hoping I wouldn't make it out of there alive. Fortunately, though, a Yella called Rosy came to my rescue and led me to safety. She was also the one who said I should seek the help of a brewmaiden, which I did. It was the brewmaiden who suggested that your condition might be the result of a potion that was only ever intended for dogs. She also told me that she'd sold such a potion to a Yella who kept winking at her. Luckily, she was able to suggest another potion that she thought might reverse the effect of the original sleeping draught. She wasn't sure that it would work, but it certainly seems to have done the trick. It's fair to say that if it hadn't been for Rosy, Your Majesty might still be asleep."

"Then she must be richly rewarded. Stella, see that she is traced and brought to the palace."

"Yes, mother. I still can't believe Ralph would do something like this. He has served our family for such a long time."

"It's very disappointing," the queen agreed. "I will take into account his long service record when passing sentence on him."

***

"Have you given up on the contact lenses, Mrs V?"

"Yes, they just aren't for me. It feels so good to be wearing my glasses again."

"For what it's worth, I think glasses suit you better."

"Thank you, dear. While you were out, Mr Bottle from down the corridor came to see you. He asked if you could drop by his office as soon as you got back. It sounded like it might be urgent."

"Did he say what it was about?"

"No, I did ask, but he obviously didn't want to tell me."

"Okay, I'll pop down there in a couple of minutes."

"All sorted," Winky said. "I've found you somewhere to stay tonight."

"Somewhere with a cat flap?"

"Of course. My old buddy, Aaron the Arrow, lives there. He's a good guy. I think you'll like him."

"Why is he called Aaron the Arrow?"

"Because he's a dead eye with the darts. It's as well you know because he'll probably try and hustle you."

"Like you once did, you mean?"

"You'll probably find this hard to believe, but Aaron is even better at darts than I am."

"Don't worry, I won't be playing darts while I'm there. I'm going there for one reason and one reason only, and that's to catch those thieves. Anyway, I'd better go and see what Talbot wants."

Talbot was pacing up and down behind his desk and was clearly stressed about something.

"Mrs V said you wanted a word?"

“Thanks for popping over, Jill. I’m hoping you might be able to do me a really big favour.”

“I will if I can. What is it?”

“One of my biggest clients is DeRosa. Have you heard of them?”

“Of course. Who hasn’t?”

De Rosa cosmetics were amazing, but ridiculously expensive.

“I’d arranged for one of the witches on my books to appear in an ad shoot for them this afternoon, but she tripped over her cat this morning, and she’s broken her leg.”

“Poor thing.”

“The company has spent a small fortune, setting up the shoot, so if I tell them the model can’t make it, they won’t be best pleased.”

“Surely, they’d understand, given the circumstances.”

“Companies like this expect results, not excuses. If they are forced to cancel the shoot, there’s a good chance I won’t get any more work from them.”

“I see, but I’m not sure how I can help.”

“I thought maybe you could do the shoot instead.”

“Me?”

“Yeah, you’d be perfect for it.”

“I’ve never done anything like that before.”

“There’s nothing to it. You just stand in front of the camera and do what they tell you. It’ll not take more than a couple of hours.”

“But won’t they wonder where the original model is?”

“No, because if you agree, I’ll call and warn them that there’s been a change. They’ll be okay, just as long as the ad gets made. What do you say?”

"I really don't think it's a good idea."

"You'd be paid one thousand pounds."

"A grand, just for a couple of hours' work?"

"Yeah. And, if they like you, they might ask you to do more work for them."

"Okay, why not?"

"Great." He handed me a sheet of paper. "The address is on there. You'll need to be there by three o'clock sharp. Any questions?"

"No. I'll be there."

As I walked back to my office, my mind began to wander. What if this turned out to be the start of a whole new career? I could picture myself as a model, not on the catwalk, but in glossy magazines. And the pay was amazing.

"Are you okay, Jill?" Mrs V asked.

"Never better, Mrs V. Never better."

Once I was back in my office, I couldn't wait to share my exciting news, so I gave Jack a call.

"You'll never guess what I'm going to be doing this afternoon."

"I bet it isn't making a Bluebottle Girl costume."

"I'm doing a photoshoot for DeRosa."

"What do you mean you're doing a photoshoot?"

"Talbot from the talent agency next door asked if I'd stand in for one of his models who has broken her leg."

"Why you?"

"Because he thought I'd be perfect for the ad."

"DeRosa? Where have I heard of them?"

"They do a range of cosmetics. Really expensive ones. And guess how much I'll get paid for a couple of hours work?"

"A couple of hundred?"

"A grand."

"That's amazing."

"I know, and according to Talbot, it could lead to other work."

"Don't get your hopes up too much."

"I won't. I'd better go because I want to tell Kathy before I leave."

"Okay. Good luck, and I'll see you tonight."

"Kathy, it's me."

"I do have caller ID, you know."

"Yeah, anyway, I have big news."

"You'll have to be quick because I have an appointment with a customer in ten minutes."

"I'm going to be a model for DeRosa."

"What do you mean you're going to be a model?"

I explained how Talbot had asked me to stand in for his incapacitated model.

"You?" She scoffed. "Why you?"

"He said I'd be perfect for it. I don't want to count my chickens but if this is a success, who knows what it might lead to?"

"Yeah, I definitely wouldn't start counting any chickens yet."

"You could at least be excited for me."

"Sorry, I'm sure it'll be great, but I really do have to go now."

I might have known I wouldn't get any encouragement from Kathy, but it didn't matter because I intended to grab this opportunity with both hands.

"You, a model?" Winky began to roll around the floor, in hysterics.

"You shouldn't be listening to private conversations. And why shouldn't I be a model? Talbot said I'd be perfect for it."

"He would have said anything to save his bacon. If you'd said no, he'd have probably asked Mrs V to do it."

"You'll be laughing on the other side of your face when I appear in glossy magazines all over the world."

"Delusional much."

Chapter 23

I didn't have time to waste arguing with Winky because I had to hightail it across town to the photoshoot. I was a little surprised to find that it was being held on an industrial estate, but then these 'arty' types often came up with weird and wonderful concepts for ads.

I arrived at the small, unmarked unit with fifteen minutes to spare. Around the back was a large metal door, which was obviously used for deliveries. Next to it, was a smaller, wooden door that was unlocked. I wasn't entirely sure I'd come to the right place until I stepped inside and saw a young woman, with a clipboard. As soon as she spotted me, she came hurrying over.

"Are you Jill?"

"Yeah."

"Hi, I'm Freda. Talbot told us what had happened to Trisha. We really appreciate you standing in like this."

"No problem."

"Talbot said we were lucky to catch you in between assignments."

"He did? Right, yeah, that was fortunate."

"He told you what the job is, I assume?"

"Yeah, he said it was for DeRosa."

"It's actually pronounced *Droza*."

"Oh, I didn't realise that."

"And Talbot said you'd be okay with the acting."

"*Acting*?"

"It isn't much, but he said you'd done a number of small parts before?"

"Err, that's right. No problem."

This was getting better and better. With an opportunity

to showcase my natural acting ability, I could potentially attract interest from other agents casting parts for TV and movies. And I was being paid a grand for the privilege.

"Great, come through and take a look at the set." She led the way through a pair of rubber doors. "What do you think, Jill?"

"It's—err—amazing."

The set had been made to resemble the aisle of a typical supermarket. The shelves on either side were stocked with what looked like real produce. There were cameras everywhere, including one on a gantry that could run the full length of the aisle, to get a bird's eye view of the action.

"Jill, can I introduce your co-star today."

Until then, I hadn't noticed the little boy, who couldn't have been more than four years of age. He was dressed in a green blazer and green shorts.

"Mummy!" the little boy threw his arms around me and gave me a hug.

"*Mummy*?"

The boy took a couple of steps back and said, "I hope you don't mind, but I feel it's important to get into character ahead of the shoot. Don't you agree?"

"Err, yeah, I guess."

"I'm Tristan, by the way, but everyone calls me Moo."

"*Moo*?"

"It was the first word I uttered, and my parents thought it was so cute that they started to call me by it, and it kind of stuck."

"Jill, Moo, are you both ready?"

"Ready and waiting," Moo said.

"Jill?"

"Err, I don't actually know what I'm supposed to be doing."

"Didn't Talbot give you the script?"

"No, sorry."

"Not to worry. It's all very straight forward. You're pushing the trolley when Timmy spots the display at the other end of the aisle."

Until then, I hadn't spotted the incredibly tall stack of toilet rolls at the far end of the aisle. It was only then that the penny dropped. This wasn't an advert for DeRosa; it was for Droza, the economy toilet roll manufacturer.

"Jill?"

"Sorry. Who's *Timmy*?"

"That's Moo. Timmy is your son's name."

"Right, so you just want me to push the trolley down the aisle?"

"Until Timmy starts to run towards the stack of toilet rolls. Then, you should abandon the trolley and run after him."

"Okay."

"Here are your lines." She handed me a single sheet of paper. "Do you want to give them a go?"

"Sure." I took a breath and then said, "Timmy, come back. Timmy, don't you dare."

"Do you think you can remember those?"

"Yeah, no problem."

"The timing of the lines is very important. When Timmy first starts to run down the aisle, you shout 'Timmy come back'."

"Okay."

"He ignores you and he takes hold of one of the toilet rolls near the bottom of the stack."

"Is that when I shout 'Timmy, don't you dare'?"

"Yes, but not until you reach the stack yourself. Okay?"

"Yeah, no problem."

"Great. If you could both take your positions, we'll start."

I put both hands on the trolley, but Moo tugged at my arm, and held out his hand for me to hold.

"Okay," Freda said. "When I say action, I want you to start walking slowly down the aisle."

"Break a leg," Moo said.

"Action!"

I started to push the trolley slowly down the aisle. I'd only gone a few steps when Moo/Timmy let go of my hand and set off at a sprint. As directed, I abandoned the trolley and ran after him.

"Timmy, come back!"

Moo/Timmy ignored me and continued down the aisle. By the time I caught up with him, he was standing next to the stack of toilet rolls and looked as though he was about to remove one from the bottom of the precarious structure.

"Timmy, don't you dare!"

The next thing I knew, several hundred toilet rolls came tumbling down on our heads.

"Cut!" Freda shouted. "Well done, everyone, that's a wrap."

"Won't we have to do it again?" I asked after climbing out from under the pile of toilet rolls. "The stack fell down."

"That was always the intention." She grinned.

"You could have warned me."

"I wanted to get a genuine reaction from you, Jill. If

you'd known in advance what was going to happen, it wouldn't have been so authentic."

Moo came over and shook my hand. "Nice working with you, Jill."

"Err, yeah, likewise."

***

Before going back to the office, I dropped in at Talbot's office.

"How did it go, Jill?"

"You could have told me the ad was for toilet rolls."

"I told you the client was Droza. I thought you'd realise."

"I thought you said—never mind."

"Did it go alright? Was the client happy?"

"I think so, but they weren't the ones buried under a mountain of toilet rolls."

"Is that what they did? Brilliant! Those guys always did know how to make an ad." He reached into the drawer of his desk and took out a cheque book. "This will make you feel better about it." He scribbled a cheque for one thousand pounds and handed it to me.

"Are you okay, Jill?" Mrs V asked when I walked through the door. "You look a little flustered if you don't mind me saying so."

I wanted to say that she would have looked flustered too if she'd just been buried under a mountain of toilet rolls, but the fewer people that knew about it, the better.

"I'm just a little tired. Nothing a nice cup of tea won't put right."

"I'll bring it through."

"If it isn't the UK's new top model," Winky said. "How did the ad shoot go?"

"Okay."

"*Okay*? Is that it? What went wrong?"

"What makes you think anything went wrong?"

"You were involved, weren't you? Something was bound to go wrong. I bet you didn't get paid, did you?"

"That's where you're wrong." I flashed the cheque that Talbot had given to me.

"How come your face doesn't look any different?"

"What are you talking about?"

"I assumed they'd make you up with the cosmetics you were promoting."

"Oh, right. Yeah, they did, but I cleaned it all off before I left the shoot."

"Why do I get the feeling there's something you're not telling me?"

"Because you judge everyone else by your own low standards. Why can't you just accept my word that everything went okay?"

A few minutes later, Mrs V brought through a much-needed cup of tea. "There you are, dear, that'll buck you up in no time at all."

"Thanks, Mrs V, you're a lifesaver."

"By the way, while you were out, Mr Brown called. He asked if you'd call him back."

"Okay, thanks."

He'd also tried calling me on my mobile phone, but when I saw the caller ID, I'd let it go to voicemail. There was only so long I could ignore him, but I really wasn't looking forward to having to tell him there was nothing I could do for his son.

Mrs V had just left the office when Winky's phone rang.

"Hey, bro. Yeah, I know, but you can't blame her. She's going to try again tonight. Yeah, Aaron the Arrow's gaff. I'll give you a bell in the morning to let you know how she went on. Okay, later."

"I take it that was Socks?" I said.

"Yeah."

"Was he criticising me?"

"Course not."

"It sounded like it to me."

"He's just upset about the money, that's all."

"If no one turns up tonight, then you're both going to have to kiss goodbye to your money."

"I know, but I have every confidence in you."

"That's not what you said earlier."

"That was just a joke. You know I didn't mean it."

"Hmm."

***

"So, how did it go?" Jack said as soon as I walked through the door.

"What?"

"The ad shoot of course. I've been telling everyone about it."

Oh bum! "When you say everyone—?"

"The Stock sisters, the vicar, Mr Ivers. Oh, and your grandmother."

"Grandma?"

"Yes, she was in the store when I popped over there for some soup. Everyone was very impressed. Well, everyone except for your grandmother, but then nothing impresses her. So, how was it?"

"A bit of a disappointment if I'm being honest. There wasn't much to it."

"But were they pleased with what you did?"

"Yeah, I think so."

"Might you get more work on the strength of it?"

"I wouldn't think so, and to be honest, I'm not that bothered. I found it all pretty boring."

"Did they at least give you any samples to bring home?"

"Samples?"

"Of the cosmetics you were advertising?"

"No, it's a brand new product range. They don't want word getting out before the launch day."

"When is that?"

"Months away."

"I can't wait to see the ad when it's aired."

"That's probably going to be months away too. What's for dinner? I'm starving."

"I thought we might get a takeaway tonight."

"Good idea. What do you fancy?"

"Florence said she'd like pizza."

"That'll do for me. Where is she?"

"She went straight up to her bedroom after she got back from CASS. I haven't seen her since then."

That set alarm bells ringing. Who knew what kind of crazy spells she might have learned at CASS.

"I think I'll go and check on her." I started for the stairs.

"I'll order the pizza. Do you want your usual?"

"Yes, please."

There were no sounds coming from Florence's

bedroom, which could be a good thing. Or very bad. It was with some trepidation that I opened her bedroom door and stepped inside. Jay was sitting on the bed but there was no sign of my daughter.

"Where's Florence, Jay?"

He didn't answer but instead looked up at the ceiling. I followed his gaze to find my daughter hanging from the ceiling like a bat.

"You didn't see me up here, Mummy, did you?" Florence giggled.

"What are you doing up there?"

"Nothing." She shrugged.

"How did you get up there?"

"I used the 'sticky feet' spell."

"The *what* spell?"

"Sticky feet. Mr Horsetrot taught us it today. Me and Kirsty were the only ones who could walk on the walls and ceilings. The others fell off the ceiling." She laughed.

"Fell off the ceiling? Did they hurt themselves?"

"No, silly, we were in the gym, and there were big cushions on the floor."

"Don't you feel dizzy?"

"No, Mr Horsetrot said that the spell stops you from feeling woozy. Do you want to see me walking?"

I hesitated, but then realised if she did fall, the bed (and Jay) would break her fall.

"Okay, but be careful."

With no obvious signs of fear, she walked across the ceiling and then smoothly transitioned to walking down the wall.

"That was fun. Why don't you try it, Mummy?"

"I don't know that spell. It isn't in the spell book, is it?"

"It's a new one." She picked up her school bag and took out a sheet of paper. "Mr Horsetrot printed it out for us. "Try it." She handed me the sheet of paper.

It looked simple enough, and I figured that walking on the ceiling might actually be fun, so I cast the spell. Nervously, I planted first one foot and then the other onto the wall. Only when I was sure they had gripped, did I begin to walk.

"You did it, Mummy!"

Once I reached the top of the wall, I hesitated, but with Florence's encouragement, I stepped gingerly onto the ceiling. Florence was right; I didn't feel the blood rush to my head as I would normally have expected.

"This is fun," I said.

I hadn't realised just how much dust there was on the light fitting, and I regretted not taking the feather duster up there with me. Speaking of dust, my nose began to tickle, and I sneezed. The next thing I knew, I dropped like a stone, bouncing off the bed, and landing with a thud on the bedroom floor.

"Are you okay, Mummy?"

Florence and Jay were looking at me with some concern.

"Yeah, I'm fine." I stood up and dusted myself off. "I don't know what happened."

"Mr Horsetrot said that anyone with a cold couldn't practise the spell because if you sneeze or cough, it breaks the spell."

Now she tells me.

"This is the last time I'm going to tell you, Florence," I said. "You are not allowed to walk on the ceiling while you eat your pizza."

"Aww, not fair." She huffed, then took another bite of pizza.

"What time do you reckon you'll be back tonight?" Jack asked.

"I have no idea. It all depends if and when the thieves come looking for the briefcase. I'm going to take a change of clothes with me, just in case I'm there all night and have to go straight into the office."

"Okay, but if you do have to stay all night, give me a call in the morning so that I know you're okay."

"Ahh, are you worried about me? That's sweet."

"I always worry about you."

"I've finished my pizza now," Florence said. "Can I walk on the ceiling?"

"Okay, but do it in your bedroom, so if you fall, you land on the bed."

Chapter 24

Aaron the Arrow lived out in The Sticks. And by that, I don't mean he lived in the middle of nowhere, but in a small village, which I'd never previously come across, called The Sticks. It was located between Washbridge and West Chipping.

It was almost eleven o'clock by the time I got there, and the streets were deserted. Out of caution, I parked a couple of streets away, and then made my way on foot to the small, terraced house, which was in total darkness.

I knocked on the door.

"Who's that?" Came a voice from inside.

"Aaron? It's me. Jill Maxwell."

"Shush, you'll wake the neighbours."

"Sorry, can you open the door?"

"I can't. It's locked."

"Don't you have the keys?"

"Why would the two-leggeds give me the keys?"

"Good point. I hadn't thought of that."

"You'll have to go around to the backdoor, the flap is there."

"There's no need. I'll magic myself inside. Stand back."

"Oh, okay."

Moments later, I was standing in the hallway, and Aaron, a pure white cat, was staring at me in disbelief.

"Winky said you were a witch, but I didn't believe him. That was pretty cool what you did just now."

"Thanks."

"What else can you do?"

"Now's not really the time."

"Sorry. I wish my two-leggeds could do magic." He

glanced at the briefcase in my hand. "Is that the cash?"

"No, it's empty, but the thieves won't know that until it's too late."

"How do you want to play this?"

"You said the cat flap is in the backdoor, can you show me?"

"Sure, this way."

The backdoor was in the small kitchen.

"What's through that door over there?"

"That's just a walk-in cupboard."

"Perfect. I'll put the briefcase on the table, and I'll lie in wait in the cupboard."

"What about me? What do you want me to do?"

"Nothing. You need to stay well out of the way in case things get nasty."

"I'm not scared. I can handle myself in a fight. Just ask Winky."

"I don't doubt it, but it would be better if I handled this alone. Why don't you go upstairs until I call you."

"What time are you expecting them?"

"I have no idea, but I believe it was sometime after midnight when they hit Socks' place."

"They aren't likely to be here for a while, then. How about a friendly game of darts to kill a bit of time? Maybe even a small wager, just to make it interesting."

"No chance. Winky warned me about you. He told me you might try and hustle me."

"That cat always did have a big mouth."

"Look, these guys could turn up any time, so why don't you make yourself scarce."

"Okay, but if you need any help, just yell."

"I will. Thanks."

Aaron had failed to mention that the walk-in cupboard was chock-full of all manner of rubbish, and I only just managed to squeeze inside. It was at times like this, sitting on an upturned bucket in the dark, that I questioned the direction my life had taken. What would my father have made of me, I wondered, if he could see me now?

Despite the discomfort of my surroundings, I somehow managed to nod off, but I was awoken with a start.

"It's there, on the table."

Someone was in the kitchen, and they'd obviously spotted the briefcase. Moments later, I heard two clicks, as the case was opened.

"It's empty."

This second voice was one that I recognised. That was my cue to make an appearance. Stepping out of the cupboard, I found three cats, all wearing masks.

"Hello, guys," I said.

"Who are you?" the cat standing by the cat flap demanded.

"How come she can talk to us?" his colleague asked.

"She must be a witch," said the cat who had opened the briefcase.

"Right first time, Billy," I said.

"How do you know my name?"

"We've met before."

"I very much doubt that."

"Let me jog your memory." I turned myself into Daisy, the cute white Persian.

"You were at the casino the other night."

"Correct. The night that Tulip won on the golden wheel."

"What's going on, Billy?" the cat by the door said.

"Maybe I can answer that," I offered. "But before I do, why don't you take off those silly masks? You aren't fooling anyone."

Billy took his off and threw it on the table, but the other two seemed reluctant to reveal their identities.

"Okay, here's my take on what's going on: My friend, Billy, with the help of one of the croupiers, is making sure that certain cats win big on the roulette table. Those winners are always new visitors to the casino. How am I doing so far, Billy?"

"That's nonsense," he said. "You don't know what you're talking about."

"That's what I would expect you to say. When the lucky winner claims their cash, they are given a briefcase in which to take home their winnings. What the winners don't realise is that there is some kind of tracking device inside the briefcase that allows you and your hired goons, to—"

"Hey, who are you calling a goon?" objected one of the other cats.

"As I was saying, Billy uses the tracking device to locate the briefcase, and then helps himself to the money."

"You can't prove any of this," Billy said.

"The fact that you're here tonight kind of proves it, don't you think? What confused me at first was why you would allow someone to win, only to steal the money back, but then it came to me: Instead of trying to walk out of the casino with cash stuffed in your pockets, you allow someone else to take it out for you, then you steal it from them. What kind of deal have you got going with the croupier? Is it a fifty-fifty split?"

"I don't have to listen to any more of your nonsense."

Billy turned to his partners-in-crime. "Come on, guys, we're out of here."

"Not so fast." I cast the 'shrink' spell on all three cats, then picked them up, put them in the briefcase, and locked it.

"Let us out!" came Billy's muffled cry.

The casino was open twenty-four seven, but I wasn't sure if the owner would be there at that hour. If he wasn't, then Billy and his colleagues would be spending a long night confined in the briefcase.

I didn't bother to change myself into a cat, but I did shrink myself, so that I'd be able to get through the door to the casino. The cat who opened the door did a doubletake when he saw me standing there.

"Who—err—what?" he stuttered.

"Is the owner in?"

"Yes, but you can't come in here. The casino is for animals only. And, how come I can talk to you, anyway?"

"There isn't time for that now. Just go and tell your boss that his casino is being embezzled for tens of thousands of pounds, and I have the proof right here, in this briefcase."

"I—err—"

"Just do it."

"Okay, wait here." He closed the door in my face.

After ten minutes, I was beginning to think that he wasn't going to return, but then he reappeared.

"Mr Healine will see you. Come with me, please." I followed him across the casino floor to a staircase that was hidden behind a red velvet curtain. "Up here." At the top of the stairs was a single door. The cat knocked and waited.

"Come in!"

The cat opened the door and stood to one side, to allow me to enter. Sitting behind an enormous, red, sparkly desk was one of the fattest cats I'd ever seen.

"Well, well, well, I never thought I'd see the day when a witch paid a visit to my humble casino." He stood up and offered his paw. "Freddy Healine at your service. And you are?"

"Jill Maxwell."

"Why does that name ring a bell?"

I shrugged, all modest-like. "Thank you for seeing me."

"Take a seat." He dropped back into his chair which groaned under his weight. "I was intrigued. Larry tells me that you have proof someone is stealing from the casino."

"That's correct."

"That's a pretty serious accusation."

"It is, and I wouldn't be standing in front of you if I wasn't sure it was true."

"Okay, I'm all ears."

He was right about that; I'd never seen such huge ears on a cat. But I digress. I proceeded to outline what I'd discovered, but I did so without naming names. He remained silent until I'd finished, and then said, "You're saying that the thief is an employee?"

"At least two employees, by my reckoning. One of your croupiers is definitely involved. He's the one who ensures the *lucky* cat goes on a winning streak."

"But that's the part I don't get. There's no way the croupier can control where the ball comes to land on the wheel; it's completely random."

"Unless—" I hesitated mainly for effect.

"Yes?"

"I believe the croupier in question is a wizard."

"But our croupiers are all cats. I hired them myself."

They say a picture is worth a thousand words and this was one of those times. I changed myself into Daisy, the Persian, and jumped on the manager's desk.

"How did you do that?" Clearly unnerved, the manager pushed his chair a few inches back from the desk.

"Any half-proficient wizard or witch can change themself into a cat. That's the easy part. Creating a spell that can accurately control the ball on the roulette table is much more challenging. If I'm right, and I'm pretty sure that I am, the croupier is a very powerful wizard, which makes them particularly dangerous."

"You said there were at least two employees involved. Who else?"

"I'm glad you asked that."

After changing back into myself, I placed the briefcase on the desk, clicked open the fastenings, and opened the lid.

"Billy?" The manager stared in disbelief at his diminutive employee. "Ricky? Mike?"

"I take it you know all three of these gentlemen?" I said.

"She's got it all wrong, boss," Billy complained.

"If that's true, maybe you'd like to explain to Mr Healine why you broke into my house tonight, to try and retrieve the cash you thought was there."

"We didn't break in," Ricky objected. "We went through the cat flap."

"Shut up, you idiot!" Billy turned on his accomplice.

"I think I've heard enough," Healine slammed the briefcase closed.

"What are you going to do?" I asked.

"I know what I'd like to do: take this briefcase and drop it into the nearest river with these three still in it."

"You can't do that."

"Don't worry. That's what I'd like to do, but I won't. Will these guys have to stay this size forever?"

"No, I'll change them back to full size once we're done here."

"And then I'll sack their sorry backsides."

"Is that it? Won't you involve the police?"

"Nothing would give me greater pleasure, but if I did that it would be disastrous for the casino. If word was to get out that someone had been fixing the results, and it would, no one would ever trust us again."

"That's your call, obviously. What about the money they stole from you?"

"Can you see this lot volunteering to hand it back?"

"I guess not. Full disclosure, though, at least one cat still has her winnings. Her name is Tulip and she helped me to set up this sting. Do you want me to ask her to return it?"

"Definitely not. She won that money fair and square, or at least she believed she did. She can keep it with my blessing."

"That's very good of you. She'll be delighted, I'm sure." I stood up. "I ought to be going now."

"Wait, please. Can I ask you something?"

"Sure."

"I don't understand how you came to get involved with all of this."

I told him about Winky, and how his brother, Socks, had won at the casino, only to have his winnings stolen from him.

"Winky and Socks were hoping I might be able to

recover their money, but I'll have to tell them that's not going to happen."

"Maybe not."

"What do you mean?"

"From what you've told me, it's clear that these three scumbags are just the muscle. The brains behind this operation is obviously the croupier."

"I agree."

"You said you think he's a wizard?"

"That would be my guess."

"If he's as powerful as you think he is, I'm worried about what he might do if I confront him. Would you be prepared to help me? I'd reward you generously. How about I pay you the same amount your cat's brother lost?"

"Ten grand? That's a lot of money."

"It would be worth it to me if it gets rid of that snake."

"What if he gets a whiff of what has happened to his partners-in-crime here?"

"He won't. I'll keep these guys on ice until you've done your thing. What do you say?"

"Why not? Wizards living in the human world are expected to keep their identity secret, and they're not allowed to do anything that might draw attention to them. If they step out of line, they are liable to be arrested by the rogue retrievers."

"The *who*?"

"Essentially, they're kind of the police, except they wear catsuits. I'm pretty sure they'd be interested in the activities of the croupier."

"Excellent. I assume you can check which croupier was working the table when Tulip won the other night?"

"I already know who it was, but they aren't on duty at

the moment. They are scheduled to work again tonight, though. Would you be able to arrange something with the rogue retrievers that quickly?"

"I'm pretty sure I can."

"Fantastic."

After leaving the casino, I made a quick phone call to Daze who confirmed that she and Blaze would pay the casino a visit that night, to arrest the croupier.

Chapter 25

By the time I made it back home, it was seven-thirty in the morning. I was so tired I could hardly keep my eyes open. When I walked into the house, I could hear Jack and Florence in the kitchen.

"Florence, what are you doing up there?" I shouted. "Jack, what were you thinking, letting her walk on the ceiling?"

"She's really good at it now. I don't think she'll fall. I made her wait until she'd eaten all her breakfast."

"Oh, that's okay, then." I looked up at Florence. "Right, madam, down you come."

"Aww!"

"This minute. If you want to walk on the ceiling, you have to do it in your bedroom, above your bed. Okay?"

"Okay." She huffed, as she walked down the wall, and then disappeared upstairs.

"I was beginning to worry about you," Jack said. "I thought you'd have been home ages ago."

"Me too. I'm shattered."

"Was it worthwhile? Did you catch the bad guys?"

"I did. The reason I'm so late is because I took them to the casino. The owner had no idea he was being robbed blind by his own staff. I thought he'd hand them over to the police, but he doesn't want word to get out about the theft in case it ruins the casino's reputation."

"What about Winky's brother's money? Did you manage to recover that?"

"No, that's long gone."

"Winky won't be best pleased."

"I think he'll be okay."

"Do you want me to get you some breakfast? I could do you a fry-up if you fancy it."

"No, thanks. I couldn't face anything at the moment. I'm going to bed for a few hours. Will you do me a favour and call Mrs V? Tell her I'm feeling a little peaky and I might not make it in today."

"Okay, will do."

I was asleep before my head even hit the pillow.

"What's all this about you being a model?"

The words swam around my head and felt like part of a weird dream.

"Hey, sleepy head. I asked you a question."

This was no dream; it was a nightmare, and the name of that nightmare was Grandma. I sat up to find her standing next to the bed.

"What are you doing here? Couldn't you see I was asleep?"

"I could, and you should be ashamed of yourself. Don't you know what time it is?"

"I've been up all night."

"That's what comes of marrying a human. They're all the same: sex mad."

"It had nothing to do with Jack. I was working on a case."

"What kind of case requires you to work all night?"

"I caught some cats who had been stealing from a casino."

"Why are you working with cats?"

"Enough questions. Why are you in my bedroom?"

"Because that's where you are. I came to find out about this new modelling career of yours."

"I don't have a modelling career."

"Jim said you were doing some modelling for a cosmetics company."

"It's *Jack*, and I did do some modelling, but it was a one-off. Why are you interested, anyway?"

"I was thinking you might put a word in with your modelling agency."

"Put a word in about what?"

"Me of course. The grey market is huge. I'm sure there would be lots of opportunities for someone with my looks."

With her looks? Did she even possess a mirror?

"Sorry, Grandma, I don't have an agency, and I won't be doing any more modelling."

"What went wrong? Did you mess up?"

"No, I didn't. It's just not for me. I'm going to stick with being a private investigator."

"Typical. Just when I think you might actually be able to help me for once, you let me down again." And with that, she disappeared.

Fortunately, despite Grandma's untimely appearance, I was able to grab a few hours' sleep. By the time I got up, just after eleven o'clock, I was starving, and trying to decide if I should have breakfast or lunch. I solved the problem by combining the two. Who knew that pizza would go so well with Strawberrycandy Pops.

What? I was starving.

I would have liked to have taken the rest of the day off, but I had an appointment with Keith Maxwell. Not an *actual* appointment because he had made it quite clear he was never going to meet with me. That was okay, though, because Edna had given me a comprehensive timetable of the man's movements. According to Edna, he went to the La Whistle restaurant every day at one o'clock. He would be accompanied by his bodyguards, but that was okay because I had yet another cunning plan.

After making myself invisible, I magicked myself backstage at the restaurant. Shortly after, a young woman came through the rear staff entrance. I followed her into the staff changing room where she opened a locker. Inside it, hung a waitress uniform. Before she could take it out, I cast the 'sleep' spell and helped her to a nearby cupboard.

"Sorry, I won't leave you there for long," I said to the sleeping beauty.

After donning the uniform, I headed for the table in the corner of the room, where Keith Maxwell was seated alone on a large semi-circular bench seat. Two of his bodyguards stood close by, but they didn't challenge me as I approached the table. It was only when I got close to him that I realised he was a sup.

After taking a small notebook from the pocket of my uniform, I said, "What can I get for you today, sir?"

Maxwell looked perturbed. "Where's Jessica? Jessica always takes my order."

"I'm afraid she called in sick."

"Who are you? I haven't seen you in here before."

"My name is Jill. I'm new here."

"*New*? I don't have time to deal with trainees. Get me the manager."

"Sorry, I can't do that."

"What did you just say? I'll have you sacked." He turned to his two henchmen. "Ron, Tom, get this woman out of my sight and go and get the manager."

Before the two stooges could carry out his orders, I cast the 'sleep' spell on both of them, and they slumped onto the bench seat, one either side of Keith Maxwell.

"You're a witch," Maxwell said.

"And you're a wizard."

"What do you want?" He looked like he would rather be anywhere else, but he was blocked in by the two sleeping uglies.

"Before I get into that, I just wanted to tell you that you and I have quite a lot in common."

"What are you talking about?"

"First, you have a brother called Jack Maxwell."

"So?"

"My husband is called Jack Maxwell too."

"I couldn't care less."

"Yes, but wait until you hear this. You're a sup who was raised with a sibling who is a human. Guess what? So am I. My sister is a human."

"Is that what you came here to tell me?"

"No, I just thought that was kind of interesting. I came here to tell you that I know it was you, not your brother, who killed your partner, Joseph."

"You're insane. My brother was convicted in a court of law for Joseph's murder. I had nothing to do with it."

"Yeah, but here's the thing. The jury could have no way of knowing that the person caught on the CCTV, going into Joseph's apartment, wasn't Jack. It was you. How could those humans on the jury be expected to know that you'd used the 'doppelganger' spell to make yourself look like your brother?" He didn't respond, but his eyes told me I had hit a nerve. "The same thing applies to the argument that Jean Longton overheard, doesn't it? That was you too."

"That's nonsense. My brother killed Joseph. I had nothing to do with it, and good luck trying to prove otherwise. Who are you, anyway?"

"This is me." I handed him my card.

"Who hired you? It was Jack, wasn't it? Where did he get the money from?"

"I'm going to leave you now, but I suggest you spend the next couple of hours considering your position. When you decide to do the right thing, and confess to Joseph's murder, give me a call."

"I wouldn't hold your breath."

"Enjoy your meal."

As I headed away, I reversed the 'sleep' spell on his bodyguards.

"What happened, boss?" Ron rubbed his forehead.

"Come on, you useless lumps. We're leaving."

Something told me that Keith had lost his appetite, and if my hunch was correct, he wouldn't be in the mood for returning to the office. If my cunning plan was to work, I would have to move fast. Edna had provided me with Keith Maxwell's home address, and I needed to get there as soon as possible. Driving there wasn't an option because, as a wizard, Keith might decide to magic himself back home. As soon as I was out of the restaurant, I magicked myself to his house.

I wasn't totally surprised to find that the woman who answered the door was a witch. It made sense that Keith would have married a sup. She looked a little confused to see me standing there, probably because I had apparently bypassed the elaborate security at the gates.

"Who are you? How did you get into the grounds?"

"I'm really sorry. I'd love to chat, but I'm in rather a hurry."

"What do you mean, you're—"

The 'sleep' spell cut her off midsentence. After taking her through to the bedroom, I used the 'doppelganger' spell to make myself look like her. And not a moment too soon because, just a few minutes later, Keith Maxwell's car came up the driveway and parked in front of the house. Moments later, he came charging through the door, red in the face, and looking like he wanted to kill someone—and that someone was most likely me.

"What's the matter, Keith?" I asked.

Although the 'doppelganger' spell was incredibly accurate in the way it made me resemble the person in question, what it couldn't help with were the mannerisms and habits of that person. For example, I had no idea whether Keith's wife would normally call her husband by his name or if she would refer to him as darling or something similar. Luckily, judging by his reaction, I'd got away with it.

"I need a drink!" He headed for the bar in the corner of the room, poured himself a large whisky and downed half of it in one.

"What's wrong?"

"That brother of mine. That's what's wrong."

"Jack? What has he done? Have you seen him?"

"No, but he's hired one of your lot."

"What do you mean *my lot*? What are you talking about?"

"A witch, what do you think I mean? And not just any witch, it's Jill Maxwell. You must have heard of her."

"Yeah, isn't she supposed to be the most powerful witch

in Candlefield?"

"Supposedly, but she's also a private investigator here in the human world."

"How can Jack afford to hire her?"

"I've no idea but he has." He chugged the rest of the whisky then poured himself another one.

"Take it steady."

"Don't tell me to take it steady," he snapped.

"You mustn't panic, Keith. She can't possibly know anything."

"That's just it. She knew I'd used the 'doppelganger' spell to make it look like Jack was the one who visited Joseph's apartment. And she knew it was me who argued with him at the office."

"Even so, what can she do?"

"What do you mean? Didn't you hear what I just said? She knows I was the one who killed Joseph, not Jack."

"Think about it for a minute. She can hardly take what she knows to the authorities here in the human world, can she? As soon as she starts talking about wizards and spells, they'll laugh in her face."

He took another sip. "Yeah, you're right. She can't do anything. Thanks, doll. I'm sorry I snapped at you before."

"That's okay." I reversed the 'doppelganger' spell. "It was worth it."

"You again!" He dropped the glass, which shattered on the wooden floor. "Where's Josie?"

"She's okay. She's just having a nap."

"I'm going to kill you."

He lunged for me, but the 'sleep' spell stopped him in his tracks.

I made a call to Daze.

"Hey, Daze, are you busy?"

"Nothing that can't wait. What's up?"

"I have a couple of characters over here that I think you'll be interested in. Any chance you can pop over?"

"Sure, we just need to book a couple of elves into custody and then we'll be with you."

"Great."

Thirty minutes later, Daze and Blaze arrived.

"What are you wearing, Blaze?" I laughed.

"I told him he looks ridiculous." Daze rolled her eyes. "But he won't have it."

"I don't care what either of you says, I think I look cool."

"It definitely must be cool around your calves," I said.

The legs in Blaze's catsuit appeared to have been cut off at the knee.

"It wouldn't be so bad if he had nice legs." Daze grinned.

"What's wrong with my legs?" he snapped. "I have nice legs."

"They're like chicken legs."

"You two are so unprofessional."

"Sorry, Blaze," I somehow managed to say without laughing. "You look great."

"What have we got here?" Daze pointed to the prone figure on the floor.

"My client, Jack Two, was recently released from prison after serving a sentence for murder."

"Jack *Two*?" Blaze said. "Is that really his name?"

"No, sorry. His name is actually Jack Maxwell, but I called him Jack Two so as not to confuse him with my Jack."

"That could only make sense to you, Jill," Daze said. "Sorry, carry on."

"This guy is Keith Maxwell, Jack's brother."

"Jack's a wizard too, I take it?"

"Actually no. I should have said that they are half-brothers, and Jack obviously has no idea that his brother is a sup. Jack, Keith and a guy called Joseph were partners in a construction business. Jack was convicted of Joseph's murder, largely on the evidence of CCTV footage and an overheard argument. When Jack first approached me, I wasn't optimistic that I'd be able to help, but once I realised his half-brother was a wizard, it all became clear. Keith had used magic to make it look like his brother was the one who murdered Joseph."

"I can understand why you'd think that's what happened," Daze said. "But do you have any proof?"

"I have this." I took out my phone and played back the conversation I'd had with Keith when he thought he was talking to his wife.

"That should do it." Daze nodded. "Can you send me a copy of that recording?"

"Sure."

"Where is his wife?"

"In the bedroom, asleep. I'm not sure if she played any part in the murder, but she definitely knew what her husband had done."

"Right, we'd better get these two back to Candlefield." She looked around. "This is a lovely house. What will happen to it?"

"I've no idea."

Chapter 26

It was mid-afternoon when I finally made it back to the office.

"Are you sure you should be here, Jill?" Mrs V said. "Jack said you were feeling a little peaky."

"Yeah, I feel fine now, but I could murder a cup of tea."

"I'll get straight on it, but before I do, there were a couple of calls."

"Okay?"

"A Mr Terry Rain called and wanted to know when the next meeting of the Washbridge Train Spotter's Society was being held. I told him he had a wrong number."

"Right."

"And Mr Braxmore called again."

"What did *he* want?"

"He seems like such a nice man, but he's got it into his head that we are stockists of compass stones. I explained to him that you're a private investigator, and that we don't sell compass stones or anything else for that matter. Hopefully, he got the message. What is a compass stone, anyway? I've never heard of them."

"Me neither. I've changed my mind about the tea. I'll have a coffee, black and strong."

"Nice of you to make an appearance," Winky said. "I've been on tenterhooks. What happened last night at Aaron's? I called him, but he said you'd left by the time he got up and that he hadn't heard anything. Did they show up?"

"They did. There were three of them, all employees of the casino."

"And?"

"I took them to Winskers where we all had a friendly little chat with Freddy Healine."

"Who?"

"He's the owner of the casino. He wasn't best pleased to discover that his business was being robbed by his own employees."

"What about our money?"

"That's gone, I'm afraid."

"Are you sure?"

"Positive. Sorry."

"Great. What am I going to tell Socks? He'll be devastated."

"Don't you want to know what happened to the thieves?"

"What does it matter? We've lost our money."

"You're totally minted. What difference would an extra five grand have made to you?"

"None, that's why I was going to tell Socks to keep the lot. Look, I know you don't like him, and he can be his own worst enemy at times, but he and his family are really struggling at the moment. Financially, I mean. That money would have been lifechanging for them. What am I going to tell him?"

"It might not be quite as bad as you think."

"How so?"

"If you'll allow me to tell you what else happened last night, you'll see. Okay?"

"Go ahead. I'm not in any hurry to tell Socks the bad news."

"Freddy Healine isn't going to press charges against the three cats I caught at Aaron's."

"Why not? They should rot in prison."

"He's afraid that the adverse publicity would impact on the casino."

"So, they get away scot-free?"

"Not entirely. They've all lost their jobs."

"Is that it?"

"No, you haven't heard the best part yet. Haven't you ever wondered how come Socks won so much money that night?"

"I assume the wheel must have been doctored."

"Not exactly. The croupier wasn't actually a cat; he was a wizard. He used magic to control the ball as it spun around the wheel."

"So, he was in on it too?"

"Yes, in fact, I'm pretty sure he was the mastermind behind the whole thing. Freddy Healine was worried about what might happen if he had to tackle the wizard, so he asked if I could do it, which I was more than happy to do."

"I don't see how any of this is meant to make me feel better."

"Because, dear friend, Freddy paid me ten grand for uncovering the theft in the first place and for sorting out the wizard problem."

"Well, that's just dandy. You get ten big ones for one night's work while Socks and I are still out of pocket. Typical. Just typical."

"If you had let me finish, I was going to say that I am going to give the money to Socks."

"Are you serious? You'd really do that?"

"Yeah."

"You're the best." Winky threw himself at me and wrapped his legs around my body. "I could kiss you."

"Yuk, you'd better not. Get off or I might change my mind."

He jumped down. "I'm going to call Socks."

"Okay, but this doesn't change anything. I still don't want to see him in this office."

Winky grinned. "You act cold and hard, but inside you're really a big softy."

"Just don't tell anyone."

Winky was on the phone to his brother for almost fifteen minutes.

"Socks says thank you, and if there's anything he can ever do for you, you only have to ask."

"I think that's unlikely."

"He really wanted to come over to bring you some flowers, but I warned him off."

"Just as well. Anyway, down to business. The deal was that I'd catch the thieves and in return you'd tell me what you'd managed to dig up about Harmony Fashion."

"Hmm." Winky frowned. "I didn't actually manage to find anything on them. I just said I had so you'd try and get the money back."

"What?" I exploded. "How could you lie about something like that? I could face bankruptcy if they go ahead and sue me."

"You should see your face." He laughed. "Of course I've got something on them." He scuttled under the sofa, then reappeared clutching a large brown envelope. "Read this."

I opened the envelope, took out a single sheet of paper, and read it.

"Are you sure about this?" I said.

"One hundred percent."

"You'd better be because if you're wrong, I'll be in even bigger trouble than I already am."

"You can take it to the bank."

***

It was quite a relief to find Florence walking on the floor rather than the ceiling or walls.

"When will I get my Bluebottle Girl costume, Mummy?" she asked as soon as I walked through the door.

"You already know the answer to that. On Saturday."

"Please let me see what you've done already."

"No, it's bad luck to see it before the day it's supposed to be ready."

"I thought that was a wedding dress." Jack grinned.

I shot him a look. "Shouldn't you be making dinner?"

"But it's your—I'll go and make a start on it."

"When I get the costume, I'm never going to take it off," Florence said.

"You know you can't wear it to school, don't you?"

"Why not? Julie did."

"Yes, and the teacher wasn't very happy about it from what I heard."

Unimpressed, she buzzed her way upstairs. Once I was sure she was out of earshot, I gave Kathy a call.

"It's me."

"I know. Do I really have to explain to you how caller ID works again?"

"I just wanted to check that Florence's costume will be ready for Saturday?"

"I promised it would be, didn't I? Have I ever broken a promise to you before?"

"There was that time you promised to share your candyfloss with me, and you didn't."

"Sheesh, Jill, I was seven at the time. Are you really still holding a grudge about that?"

"No, I was just saying."

"The costume will be ready on time."

"Thanks, it's just that Florence is counting the days."

"You can relax. Your ever reliable sister has it all in hand. I thought you might have given me a call to let me know how the modelling went."

"There wasn't much to say about it. It was all pretty boring really."

"Still, getting a makeover from a professional makeup artist must have been nice. Have you got any photos?"

"What do you mean?"

"You know: before and after."

"No, I never thought to."

"Do you reckon you might get any more assignments on the strength of what you did?"

"I wouldn't think so. It was just a one-off."

"What about free samples? They must have given you some. I hope you're going to share."

"I didn't get anything. It's a completely new range, so they weren't allowed to give away samples until it's actually launched."

"What a disappointment."

"Anyway, I have to go. Dinner is nearly ready."

After dinner, Florence went up to her bedroom, so that she could walk on the ceiling. It was nice not to have to go out in the evening for once, and I intended to make the most of it by chilling out in front of the TV.

"Do we have to have the TV on?" Jack said when he joined me on the sofa.

"Yes, I hardly ever get to watch TV."

"You'll just fall asleep."

"No, I won't."

"I thought we might do something more interesting." He grinned.

"You do realise Florence is not in bed yet, don't you?"

"I didn't mean *that*." He stooped down and reached for something under the sofa. "Voila!"

"*Scrabble*? Are you serious?"

"There was a jumble sale at the church hall today, and I got this for fifty-pence."

"You were robbed."

"I used to love playing this when I was a kid."

"That was because you were a boring little nerd."

"There's nothing boring or nerdy about Scrabble. It's a test of your vocabulary."

"My vocabulary is just fine, thanks."

"Well, if you're afraid of losing."

"To you?" I scoffed. "Do me a favour."

"Would you care to put your money where your mouth is?"

Damn that man. He knew just how to press my buttons.

"Okay," I agreed. "A fiver says I win, but I'm only playing one game."

"You're on."

So much for my relaxing evening in front of the TV. Still, whupping Jack at Scrabble and picking up a fiver in the process did have a certain appeal.

Twenty minutes later:

"Best of three," I said.

"You said one game only."

"That was before I knew you were going to cheat. You only won because you used made up words."

"I didn't make up any words, and you know it."

"Bezique?" I scoffed. "Really?"

"It's a nineteenth-century French melding and trick-taking card game for two players. You saw for yourself when you insisted on checking Wikipedia."

"Yes, but how could you possibly have known that?"

"I have a very wide vocabulary. Where's my fiver?"

"Best of three."

"Only if you make it a tenner."

"Okay. Let's rumble."

One hour later:

"Hand over the money." Jack held out his hand.

"I don't have any cash. I forgot to go to the ATM."

"Liar. Show me your purse."

"Okay." I slapped a tenner into his hand. "But I never want to see that stupid game again."

"You always were a bad loser." He grinned.

I grabbed the remote control and switched on the TV. Sensibly, Jack made himself scarce, leaving me to stew.

"That was entertaining," Wanda said.

"Do you mind? I'm trying to watch TV."

"Best laugh we've had in ages, wasn't it, Mabel?"

"Hilarious."

"And the best part is she has no idea."

"What are you two talking about?"

"Nothing, we wouldn't want to disturb your TV viewing."

I got up off the sofa and went over to the fish tank. "What did you mean when you said that *I had no idea*?"

"Bezique."

"What about it? It's a real word, I checked."

"It may be, but how do you think your hubby came up with it?"

"Jack reads a lot of books and watches a lot of documentaries. He probably came across it there."

"Yeah, I guess so." Wanda bubbled.

"I've got a great word for Scrabble," Mabel said.

"What's that?" Wanda asked.

"Gullible."

With that, the tank filled with bubbles, as the two fish rolled around in hysterics.

"What do you two know that I don't?"

"What's it worth?" Wanda said.

"What do you want?"

"A new ornament wouldn't go amiss. Just to brighten the tank up a little."

"Okay, I'll buy you an ornament. Now, tell me what you know."

It was Jack's turn to take Florence up to bed and read her a bedtime story. Afterwards, when he came downstairs and joined me in the lounge, he did a doubletake.

"What's all this?" he said.

"I just thought you'd like a cup of tea."

"You always wait for me to make it."

"It's my way of saying sorry for being a bad loser."

"And a bun too?" He joined me on the sofa.

"I picked those up on the way home. I've already eaten

mine. They're delicious."

He took a bite. "Hmm, you're right. This is amazing. What is it?"

"Waddle berry."

"I've never heard—wait a minute." He put what was left of the bun back onto the plate. "Isn't that—?"

"Yeah." I grinned.

"You've poisoned me."

"Don't be so melodramatic. It isn't poison and it won't make you ill. Just a bit spotty. Green spotty."

"Why would you do that?"

"Bezique."

"What are you talking about?"

I picked up his phone, which he'd left on the coffee table when he took Florence to bed.

"This is why!" I opened the word solver app that was installed on his phone.

"I—err—I didn't use it."

"The fish saw you. You were checking it while I was studying the board."

"Okay, I admit it." He sighed. "You can have your money back." He handed me the tenner.

"Thanks."

"This isn't really a waddle berry bun, is it?"

Chapter 27

"Not fair," Florence said as the three of us ate breakfast. "Mummy had green spots, now Daddy has them, why can't I have them?"

"Green spots aren't a good thing, pumpkin." Jack glared at me.

"Do you think I'll get them soon?" she persisted.

"No, darling, children can't get green spots," I said. "Only grown-ups get them."

Once she'd finished her breakfast, and still pouting because she wouldn't be getting any green spots, she went back to ceiling walking in her bedroom.

"I can't believe you did this to me," Jack said.

"I couldn't believe you would cheat at Scrabble and steal ten pounds from me, so I guess that means we're disappointed in one another."

"How long will the spots last?"

"Mine were pretty much gone within twenty-four hours."

"Good."

"But then, I am a super powerful witch and you're just a mere human, so who knows how long you'll have them."

"You're enjoying this, aren't you?"

"More than you'll ever know. Plus, I think our daughter has learned a valuable lesson today, don't you?"

"What's that? Don't cheat, I suppose."

"No, it's don't get caught cheating."

Anyone who saw me on my drive into the office would probably have thought I'd lost my mind because I kept thinking about Jack's green spots and breaking into laughter.

What do you mean I'm cruel? A cheat must never be allowed to prosper. I think he got off lightly with just a few green spots.

"That hubby of yours is such a sweety," Mrs V said.

"Sorry?"

"I love Armi to bits, but he would never send me flowers at work."

"*Flowers*?"

"They're on your desk."

"And they're from Jack?"

"There wasn't a card with them, but who else would they be from? Tea?"

"Yes, please."

The bouquet of flowers on my desk was one of the largest and most beautiful I'd ever seen.

"Socks knew you didn't want to see him, so he had these delivered for you," Winky said.

"They're lovely. Tell him thank you."

"I will. You did a really nice thing giving him the money. He'll be able to buy that sports car he's had his eye on for ages."

"*Sports car*?"

"Joking. I'm just joking. It will make a world of difference to him and his family."

Mrs V came through the door carrying a vase. "Shall I put them in water for you?"

"Yes, please."

"I hope you're going to call Jack and say thank you."

"I would but I happen to know he has a *spot* of bother he has to deal with this morning." I laughed.

A little confused by my reaction, she said, "Nothing too

serious, I hope?"

"No, he'll be fine *berry* soon."

"O—kay. I'll go and make that tea."

"What's really going on?" Winky said.

I told him about the Scrabble and the waddle berry cakes.

"Remind me never to cross you." He grinned.

"Do you think I overstepped the mark?"

"Course not. I'm proud of you. Green spots for the win."

As we high-fived, I did wonder for a moment if Winky's endorsement was actually a good thing or not.

When I'd finished my cup of tea, I made the telephone call that I'd been dreading.

"Jill, do you have something for me?" Jack Two said.

"We need to talk, Jack, and it would be better if we did it face to face in my office."

"I'm not sure that's safe."

"You don't need to worry about Keith. I give you my word on that."

"Has something happened?"

"I really need to have this conversation with you in person."

"Okay, if you say it's safe, I trust you. I'm in London at the moment, but I can probably get to you about one o'clock."

"Perfect, I'll see you then."

The conversation with Jack Two wasn't going to be easy, but it had to be done, even though I had no way of knowing what his reaction would be.

When Mrs V came through to my office a few minutes later, I assumed she had come to take away my cup, but when she closed the door behind her, I knew someone must be in the outer office.

"It's Mr Brown, Jill. I think he's fed up with not being able to get hold of you on the phone. What shall I tell him?"

"Send him in, please."

Charles Brown's expression caught me off-guard. I'd expected him to be fuming that I'd been giving him the runaround, but he was beaming.

"I'm really sorry to just turn up like this, Jill, I know how busy you are."

"Not at all. I'm the one who should apologise for not returning your calls. It's been pretty manic around here. Please, have a seat. Can I get you something to drink?"

He sat down but declined the offer of a drink.

"I'm glad you dropped by, Charles. I'm just sorry I haven't been able to come up with any answers for you about Max. I know how worried you are about him."

"It's okay, honestly. You were right. Everyone was. Except me."

"Sorry, I don't—"

"It was just a phase he was going through."

"Right?"

"We all go through periods of our life when things get on top of us, don't we? I know I did. Max was just going through a bad patch. All he needed was time and understanding."

"And he's coming out of that now?"

"Absolutely, he's practically back to his old self. He no longer spends all day locked away in his room. And he and I are talking again, just like we used to."

"That's fantastic."

"He's even started playing sports again. And he's looking for a job."

"I'm so pleased. For both of you."

"I'm just relieved he doesn't know that I'd hired you to check up on him. He won't find out, will he?"

"No, you don't have any worries on that score."

"Anyway, while I'm here, I'd like to settle your bill."

"I—err—don't really feel right about charging you. I didn't actually do anything to help."

"Rubbish. You did exactly what I asked you to, which was to follow Max and find out what was the matter with him. The fact that there was nothing to discover wasn't your fault."

"Okay, if you're sure."

"I am."

I fired up my laptop and consulted my time recording system to verify the hours I'd spent on the Brown case, printed out a bill, and handed it to him.

What? Of course I don't have a time recording system. I just tapped away on the keyboard while I came up with what I thought was a reasonable number.

Charles wrote out a cheque there and then and handed it to me.

"This is too much."

"I've included a small bonus as a sign of my appreciation for everything you've done."

"Thanks, that's very kind."

"See that, Winky?" I said after Charles had left. "Yet another satisfied customer."

"When are you going to move out of the stone age?"

"What do you mean?"

"I mean when are you going to start accepting card

payments?"

"What's wrong with cheques? I like cheques."

"Dinosaur."

Ignoring Winky, I reflected on what Charles had said. Although life would never actually be the same for his son, it did sound as though he was doing his best to adapt to being a vampire. The fact that he was able to take part in sports and had begun to look for a job proved that he must be drinking synthetic blood. That didn't make what had happened to Max any less of a travesty. If it was up to me, those responsible would spend the rest of their lives in jail in Candlefield.

"Right, Winky, I'm going to pay a visit to Harmony Fashion."

"Good luck."

"What do you mean, *good luck*? This information of yours had better be solid."

"It is. One hundred per cent."

Despite Winky's reassurance, I was really nervous as I walked into Harmony Fashion. If this didn't pan out the way I hoped it would, I might lose everything.

Candy, the assistant who had served me during my previous visit, was on duty. Her face fell as soon as she spotted me.

"Hi." I tried to sound bright and breezy, as though I didn't have a worry in the world.

"What are you doing here? You have to leave."

"Sorry, but I can't do that. I'd like to speak to your manager, please."

She glanced around nervously, unsure what to do.

"Candy, if you don't go and get her, I'll go and find her

myself."

"Okay, but you have to wait here."

A couple of minutes later, she returned with her manager. The last time I'd seen Greta, she'd been all smiles and couldn't do enough for me. Today, she had a face like thunder.

"You've got a nerve coming here." She practically spat the words at me.

"I just want a friendly talk, that's all."

"You're unbelievable." She scoffed. "Do you have any idea how much damage you did to Harmony?"

"I really am sorry about that misunderstanding."

"*Misunderstanding*? You told us that you wanted the outfit because you were being presented with a medal by the king. That wasn't a misunderstanding, it was an outright lie."

"Technically, it wasn't, but I understand why you would think that."

"You'd better leave. Now. We'll see you in court."

"I'm afraid I can't do that."

"Then you leave me no choice but to call the police."

"Before you do, I think you should read this." I handed her the brown envelope that Winky had given me.

"What is it? If they're papers related to the court case, these should be handed to our solicitors."

"It has nothing to do with the case. Take it out and read it, please."

"Do you promise to leave if I do?"

"I promise."

She took the sheet of paper out of the envelope and began to read it. Within moments, the colour had drained from her face. If there had been any doubt that Winky had come up with the goods, her reaction had dispelled them.

"Where did you get this?"

"That's not important."

"These are all lies. You can't prove any of this."

"In that case, you won't mind if I take it to the press. I'm guessing the fashion magazines will find this of particular interest."

"You can't do that. It would ruin us."

"Not my problem." I turned and started towards the exit.

"Wait!"

"Yes?"

"If Harmony were to drop the case against you, would you promise not to pass this information onto anyone else?"

"Are you offering me a deal?"

"I can't authorise it myself, but I'll check with our CEO."

"How long will that take?"

"I don't know. She's an extremely busy woman."

"You have until end of business today. If by then you haven't confirmed that you'll be dropping the case against me, I will take this to the press."

"Okay, fine."

"Well?" Winky said. "How did it go?"

"You should have seen her face when I showed her the paper you gave me. I thought she was going to have a seizure."

"Does that mean they're dropping the case against you?"

"She said she had to check with the CEO, so I told her

that I needed an answer by end of business today. I'm going to be on tenterhooks until then."

"There's nothing to worry about. It's a done deal. No way they can risk you handing that information to the press."

"I hope you're right."

"Didn't you know? I'm always right."

Chapter 28

I wasn't expecting Jack Two until one o'clock, but just after twelve-thirty, Mrs V came through to my office.

"The other Jack Maxwell is here, Jill, and he seems a little agitated."

"Send him through, please."

"What's going on, Jill?" he asked as soon as he walked through the door.

"Please take a seat, Jack."

"I'd rather stand."

"Please. Trust me, when you hear what I have to say, you'll need to be sitting down."

"Okay." He took a seat.

"First, you need to listen to this." I played part of the recording I'd made at Keith Maxwell's house when he had thought he was speaking to his wife:

Didn't you hear what I just said? She knows I was the one who killed Joseph, not Jack.

Jack Two stared at the telephone in disbelief. "That was Keith, wasn't it?"

"It was."

"He just confessed to the murder. Surely, that's enough to get my conviction quashed, isn't it?"

"Normally, it would be, but these aren't normal circumstances."

"I don't understand."

"What I'm about to tell you is going to blow your mind. Are you ready?"

"I think so."

"Your half-brother isn't human."

"You're telling me. What he did to me was inhumane."

"That's true, but I meant he isn't a human being."

I wish I could adequately describe the expression on Jack's face, but I don't have words that would do it justice.

"I don't understand."

"Before I try and explain, I need you to give me your word that what I'm about to tell you, you won't share with anyone outside of this room."

"Okay."

"I need to hear you say it."

"I promise not to share what you tell me with anyone else."

"Your half-brother is a wizard."

It was at this point that I'm pretty sure Jack thought I'd completely lost my mind, or that I had been smoking funny cigs, so I made myself invisible.

"Jill?" He looked all around the room. After a minute, I reversed the spell. "What just happened?"

"The reason I know that Keith is a wizard is because I'm a witch, and I just used magic to make myself invisible."

"I don't believe you. How did you really do it?"

He clearly wasn't convinced yet, so I levitated to the ceiling and then lowered myself back into my chair. Finally, I shrank myself, and mini-me walked across the desktop towards Jack.

"Now, do you believe me?"

"I guess so."

After restoring myself to full-size, I returned to my seat.

"As soon as I got close to your half-brother, I realised that he was a wizard. Everything made sense then. There is a spell, called the doppelganger, which allows witches and wizards to change their appearance, so they look like someone else." To illustrate the point, I changed myself into Jack Two.

"I—err—" Was as much as he could manage. His mind was clearly blown.

After reversing the spell, I continued, "Once I knew Keith was a wizard, it was obvious that he'd used the 'doppelganger' spell, to look like you, when visiting Joseph's apartment. He knew he would be caught on CCTV. He did the same thing when Jean overheard the argument earlier that day."

"I don't know what to say. I always felt like Keith was different, but I could never put my finger on why. Are there others like him here?"

"The short answer is yes. Sups, that's short for supernaturals, have lived amongst humans since the beginning of time. For the most part, they do so peacefully. Any sup who breaks the laws of the human world is likely to be taken back to the sup world and never allowed to return."

"There's a sup world?"

"Yes, but we don't need to get into that. The reason I wanted to talk to you face-to-face was to explain that there's no way to get your conviction overturned."

"But what about the tape you just played to me? He confessed."

"I only played you a part of the recording." I took out my phone. "Listen." I pressed play:

"What's wrong?"

"That brother of mine. That's what's wrong."

"Jack? What has he done? Have you seen him?"

"No, but he's hired one of your lot."

"What do you mean my lot? What are you talking about?"

"A witch, what do you think I mean? And not just any witch, it's Jill Maxwell. You must have heard of her."

"Yeah, isn't she supposed to be the most powerful witch in the world?"

"Supposedly, but she's also a private investigator here in the human world."

"How can Jack afford to hire her?"

"I've no idea but he has."

"Take it steady."

"Don't tell me to take it steady."

"You mustn't panic, Keith. She can't possibly know anything."

"That's just it. She knew I'd used the 'doppelganger' spell to make it look like Jack was the one who visited Joseph's apartment. And she knew it was me who argued with him at the office."

"Even so, what can she do?"

"What do you mean? Didn't you hear what I just said. She knows I was the one who killed Joseph, not Jack."

"Think about it for a minute. She can hardly take what she knows to the authorities here in the human world, can she? As soon as she starts talking about wizards and spells, they'll laugh in her face."

"Yeah, you're right. She can't do anything. Thanks, doll. I'm sorry I snapped at you before."

"Who was he talking to?" Jack asked.

"He thought he was talking to his wife, but he was actually talking to me. I'd used the 'doppelganger' spell to make myself look like her. Do you see now why you can't take this to the police?"

"Yeah, like she—err—you said on the tape: they'd laugh at me."

"I know this must be hard for you to swallow, but if it's any consolation, Keith will be punished."

"How, if there's no way to present the tape as

evidence."

"There's no way to punish him in this world, but he and his wife have already been taken back to the sup world where they'll spend the best part of their lives behind bars."

"Honestly?"

"Yes, and you don't have to take my word for it. It will soon get out through the media that Keith and his wife have mysteriously disappeared."

"If I'm honest, I don't know what to do with any of this."

"That's hardly surprising. You'll need time to process all of this, but hopefully, when you have, you'll be able to start living without always having to look over your shoulder."

"I must admit that would be nice."

"You'll probably have some questions over the next few days and weeks. If you do, you can call me at any time."

"Thanks, Jill, I may take you up on that offer." He stood up.

"Are you going to be okay?"

"Yeah. Yeah, I think so."

"Don't forget, Jack, not a word of this to anyone."

"I promise. Who would believe me, anyway?"

"And one last thing before you go."

"Yes?"

"Can I ask how you came by the compass stone?"

"A couple of days after I was released from prison, I was in a bar, drowning my sorrows. This guy came and sat with me, and we got chatting. I ended up telling him what had happened to me—how I'd been sent to prison for a murder that I didn't commit. He said he knew someone who would be able to help, and he gave me your name. I told him I couldn't afford to hire a private investigator. That's when he handed me that stone thing. He said if I brought it to you, that you'd agree to help me without any other payment. If I'm honest, I thought he was a bit of a nutter, but I figured I had nothing to lose by trying."

"And you say this man was a complete stranger?"

"Yeah, but he did tell me his name just before he left. Braxmore."

"Are you okay?" Winky asked me after Jack Two had left.

"Err, yeah."

"Are you sure? You look like you've just seen a ghost."

"I'm fine."

In fact, I was feeling anything but fine. If what Jack Two had said was true, he had been given the final compass stone by Braxmore. According to Martin, the compass stones would act as a kind of kryptonite against Braxmore, but how could that possibly be true if he had handed one of them to Jack?

I was just about to call it a day when my phone rang.

"This is Greta from Harmony Fashion."

"I was beginning to think you weren't going to call. What have you decided?"

"We're going to drop the case against you."

"Good decision."

"We need you to go into our solicitors' offices, to sign an agreement that you will not pass on the information you have to anyone else."

"Nah, I'm not going to do that."
"But you have to."
"No, I don't. You'll have to trust me, just like I'll have to trust you not to sue me. Sorry, I have to go now."

***

Jack waited until Florence was in bed before asking the question that had obviously been troubling him since I arrived home.
"What happened with Harmony? Are we going to lose the house?"
"Of course not. I would never let that happen."
"Does that mean they're not going to sue you?"
"No, once they saw what Winky had managed to dig up on them, they decided to drop the case, in return for me agreeing not to take what I know to the press."
"Which was what?"
"Their award-winning summer collection from last year was stolen from a nineteen-year-old student from Thandringham College of Art and Design."
"If that's true, how come the student didn't sue them?"
"Apparently, she sent her designs to Harmony, hoping for some kind of feedback. She never heard back from them, but the following year, several of her designs had been copied in Harmony's summer collection. Understandably aggrieved, she contacted the company to try and get some kind of explanation. Harmony disputed her claims, and threatened legal action if she repeated them."
"How did Winky find out about this?"
"I have no idea, but that cat has contacts everywhere."

"Why didn't the student go to the press?"

"I don't know. She should have done."

"So, that's it?"

"Yeah."

"Phew! I've been really worried about this. You must have been too."

"Me? Worried? Not for one minute," I lied. "Incidentally, your namesake came to see me today."

"How did he take the news about his half-brother being a sup?"

"It kind of blew his mind, but not nearly as much as what he told me blew mine."

"What do you mean?"

"When I asked him how he came by the compass stone, he said someone had approached him in a bar, handed it to him, and told him to contact me because I might be able to prove his innocence. Guess who the man in the bar was."

"I've no idea."

"Braxmore."

"That doesn't make any sense. I thought the whole idea of these stones is that they'll help you defeat Braxmore."

"I thought the same, but now I'm beginning to wonder if I've been on a wild goose chase."

"Have you told Martin this?"

"I tried to, but as always, I can't get in touch with him."

Chapter 29

When Kathy called me on Friday afternoon, I feared the worst.

"Please don't tell me you aren't going to have the costume finished by tomorrow."

"Oh, ye of little faith. I promised it would be ready and it is. In fact, the reason I'm calling is to tell you I got it finished last night."

"That's brilliant. I'll pop over now and get it."

"You can't. The kids are going to Pete's parents for the weekend, and he and I are having a couple of days away at the coast."

"It's alright for some, but what about the costume? I promised Florence she'd have it tomorrow."

"Don't panic. We'll be driving by Middle Tweaking, so I'll drop it off with Jack in about half-an-hour."

"He won't be in. He's meeting an old cop buddy for lunch. There's a key under the third plant pot from the right, next to the door. You can let yourself in with that and leave it in the hall."

"Why would you leave a key under a plant pot? Don't you know that's the first place burglars check?"

"Will you do it?"

"Of course I will. I hope Florence likes it."

"She's going to love it. Thanks, sis. You're the best."

I was going to kill that sister of mine.

I had just arrived home and opened the box with the costume in it. I was holding it in front of me when Jack walked in.

"What's that?" he said.

"Kathy dropped it off before I got back."
"It's a bumble bee."
"Thanks, Jack, I hadn't noticed that until you mentioned it."
"Why has she made a bumble bee costume? Didn't you tell her it was supposed to be Bluebottle Girl?"
"Of course I did."
"Then, I don't get it."
"When I went over there to ask her to make the costume, I made her make a note in her diary so she wouldn't forget. She told me that she'd written *BB superhero costume for Florence*. I can only think that when she got around to making the costume, she saw the BB and thought it referred to Bumblebee."
"I didn't realise there was a Bumblebee Girl."
"Neither did I until I just checked."
"What are we going to do? I have to collect Florence from school in twenty minutes."
"I have no idea."
"Can't you change it?"
"Why didn't I think of that? I'll get out my needle and thread."
"I meant can't you use magic to change it?"
"With the old *change a Bumblebee Girl costume into a Bluebottle Girl costume* spell, you mean?"
"You told me that you can create your own spells."
"I can, but it isn't easy."
"She's going to be crushed."
"Thanks, Jack, that really helps. You're going to have to buy me some time by keeping Florence away while I try to come up with a spell."
"What do you want me to do?"

"I don't know. That's your problem. I've got enough on my plate, don't you think?"

"Okay, I'll think of something."

I rushed upstairs and took out the spell book. With the limited time I had available, I would have to try and find a spell that I could modify because coming up with one from scratch would take much too long. I spent over an hour, just flicking through the pages of the book, desperately hoping to find a spell that might fit the bill. I had no idea what Jack would be doing with Florence, but I was sure it wouldn't be long before the two of them returned.

I was beginning to think that it was a bust, and that I'd have to confess to Florence that I hadn't made her costume, and that her Auntie Kathy had made a terrible mistake. Then, I spotted a set of three spells that collectively were known as the 'Cinderella' spell collection. One of the spells was the one that had attracted Florence's attention recently, and which had resulted in her trying to come by a pumpkin and mice. But it was the 'Cinderella's dress' spell that caught my eye. The spell allowed you to transform an ordinary dress into an elaborate ball gown, fit for a princess. Although, a ball gown wasn't exactly a superhero costume, I figured I might be able to make it work.

"Mummy, you did it!" Florence grabbed the costume and held it in front of her.

"Do you like it, darling?"

"It's fantastic. Thanks, Mummy, you're the best. Can I go and try it on?"

"Sure, but you'd better be quick because it will soon be

time to go to CASS."

"Yay!" She went rushing upstairs.

"Well done, you." Jack gave me a kiss. "How did you manage it?"

"Let's just say I had some help from Cinderella."

"Huh?"

Before I could elaborate, my phone rang.

"Martin? I've been trying to get hold of you for ages. Where have you been?"

"Never mind that. I've tracked him down."

"Braxmore? Where is he?"

"I'm not sure knowing is going to help."

"Just tell me."

"I have it on good authority that he's in Sunville, but I have no idea where that is or how to get there."

"That's okay. I do."

ALSO BY ADELE ABBOTT

The Not-A-Date (a sweet romantic comedy)

I'd just been fired, so the last thing I needed was some guy hitting on me, and I told him so in no uncertain terms. Then he goes and offers me the job of my dreams.

Pushing All My Buttons (a sweet romantic comedy)

I got stuck in a lift with this guy who then tried to hit on me, so I told him he was a jerk. A few days later, I started a new job and discovered he was my boss.

So Not The One (A sweet romantic comedy)

I was devastated when my old boss had to take early retirement. But that was nothing compared to how I felt when I discovered who his replacement was.

The Witch P.I. Mysteries (A Candlefield/Washbridge Series)

Witch Is When... (Season #1)

Witch Is When It All Began
Witch Is When Life Got Complicated
Witch Is When Everything Went Crazy
Witch Is When Things Fell Apart
Witch Is When The Bubble Burst
Witch Is When The Penny Dropped
Witch Is When The Floodgates Opened
Witch Is When The Hammer Fell

Witch Is When My Heart Broke
Witch Is When I Said Goodbye
Witch Is When Stuff Got Serious
Witch Is When All Was Revealed

Witch Is Why... (Season #2)
Witch Is Why Time Stood Still
Witch is Why The Laughter Stopped
Witch is Why Another Door Opened
Witch is Why Two Became One
Witch is Why The Moon Disappeared
Witch is Why The Wolf Howled
Witch is Why The Music Stopped
Witch is Why A Pin Dropped
Witch is Why The Owl Returned
Witch is Why The Search Began
Witch is Why Promises Were Broken
Witch is Why It Was Over

Witch Is How... (Season #3)
Witch is How Things Had Changed
Witch is How Berries Tasted Good
Witch is How The Mirror Lied
Witch is How The Tables Turned
Witch is How The Drought Ended
Witch is How The Dice Fell
Witch is How The Biscuits Disappeared
Witch is How Dreams Became Reality
Witch is How Bells Were Saved
Witch is How To Fool Cats
Witch is How To Lose Big
Witch is How Life Changed Forever

Witch Is Where... (Season #4)

Witch is Where Magic Lives Now
Witch Is Where Clowns Go To Die
Witch Is Where Squirrels Go Nuts
Witch Is Where Rainbows End
Witch Is Where Unicorns Cry
Witch Is Where The Lights Went Out
Witch Is Where Fairies Wing It
Witch Is Where Roses Bloom Early
Witch Is Where Decisions Are Made
Witch Is Where Gnomes Rules
Witch Is Where Cats Always Win

Susan Hall Investigates
(A Candlefield/Washbridge Series)

Whoops! Our New Flatmate Is A Human.
Whoops! All The Money Went Missing.
Whoops! Someone Is On Our Case.
Whoops! We're In Big Trouble Now.

Murder On Account (A Kat Royle Novel)

Her boss has been murdered. Now she must find his killer. Smart, sassy and kickass tough, private investigator, Kat Royle, is nobody's fool, but does she have what it takes to keep the agency afloat, and find the murderer?

Web site: AdeleAbbott.com
Facebook: facebook.com/ AdeleAbbottAuthor

Printed in Great Britain
by Amazon

37526177R00179